Rise of the Dragonfly

'A Legend Remembered'

By
I.A.W.Offor

Dedicated to my beautiful family

This is a work of fiction. Names, characters, places and incidents are either the product of the authors imagination, or are used ficticiously. Any resemblance to actual persons living or dead, events or locals is entirely coincidental.

Copyright © 2020 By Iain Adrian Wolfe Offor

All rights reserved. No part of this book may be reproduced or used in any manner without written permission of the copyright owner except for the use of quotations in a book review.

First paper back and ebook edition March 2020

ISBN 978-1-9161713-1-2

Chapter 1

'Brother, where are your useless bears?' Leilani shouted as she burst out from the small, falling apart, iron garden gate that Lanny's bears had thrown aside as they left in search of transport.

'I don't know!' Lanny replied. Having left their own Dragonfly Manor through its unexpectedly, splendidly, wonderfully perfect, magical big red front door, and arriving at a small Dragonfly cottage in a remote part of the Scottish Highlands, they were as desperate as each other to get to the loch where they were sure the hidden island would be found. The island the siblings were convinced would give them everything.

Although she was still an old woman, the reality, as she saw it, that all would come her way had Leilani feeling revitalised. However, her frail body was in no way capable of carrying her far, let alone at the speed she wanted, to make sure she was the first to arrive at the island. Of course her haste in searching for transport was pointless! Unknown to her the race was lost - Alex and Sophie had already found what Leilani and Lanny were so desperate to - the island and its ancient dragonfly.

Following Leilani out the gate, Lanny in his anger, kicked it off its old, rusted, just hanging on hinges. With no sign of his bears in any direction, he looked back at the place they had come from, 'What type of rotten hole of a place is this anyway? Look at it. The cottage or should I say shed, it's a disgrace!' A red mist had fallen and taken over his mind, which made sensible thought or focus on what was important quite difficult. Adrenalin and rage were in control. His state of mind found him forgetting himself as he shouted to Leilani, 'You are on your own!' and disappeared down the hillside. The adrenalin pumping through his veins produced more than enough power to carry his legs, far younger than Leilani's, at great speed for a good distance. Far enough to find his bears and to make his way to the loch, the home of the hidden island.

As he ran down the hillside leaving his sister far behind, the remains of old branches from felled trees long since removed, harsh brush and hidden thorns clawed at his legs, ripping his clothes and tearing his skin. Being focused on where he was going, the pain from his bleeding lower limbs didn't register.

The fresh morning air was clear enough for Lanny to see for miles, although frustratingly the shadowy hills that towered over him hid the loch beyond, and the thick forest at their base. Having made his way down the open hillside, he arrived at the edge of the forest. Still at full speed, out of nowhere a fallen tree rose up from the ground. Lanny slammed into its thick moss-covered trunk with such force, it sent him spinning round and crashing to the floor. Having witnessed her brother's collision, the cackling laughter of Leilani echoed down the valley reaching the throbbing, buzzing head of Lanny.

'Oh my brother, you seem to have forgotten what you created!' Leilani screeched through her laughter. She had discovered much over her unnaturally, and at times dragging days of long life. Discoveries that her brother knew of. Not necessarily how she came about what she could do, but certainly of their effects.

Accidentally having combined her crystal with Lanny's gold and the blood of the poor creature in one of his storage places being her starting point, progressing to the damp and dark room within Dragonfly Manor, where she created her own tree trunk cauldron. She learned to manipulate people with selfish minds back on Earth, such as the weasley Mr Sullivan, to do as she pleased. She was convinced she could do so much more. After years of frustrating failures experimenting with different quantities, applications and consistencies of the blood, gold and crystal mix to see what other powers she could tap into, one morning Leilani woke from a dream where she had used a ruby instead of her crystal. At first she was angry with herself for not thinking about such an obvious option much sooner. But it didn't take long for her to get over it and start searching for different gems to add to her experiments.

Thanks to Lanny and his obsession for gold mining, it wasn't long before a discovery was made. Having been sent through the smallest of gaps found deep in a cave, a young cub, born to one of his army of bears, came across a small open area. He reported back his find, which although did not indicate gold, did tell of white stones protruding from the dark walls. Unknown to Lanny, Leilani had been keeping a very close eye on every find he made. The find, of no interest to her brother, was of great interest to her. Secretly she sent Earl to retrieve the white stones. They were not crystals. They were diamonds!

Leilani took them to a secret place Lanny had come across many years earlier, a Dragonfly home. He found it deep in a very special forest that had been part of Heart and Earth since their beginning. Appearing to have never been used for its intended purpose, with there being no sign of a dragonfly and no useful humans or animals for Lanny to use in his mines, it was long forgotten by him. Hidden deep within the Bristlecone Pine Forest of California, over thousands of years, the home had become engulfed by the tree that was its centre. Growing around and beyond the Dragonfly home's small and basic walls, there was no way out to explore the forest that surrounded it, and crucially, no way in for anyone who may have stumbled across it. The only way in or out was through its faded red, covered in pinpricks of light, old door. It was the perfect place for Leilani to carry out her experiments without discovery.

Although the tiny Dragonfly home was the perfect place for Leilani to stay hidden, it was not a place she cared to stay for long. Claustrophobia occasionally would get the better of her, causing her to lose focus. Then panic would set in, which more often than not turned into anger, resulting in some sort of violence. It was on one of those days that the cycle had worked in her favour. Leilani had swiped her gems off her work table across the incredibly revitalised, energy-filled, fresh tree smelling, damp, muddy-floored, tiny room. Watching as the discarded gems sank into the mud, fear of losing them instantly refocused her. She moved quickly to collect them before they were gone.

On her knees as she took hold of the diamond closest to her, the gold bracelet she was wearing made contact with it at the very same moment her boney fingers did. In that moment, she was hit with a surge of energy which pulsed up through her hand and spread to every part of her body. Although she got a fright, she did not let go of the diamond and continued to pull it out of the mud as she recoiled and sat back on her bony heels. The surge passing, she looked to see if the delay had caused her to lose the rest of the diamonds. Her eyes popped wide open as she saw that not only had she not lost them, but they were in fact rolling towards her. Leilani's initial reaction was to stand up and back away from the sharp, fast approaching stones. As soon as she did, the gems shot in the opposite direction! They bounced off the wall farthest from her and fell back down to the muddy floor.

A clever woman, it only took Leilani a couple of seconds to realise that the gold, the mud and the diamond combined with her touch, along with the thoughts of collecting the discarded gems, was what brought them to her. And her action of stepping away to protect herself, was what made them shoot back across the room. Yet again, just as she did with her window to Earth, thanks to an accident she had discovered a connection with an energy, a power from nature she knew would be very helpful.

Feelings of claustrophobia completely gone, Leilani removed her bracelet from her wrist, wrapped it round the diamond and purposely bent down. Placing them on the muddy ground, she rested her hand over the top of them. This time the pulse of energy did not take her by surprise. This time she embraced the feeling. She looked up at the table and as quick as she thought it; it moved towards her!

Leilani spent several hours playing with her newfound power. As excited as she was, the crouched position caused her old creaking body to ache. Trying to relieve the pain by standing, the small room echoed with the cracks from her seized joints. She had to find a way to use the energies without being in that position. Her mind worked quickly. The pain was one thing, but being seen bending to the ground every time she wanted to use what she had discovered, that would give away the truth behind what she could do, and that was not acceptable to her. A plan was formed.

Her love of jewellery and her brother's love of gold would be the key to keeping her secret. She returned to her Dragonfly Manor, and under the guise of opening her window to Earth, she got her brother to deliver her some liquid gold. Once alone, she smashed one of her diamonds into tiny pieces, added them to some of her brother's liquid gold and created herself a long, fine, golden, jewel-encrusted rope.

Split into twelve carefully measured lengths, Leilani wrapped a section of the rope around each of her ankles, melting their ends together so they would not accidentally be lost. She then added five lengths to each of the ankle bracelets, the ropes running down the top of each foot and wrapping around each of her toes. The pain she suffered from soldering the gold together on her ankles and feet was a price she was happy to pay. It was the most perfect of designs because in a moment's notice, without discovery, by simply keeping her feet in contact with the ground, the energy from nature could be used. Although many wondered, no one dare question the reason Leilani suddenly stopped wearing shoes, except for the old slippers she wore inside her Dragonfly Manor - the only place her hardened feet received any comfort.

With the years passing, the jewellery which fitted well when first put in place, no longer did. As old as she was, her feet and ankles were just skin and bone, wrinkled. The gold ropes around her toes were loose. The movement rubbed her tired feet with every step she took. Even so, with her feet in constant pain, there was no way she was ever going to remove her secret weapon. The weapon that made it possible for her to cause the tree her brother collided with, to rise up in front of him.

Her goal achieved, her brother stopped, Leilani's theatrically and pointlessly raised arms dropped back to her sides. The dramatic action of her raised arms was nothing more than a distraction, another way to keep the truth of her actions from onlookers, to keep everyone thinking the power came from her. As her arms fell to her sides, so the risen tree fell back to its resting place. Her final act was a hidden one. She pulled her gold covered toes out of the soil she had dug them into. The gold, the diamonds, herself, all being part of nature's soil, connecting to all things in and on the ground, making what she did possible.

The impact of the huge tree trunk hitting the ground bounced Lanny up into the air. Coming back down, he landed in a seated position right in front of the jagged stump the trunk had been torn from on a day of extremely strong winds. Its roots, not wishing to let go of the earth they lived in, gave the trunk no choice but to snap. The snap resulted in the stump becoming a mass of jagged, sharp, long protruding splinters, which on this day found their way into Lanny! In his effort to lesson the impact of his landing, Lanny had thrown his hands back. Both hands became the victims of the tree's spear-like splinters. The pain was far worse than the scratches he had paid no attention to as he ran down the hill and he let out a scream. Fully aware of who had caused the incident, he slowly turned to look up the hill towards his sister. Annoyed he had showed weakness with his scream, gritting his teeth, Lanny pulled his hands free. If he had power like his sister, the look he threw up at her would have cut her down. Blood dripping from his hands, he stood himself up. Not losing eye contact with his smirking sibling, he felt a pressure on one of his wounds. Looking down he saw that two familiar faces had returned - George and Gregg.

'Boys, nice to see you. So what did you find?' They shook their heads. 'I thought so. You do realise that because of your failure, we are going to have to do the hard work and carry the skeleton woman.'

Distracted by trying to shut away the pain of his falls, he was being surprisingly lenient on his generals. Realising, George and Gregg looked at each other and with a nod between them, disappeared out of sight, knowing they would suffer at some point if they did not find transport.

Lanny, accepting his fate, dragged his aching body back up the steep hill to rejoin his sister. Although it only took him thirty seconds to make his way down, it took him a full ten uncomfortable minutes to get back up.

'You stupid old man, you have wasted time we do not have!' Leilani shouted, as the out of breath Lanny sat down on the low wall of the garden and looked down at his injured hands. After a deep breath to help him stay calm, he replied,

'George and Gregg will be back soon enough.'

'We don't have the time for those useless creatures. Earl, come on, you need to...' For the first time, Leilani realised her loyal companion was not at her side. Looking back towards the small run down Dragonfly cottage, her eyes searched the garden for signs of her loyal friend. There were none, so she returned to the cottage to find him.

'This place looks familiar,' Leilani said as she made her way up the barely visible, wobbly cobbly footpath, covered in long, flattened, dead grass. From her experience, since becoming forgotten, every Dragonfly home's garden was overgrown with tall trees and thick bushes, so it was strange to see this one with just the long dead grass covering everything. Leilani shuffled her way back to the sad looking front door, her hardened feet not feeling the coarse grass under them. 'Earl, are you hiding in here?' Leilani screeched. After pausing for an answer and not getting one, she stepped into the cottage and remembered why she recognised the place. It was the very Dragonfly home she had found the most enlightening of papers in, hidden in a concealed drawer high up in one of the room's walls.

'So close brother. We have been so close all along!' she said. With anger growing inside at her realisation, she turned to look at the doorframe. Leilani had assumed the cottage they were in was the closest Dragonfly home to the loch. Squinting to see the tiny intricate and detailed carved stories, she hoped to find something about the island. There was no reference to the island, not even a reference to the loch she so desperately wanted to get to. However, there was something else that stood out. A carving that was repeated. It was of a long driveway surrounded by trees, with a woman standing at its end. Each carving had the same driveway and line of trees. However, the thorough Leilani noticed that the woman in each one, although very similar, appeared to have slight differences. Looking out the open door towards her brother, she said,

'Interesting. Lanny, remember the family you said I couldn't get control of. The ones I couldn't see where they lived. The ones that were in the place of the loch, the island, the meteor strike?' Lanny was still sitting on the garden wall, attempting to stop the flow of blood from his hands with material he had torn from his top. He really wasn't paying much attention to his sister,

'Yes,' he eventually replied.

'Well, I think they are more important than we thought. There are carvings of generations of women here. They are all in the same place. I think there is a Dragonfly home we do not know of, one we have never been to!' That got Lanny's interest. If there was a hidden Dragonfly home, and they had not been to it, it would most likely still have its dragonfly. His urgency to leave the cottage, to find his bears, to get transport, was once again his priority.

'George!' He shouted as loud as he possibly could. His shout to his companions reminded Leilani of the reason she had initially returned to the cottage,

'Brother, have you seen Earl?'

'He left!' The reply did not come from her brother, it was George,

'What do you mean?' Lanny replied,

'I tried to tell you back at Dragonfly Manor, he was acting strange. He was going back and forth from the forest, and then he didn't come back at all.' Hearing his words, Leilani stepped out of the cottage, slammed the door behind her, made her way over to the cowering bear and grabbed him by his thick furry neck,

'You ragged piece of matted mess, you better have found me a way to get to the island in the loch!' The tight bony grip Leilani had round George's neck meant as much as he tried, he couldn't give her a verbal response. As he was about to lose consciousness, he saw Gregg and gestured in his direction. The gesture was just enough to get Leilani to look. Gregg was coming up the hill with a huge stag. His razor-sharp claws were firmly placed on the beast's chest and sunk through his thick winter fur, piercing the skin just above his fast beating heart. As they arrived at the opening in the wall where the gate once hung, and the stag realised who he was being taken to, the beautiful creature had a fleeting thought that it would be better for him if the bear would sink his claws a little deeper. Leilani dropped George, his neck letting out a loud crack as he bent it to one side to release the tension from the surprising grip of the old frail woman.

Pushing Gregg to one side, Leilani looked deep into the stag's eyes and gave the speech she did to all who were unlucky enough to be alive in her presence.

'You have two choices. The first, is you will do as I ask and be happy to? The second, is you will not be happy to, in which case you will still do as I ask and suffer.' Without a word, his hot breath filling the air from his flared nostrils, the stag lowered himself to the ground. 'Good,' Leilani said, climbing on to his steaming back.

Lanny was quick to follow, reaching up to take hold of the stag's back. A swift kick to his shoulder told him that was not going to happen, and just in case he hadn't got the message, Leilani said,

'You have proven you have more energy than sense, you can run!' She pulled on the stag's muscular neck, turned him in the direction she knew she had to go, bent forward and whispered in the stag slave's ear. 'If we don't get to the island in time, you know you will pay.' Sitting high up on the stag, she repeated the same words to her brother and his bears. The four legs under her and the ten legs beside her were given their incentive to move quickly. She dug her gold covered feet into the ribs of the stag who took off. Having reached full speed within a couple of strides, he glided over the dead brush and fallen trees scattered down the hill as though they weren't even there.

Off the hill and into the sparse forest, Leilani from her high vantage point could see eyes watching, eyes belonging to the stag's family and friends. Darting from side to side, pretending to avoid the standing trees and jumping over the fallen ones, the stag did all he could to keep Leilani focused on not falling from his back, to keep her from screaming out an order to her brother or his bears to do anything to the worried eyes watching. Also by carrying on at the speed he was, Lanny and his bears wouldn't stop to attack the watching eyes, knowing if they lagged behind their punishment would be unpleasant. Managing to make eye contact with one of his loved ones, the great stag whipped his head signalling for them to leave, not to follow.

The Dragonfly cottage that Leilani and her fellow travellers had arrived in was some ten miles to the east of where they expected to find the loch. The cold of the morning and the fast moving wind rushing past her as the stag continued, meant Leilani was freezing. The old coat she was wearing offered no comfort, as with her old dressing gown, it was well used. The deep red colour fading to an almost pink at points, the velvet material and padding thinning, riddled with holes, the wind just whistled through to her body.

'Lean forward on to me, you will find my warmth will help.' The gracious stag felt her shivers, and as with all who were born of Heart would do, he wanted to take away any discomfort, pain or suffering. Even with the evil that Leilani could do, would do and had done, the desire to help her was not reduced in any way. Stubbornly, not wishing to show any weakness or requirement of another, shivering, her rotten teeth chattering, Leilani stayed upright.

The speed in which they travelled, through the valley, up and over the frost-covered hills, meant the group made very good time. The area in which Leilani had calculated the loch should be, was going to be over the rise of the next hill. She pulled on the neck of the stag who, after skidding several feet on the damp and frosty ground, came to a halt. The steam that was rising into the air from every part of his exhausted body rolled away from him as Leilani lifted her leg over from one side and slid herself down to the ground.

Appearing from the mist of his body, she stepped up to the brow of the hill. Standing on a large rock she looked down into the valley where finally, she could see the beginning of the loch. At the closest end of the water-filled crater, created many thousands of years earlier, were a few stone properties scattered around the water's edge and up into the surrounding hillside.

'You don't look well sister!' Lanny's tone did not sound as concerned as his words may have suggested. He was right - her lips were blue and she couldn't move or feel her hands or feet.

'Don't get too excited!' Leilani stepped off the rock. Sinking her feet into the brown winter heather that surrounded them, she found soil. With a moment's concentration, her toes and their gold forced their way just a millimetre into the frozen mud. It was just enough. Before the watching eyes, her blue lips turned back to their pink, cracked state. Her hands and feet, with a sound of breaking bones began to move, and all feeling returned to them. Looking away from the loch she turned to her brother who had made his way to her side and took hold of his hair. Pulling him down to her height, in an eerily quiet voice she said,

'Brother. You may think your opportunity is coming. It is not. I will have whatever power that unseen island will provide. I will find a way back to our Earth home, and I will be the one who will own all that there has ever been, not you!' After letting him go, Leilani pointed towards a house that looked quite different to the rest of the old scattered buildings. It was newer, grander looking, and leading up to it was a long driveway lined with trees, 'And, no matter what happens at the island, we still have that house!'

Her attention elsewhere, the stag thought it was the perfect time to make his escape. Carefully placing his hooves to stay as silent as possible, he took off. As careful as he tried to be, the crack of the tiniest twig gave his attempted escape away. Leilani's head whipped round to see the hind legs of the stag disappearing down the hillside. Her feet, still connected to the earth, meant she didn't hesitate to use what she knew she could. It did not matter the speed in which the stag tried to make his escape, Leilani was able to send the weeds that burst up from the ground and wrap them round the stag's front legs. Gripping them tightly, they brought the stag to an instant stop. His rear end overtook his front as his back legs were thrown over his head, forcing his antlers into the ground causing them to snap!

'So you have decided to take the second option!' Leilani said with a sinister smirk. With the weeds still wrapped around him, happy her transport could go no further, she looked back towards the loch for any sign of the island where the legend, the reality of Shuing and his dragonfly began.

Their arrival could not have been timed better to witness what was about to happen. Far off in the distance, a section of the clear, fresh, loch water began to swirl as though the ground far beneath its surface had fallen away. A hole appeared at the centre of the swirl, getting larger and larger, finally resulting in the largest whirlpool any of the onlookers had ever seen. Only lasting for a moment, the hole was suddenly filled with an explosion of water and light that shot high up into the sky. The dull, silent morning transformed, as the whole valley lit up and the sound of thousands of gallons of rushing water echoed through the hills. Leilani, her bare feet still connected with the ground, was instantly aware of a massive change in the energy she was feeling. It took her breath away!

With a massive boom that shook the ground beneath her, the ear-piercing sound of rushing water rising up came to a stop. Having reached their height, each droplet of water taken from the loch fell back down, sending massive waves crashing towards its shore.

Along with the waves of water, a wave of invisible energy coming from the centre of the vanishing whirlpool spread out across the valley. Travelling up the hill to where Leilani and her brother were watching excitedly, its force knocked Leilani to the ground. Unfazed and sitting comfortably in the coarse heather, with a sparkle in her eyes, Leilani said,

'I think we have found our island.'

Chapter 2

'What do you mean, "the first dragonfly has awakened"?' grandmother asked Sophie. Alex released his mother from the tightest of hugs and lifted his top off.

'This is what she means!' turning to show what had become part of him. The muscles on his back, creating a cavern down his spine was where the shimmering body of a dragonfly lay. Its forward wings stretched over his shoulders on to his chest, whilst the rear wings made their way under his arms, hugging his waist. Alive, the dragonlfy's colours pulsed through its wings, its body mirroring every movement of Alex's.

'Oh my goodness, it's beautiful. I've never seen anything like it,' Alexandria said,

'We have!' Vicky said, sitting on the soft grass with Bart and Anchor. She was right, the night before back at Dragonfly Manor they had all witnessed something similar. Although unlike the Dragonfly Manor's dragonfly, this one stayed!

'It looks different somehow. Older maybe. Look at its back, it's cracked,' Melissa said. Hand in hand with Sophie, grandmother walked over to Alex to get a closer look. As the two arrived at his side, grandmother let out a yelp. She felt a repulsion of energy forcing her hand out of Sophie's.

'What was that?' Sophie said.

'It came from you!' grandmother replied.

'Your neck, the colours, look!' Vicky excitedly shouted as she got to her feet. The rainbow of colours swirling around Sophie's neck, and the ones out of sight under her top, were changing position, moving to the side of her body Alex was standing on. Vicky was quick to figure it out, but wanted to check before announcing her theory. She pulled Sophie away from Alex. 'I was right!' she exclaimed, as having pulled her only a couple of feet away from him, the colours on Sophie went back to their central position.

'What are you right about Vicky?' Alexandria asked.

'Watch,' she replied, shoving Sophie back towards Alex. Again the colours swirled towards him, and this time it was Vicky that received the jolt of energy that grandmother had previously. Sophie was desperate to see what everyone else was. She slipped her yellow jacket and warm jumper off to get a better look. Standing in the still, cold air wearing just a vest, she peered over her shoulder.

'Wow! I would go as far as saying that is even more beautiful than your dragonfly Alex,' Vicky said. The colours emanating from the dragonfly bite covered every visible part of Sophie's back, neck, shoulders and arms. They were not stationary like a tattoo, they were alive, slowly blending together making different colours as they did. Getting closer to Alex, the colours not only moved towards him like metal shards to a magnet, the movement became fast, frantic, the colours clashing with each other, exploding like looking out into a changing galaxy in fast forward.

'It's not just Sophie that changes when they get close,' Melissa said.

'I know, it kind of tickles,' Alex replied. As Sophie got closer, the dragonfly's wings sped up, and its massive eyes filled with light.

'Could you two be any more connected?' Vicky asked sarcastically.

'I have a few questions. For starters, what happened to you both in the house? How did the colours and dragonfly join with you? What does this all mean? And what the heck was that explosion of water and light we saw?' Melissa asked.

'Explosion of water?' Alex asked.

'Yes. The island disappeared when you two and Troy stepped onto it. Even Vicky couldn't see it. Alexandria found a boat which is how we are here. Literally just as we got in the boat there was a huge explosion. It was like a bomb had gone off under the water. Honestly, I thought the worst!' Melissa said. Reliving the emotions she'd had in that moment, a tear appeared in her eye.

'We all did!' Alexandria interrupted. She had generations of her family history taught to her, years of visiting the hidden island, but had never seen or heard of anything like that happening before. Sophie and Alex looked at each other,

'Oh, maybe it was when we were in the lake and the dragonfly came down,' Sophie said,

'In the lake! Do you mean the loch?' Alexandria asked,

'No, we were in a lake, underground,' Sophie replied. Once again they were passing on information to Alexandria which, to her surprise, had no idea what or where they were talking about. Her experiences and knowledge started and finished with the beautiful island and the small stick and mud cottage built round the island's tallest tree. The house whose handmade, perfectly incredibly inviting bright red front door, was led up to by the shortest of wobbly cobbly footpaths.

Shuing's home, the first Dragonfly home to open its door to Heart.

'Show me!' Alexandria said, unconvinced that the cave or lake existed. With her family having been part of the island since the day Shuing found himself there, she could not believe that there hadn't been stories told or written about it. Alex looked down at the ground. The group was standing exactly where the grass had opened up and lowered him into the cave. He got down on his knees and felt around for the hidden access point. 'What are you doing?' Alexandria asked.

'If you want to see the lake, there is a way in somewhere round here. I fell through it!' Alex replied. Everyone joined him in his search. As hard as they looked, kicked grass to the side, pulled at the scattered meadow flowers, there was nothing. Just grass, no indentations, no hidden holes, no access. 'Hang on. Sophie, you didn't go through the same hole I did, how did you get in the cave?' Alex asked. Sophie looked back towards the cottage and tried to remember. She couldn't, so she replied,

'I was just there. One minute I was looking at the tree, the next minute I was laying underwater looking up at the roots covering the roof of the cave.'

A confused Alexandria made her way to the cottage she had visited almost every day of her life. Being the direct descendant of Shuing charged with being the island's caretaker, she thought she knew the dragonfly island's every nook. As she passed Melissa, she grabbed her hand and said,

'Let's see if we can find the cave and lake they think they have seen!' As well as her proud need to prove she did in fact know every part of the island by disproving Sophie and Alex's story, she wanted to get

Melissa alone. She had questions she wanted answers to.

Alex wasn't ready to return quite yet. He needed a moment to gather his thoughts, so he walked in the opposite direction. Coming to a stop at the water's edge, Alex watched as the clear water made its way gently up the sand towards his toes, returning to where it had come from just before making contact.

'The questions your mother asked, they will be answered. But first you must continue your journey. There are many that need your help. There are more than many!' The words were heard inside his mind, coming from the now familiar voice of the ancient dragonfly. Just as Alex could hear the dragonfly, the dragonfly could hear Alex, so there was no need for him to speak out loud, but he did.

'What am I supposed to do?' Alex asked, unaware of Vicky who had just arrived at his side. Assuming the question was directed at her, she was about to respond when she was distracted with the realisation that the loch and the shoreline in the distance looked blurry. Curious, she looked back towards the house. It was crisp, full of detail, with not the slightest hint of a blurry line.

'Well, that's interesting!' Vicky said.

'Oh, I didn't see you there,' Alex said.

'It's ok. Hang on. Who were you taking to then?' Vicky asked. Far beyond caring if he was seen as mad for saying it, Alex told her he was talking to the dragonfly. Vicky patted him on the back and said, 'Well, beginning to think anything is possible, so why not?' She left her hand comfortingly on his topless back and examined the colourful dragonfly as she did. 'Ooo, that's weird!' she said, instantly taking her hand off him. She felt what could best be described as a ripple under her hand as the dragonfly moved. 'Did you feel that?' She asked.

'Feel what?' Alex replied.

'I guess not then. The dragonfly was moving,' Vicky replied. Alex hadn't felt the movement. The dragonfly's attachment to him was no different to the unconscious process of blood passing through his veins. 'Ok then! So, going back to your question about what you are supposed to do. I think you should just do whatever you think is right. It seems to me that everything has got you to where you are supposed to be so far! I have never been a believer in destiny, but I have to say, that worldview is changing! Look over there.' Vicky pointed to Alex's two mums disappearing into the house and Sophie, her grandmother, Anchor, Bart and Troy standing chatting. 'We are all a part of whatever you are supposed to do, as much as you are a part of what we are supposed to do! So just go with it!' Alex turned to Vicky, pulled her in close, and gave her a hug which made the pale winter skin of her face turn as red as if she had been sunburnt. 'You ok then?' Vicky asked.

'Yeh I'm fine. Come on, let's go and see if we can find the way back into the cave. That seems like a good place to start hey,' Alex said letting go of the embarrassed Vicky. Together they made their way back up to where a jealous Anchor was watching Sophie stroke the thick, winter, fur- covered neck of Troy, Alexandria's horse. 'Are you lot coming?' Alex said as he passed them. Bart was on his feet and at Vicky's side in a flash. Happy to be wanted by someone, Anchor dashed over and jumped up at Alex, slobbering all over the arm he had raised just in time to stop the scratches he would have received from the claws of the over-excited Anchor if he hadn't. Using his jumper, Alex wiped away Anchor's saliva before putting it back on, covering up the fluttering dragonfly. Troy was more than happy to stay and eat the lush grass, so didn't follow as Sophie and grandmother joined the adventurers heading for the cottage.

Inside, Melissa and Alexandria were looking around the trunk of the tree Sophie had said she was standing at before finding herself underwater. It wasn't a part of the house Alexandria had paid a huge amount of attention to on her visits. Her focus was always on the walls.

'What exactly am I supposed to be looking for?' Melissa asked, having done a full circuit of its trunk.

'I am not sure myself,' Alexandria replied, after carrying out her own circuit and finding nothing that hinted at a way to the cave. She looked down at the uneven floor made from the same cobbles that the short, wobbly cobbly path leading up to the cottage was made of. Still with no sign of any sort of an entrance, she decided to start on the questions she had for Melissa before the others appeared.

'Why did you bring him back here?'

'I didn't. He brought us. He had some crazy vision about this place, and a man who lived here. I really didn't want to come, especially after his reaction to…' Melissa stopped. She considered for a moment whether she should say anything about what had happened back in the square, to the policemen, the suited woman and the weasely Mr Sullivan.

She had to. 'His body reacted to me being taken. He, he sent everything, everyone, flying, without touching anything!' Alexandria sensed fear in Melissa's voice as she told the story, so she interrupted,

'You don't have to be scared of him. You know that right?' Alexandria said.

'Scared of him, don't be silly!' Melissa said. But she was. She loved her boy more than anything, but what she had witnessed and suffered herself back at the square, it had unnerved her.

'Good,' Alexandria said, well aware that Melissa was not being completely honest. 'What you really need to be scared of is if grandmother's grandchildren have got wind of his existence, have seen him, have seen anything about him! With him being here, just as you could see it for a short time from the loch side, they may have seen this island. What I said to you in my letter about keeping him hidden, is more important now than ever,' Alexandria said.

'I don't think we are going to have much say in that I am afraid.' Melissa paused for a moment, before coming back with her own question. 'Why did you choose me?' The question stopped Alexandria's search for the entrance she was sure didn't exist, and she snapped back at her,

'That's a question for another time.'

Looking back towards the approaching adventurers, Alexandria realised she had missed something. The door and its frame did not light up or come to life as they entered, as it usually did. Also, she didn't know how, but she had missed the fact that the walls' images were not full of life, they were not moving at all. 'Oh no!' Alexandria exclaimed, running to the door. 'What have you two done?' she shouted out at Alex and Sophie, who were just stepping off the grass and onto the first wobbly cobble of the path. They looked at each other confused.

'I don't know, what have we done?' Alex asked.

'The house, it's gone dark!' Alexandria said, whilst frantically looking over the doorframe, touching it at every point, hoping to find its magic.'Wait a minute. It's not you at all. You have the dragonfly Alex, that's why,' she said, answering her own accusatory question. And proving her point, as soon as Alex stepped through the door, the room came to life. The door lit up, the floor around the tree Melissa was standing next to moved, the cobbles individually raising and falling, creating a cobbled wave. Melissa jumped back and found a non moving area of floor to stand on.

'That's new!' Alexandria said. The wall, the window to the Dragonfly island on Heart that wrapped around the cottage, was not showing its usual, familiar view. What was there now was quite different. The view was changing. It was as though the cottage was flicking through a photographic library of places. The images spun round the room, one crashing into the next with a blur. Sophie was a few steps behind Alex, and the others a few steps behind her, so none of them had seen what was happening inside. Stepping in and seeing the fast spinning images on the walls, Sophie instantly felt motion sick and grabbed hold of the front door's handle to steady herself. As soon as she did, the walls stopped their mass of colliding images and focused on one very familiar view.

'It's your garden Sophie,' Alex said. Grandmother, Vicky, Anchor and Bart had made their way past Sophie and into the room.

'Looks like they are still there then,' Melissa said. Bouncing off the garden's alive trees, bushes and unseasonable blooming flowers, were the flashing blue lights of the police vehicles that appeared to still fill the square, their home.

'Guess we won't be going back home in a hurry!' Vicky said. The motion sickness passing, Sophie let go of the handle. The live action view into grandmother's Dragonfly Manor garden remained.

'How did you end up there?' asked Alexandria, directing the question at Melissa.

'Trying to stay hidden, like you asked,' Melissa replied. Vicky laughed and said,

'Good job! You are about as far from being hidden as you could be.' Sensing a little awkwardness, grandmother returned the focus back to the search for the cave.

'The floor is moving. There, by the tree.' Grandmother was pointing towards the spot Melissa had jumped away from.

'I know. It started when Alex came in,' Melissa said. Alex walked over to the wobbling cobbles, squatted down and reached out to touch them. As soon as his hand made contact, the movement stopped.

'I am sure that's where I was standing,' Sophie said. She walked over and joined Alex to get a closer look. 'Yes, this is the spot. I was looking at that hole in the tree.' Standing next to Alex, she said quietly for no one else to hear, 'We aren't crazy are we? This is all happening right?' Alex stood up.

'Why are we looking for the cave? Should we not be focusing on why we came here in the first place?' he asked.

'What was that reason?' Alexandria asked.

'Actually, I don't really know. We were led here by last night's events. It just seemed right,' Alex replied.

'We are here to do what we can, to bring help to those that need it. We are here, as Alex, Sophie, the two of you are the tomorrow today. You are the beginning of what Earth and Heart need. What we need to do now is find out what you can do, together.' Grandmother's wise words brought all back to the reality of why yesterday's journey had begun. 'Alex, you have the dragonfly with you. Sophie, you have something very new. Given to you both by the first, the one that no one has seen since Shuing. The one who made the healing of Earth possible. This is not something that can be taken lightly. Alexandria, I know you want to keep your son hidden, but you must see, that is not the way forward.' She looked over for some sort of confirmation from Alexandria who was staring at Alex, the baby she had left with Melissa sixteen years ago.

'But if he doesn't stay hidden, if they find him, if they get hold of him, they will kill him for what has become part of him. My heart will not survive losing him again!' Alexandria said, tears running down her face, showing the first sign of vulnerability since they had all met. Melissa made her way over and took her in her arms. She felt her pain. She had lived through sixteen years of fear of making the wrong move, the fear that whatever she was hiding him from would find him. The sixteen years of mixed emotions, love, loss, continual change, had left her tired.

'We have no choice,' Sophie said confidently. For the first time in her life, she actually felt as though she was where she was supposed to be, with people she was supposed to be with. She was comfortable and ready for whatever was to come next. Going backwards was not an option for her. Anchor suddenly broke the reflective moment as he started bounding around the tree, intermittently jumping up at it, pushing himself off it, running to Sophie, back to the tree again and repeating the process.

'You need the toilet boy?' Vicky asked, getting a laugh from the others. It made him stop, throw an evil look in her direction and bark his response, which this time was understood, not only by grandmother but also by Sophie and Alex.

'There, you think we should go there?' Sophie said. Grandmother smiled.

'You have it don't you, you have the ear to hear on Earth?'

'Ear to hear?' Melissa asked.

'Yes, they understand him,' grandmother replied, pointing at Anchor. The "there" Anchor was excited about and that grandmother had correctly realised was understood by Sophie and Alex, was Heart. The group hadn't noticed, but the wall surrounding them had changed again. The view was now of the island on Heart.

'But how, how could we possibly get there?' Sophie asked.

'The dragonfly. You have the key so try it,' grandmother said, pointing to the closed big old door. Alex cautiously walked over to it, took hold of the handle and opened the door. Nothing. The pinpricks of light that had returned as Alex and Sophie had entered, although still alight, were a dull light, and the door frame, although alive, was calm. Grandmother joined him. She purposely closed the door, and then took hold of his right hand, the one with the mark that he had thought was a mole for so many years, and placed it back on the handle. Taking his left hand she told him to point to and touch one of the dulled lights. As soon as he did, all the pinpricks of light shone bright. Laser thin lights shot across and bounced off the walls of the room. Letting go of his hands, she said,

'Now turn the handle in the opposite direction to the way you would think to open the door.' Slowly he did as instructed. The handle squeaked. There was a clunk, and the door was free to open again.

'Pull it open then!' Vicky said, standing at what she considered was a safe distance. Slowly Alex opened the door.

'I don't understand,' grandmother said. The view beyond the door was no different to the one she had closed the door to.

'If he is supposed to be the one, why has nothing changed,' grandmother questioned. She was so sure of what was going to happen.

'Things are not the same as they once were Alex. You have more than before, but remember only as two. You know what to do.' The voice of the dragonfly echoed around his head. He left the door and went over to Sophie and said,

'Come with me.' Taking her hand, he walked, not over to the front door, but to the tree. Lifting his right hand and her left, he placed them on the tree. They were standing exactly where Sophie was convinced she had been standing when she blinked and was suddenly under water in the cave. 'Ask yourself where it all started. It was not with a red front door. This is the place it all began.' With their hands on the tree together, the lights shining from the front door disappeared, lost, as wobbling, twisting, incredibly bright, colourful lights appeared in the grooves of the bark of the tree. So bright, it forced the onlookers to squint their eyes to have any chance of being able to watch the show.

'Where do you want to go?' The dragonfly spoke to Alex.

'The cave,' Sophie replied, having heard the question as Alex did. As soon as she said that, the cobbles beneath all of them wobbled violently, a bright white light shone up and around each of them. The room heated up, the red front door's lights, the doorframe's lights, the tree's lights, the floor's lights, all came together and swirled around the onlookers, dancing between them, brushing their skin, making them tingle. They were all aware of a loving energy that was hugging them, building up to something they were convinced was going to be wonderful. Bart and Anchor sat motionless, watching all that was going on. Vicky was spinning, her arms out, splitting the colours as they swirled around her. Alexandria was still in Mellisa's arms, whilst grandmother was watching with a huge smile on her face, taking in a magic she had never seen. Sensing the energies were about to reach their peak, Alex and Sophie took their hands off the tree. In an instant they were somewhere else. The cave.

'Where have they gone?' Melissa screamed in a panic. Only two had returned to the cave, Alex and Sophie. The rest left behind in the now dark, quiet, cold, motionless Dragonfly island cottage. 'Alex!' Melissa shouted, there was no response. She ran out of the house, out on to the grass. 'Alex!' She screamed again as loud as she could.

'He will be fine. They will be fine,' Alexandria said having followed Melissa. It was her turn to become the comforter.

'They can't be left alone. If what you said, "if they find him they will kill him" is true, we have to find him,' Melissa said, panic and fear turning into rage.

'Calm down my dear. All will be well,' Grandmother said, who along with the remaining others had also left the cottage. Melissa needed a moment. Before they could comfort her any further, she walked away from the arriving group and into the wooded area behind the cottage.

'So what now then?' Vicky asked.

'They are together, they are where they need to be. We just need to get to where we need to be,' grandmother said.

'But where is that?' Alexandria asked.

'Not here. With Sophie and Alex gone and having taken the dragonfly with them, this place may no longer be hidden. There is a chance that my grandchildren could see us and this island if they are looking,' grandmother said.

'She is right. Melissa, we are leaving. Come on, you have to come with us,' Alexandria shouted in the direction Melissa had disappeared. With no response, Anchor, his nose to the ground, went off in search of the missing party.

It didn't take him long to find her. She was sitting on a rock the other side of the small island, looking out over the south side of the loch, off towards the mountains in the distance. His huge paws thumping on the ground, Melissa could hear him coming from quite a distance, so she didn't get a fright when he arrived at her side, giving her hand a nudge as he did. Wiping the tears she had been crying away, she hugged him round his thick, furry neck. She knew she had to return to the group; she knew that whatever was coming next she had to stay strong and be confident that Alex was going to be fine. She knew him well. He was strong; he had been her rock as much as she had been his over the years. He had only been gone for a few moments, but Melissa missed him already.

Chapter 3

Back in the cave they both first saw in a dream, the cave that on their first visit had the dragonfly join with them, Sophie and Alex were once again alone.

'Why haven't the others come with us?' Sophie asked. Alex, wondering the same thing, had no answer for her. However, seeing as it was Sophie that had answered the question from the dragonfly, he also had a question for her,

'Did you hear the dragonfly?'

'Of course, that's why we are here!' Sophie was a little confused why he had asked. She assumed everyone had heard, and that she was just the first to answer. Alex informed her that that was not the case at all. Trying to figure out how Sophie had heard the dragonfly, they went over the sequence of events that led up to them finding themselves back in the cave. Two things stood out as being different to all the other times the dragonfly spoke to Alex. Firstly, their hands were on the tree, and secondly, their hands were on each other's. Their conclusion reached, another questioned popped into Alex's head,

'Sophie, how do we get out of here? There are no doorways or trees, and I don't think the way we did before is an option!'

'I hadn't thought about that,' Sophie replied. Looking around, everything was just as it was on their last visit. The small, freshwater stream Alex had followed to the underground lake, which was full again, was flowing freely. The gems, sparkling in the opening of a tunnel at the far end of the lake, were still giving out a gentle light to the cave.

'That could be a way!' Alex said, pointing at the tunnel. Sophie didn't respond, she was heading carefully up the rocky stream.

Still not completely sure how communication with the dragonfly worked, Alex asked the "how do we get out of here," question in his head, hoping for clarification that they were heading in the right direction. The ancient dragonfly was limited in what help he could give. Having found Alex and Sophie, Heart's continued existence was still by no means a certainty. As much as he wanted to, the dragonfly could not intervene. The choices had to be Alex and Sophie's.

'This is your journey Alex. Your heart and instincts have found this place. Your mind holds the answers, the memories from thousands of years of your families generations that have come and gone. You need time to grow, learn and understand what has gone before and what can be. Listen to all that is around you, take in what you see, and remember, every door needs a key.' The dragonfly went silent. His thoughtful words buzzing around Alex's head, Alex was curious,

'Did you hear that?' he asked Sophie. She hadn't, which confirmed that either their hands on the tree, or on each other's, was definitely how she had heard the dragonfly before.

'What did you hear?' Sophie asked. Alex repeated the words exactly. 'So he didn't give you a way out then?'

'Nope! Well actually maybe he did.' Alex was referring to the dragonfly's last words, "remember, every door needs a key." Both Alex and Sophie went silent thinking about what the dragonfly had said, but also to concentrate on not falling as they walked along the slippery, uneven ground of the stream. Arriving at the edge of the lake, Sophie stopped and gestured towards the place she had been laying under the water,

'That must have been really creepy to see!' Sophie said.

'It really was. Especially with your eyes being open,' Alex replied. The tunnel leading away from the cave that the two had decided was to be their escape route, was not easy to get to. Their choices were to swim across the lake and make the short climb up to it, or they could somehow make it along the rock face which extended along the far side of the lake. Having dried off from their first dunk into the cold water, they decided that staying dry would be preferable.

Alex was fit, always at his sports, Sophie not so much. Living her life with her head always in a book, her body was more used to sitting, curled up on a nice soft chair, her bed, or one of the old extremely uncomfortable chairs in the school's library reading. The most exercise she got was pushing an over excited Anchor off her whenever she returned home. So, she was a little nervous about the rock wall traverse. Having made their way along the side of the lake to where the slippery moss stopped and the rock face began, Alex said,

'Look, there is a ledge we can use.' It was about five foot up from where they were standing. Alex jumped up and grabbed at an indentation in the rock face a couple of feet above the ledge itself, and pulled himself up. Once he had got his footing on the skinny ledge, he reached down to give Sophie a hand. She was looking around trying to find a way to climb up herself. There was no way, being short, she was going to be able to repeat Alex's gymnastics.

'I am fine, you go ahead,' Sophie said, not wanting to be seen as a damsel in distress.

'Come on, just take my hand. You are the one with the brains, let me be of some use,' Alex said. Sophie ignored him. As keen as he was to impress her, so she was him, so she persisted with her search for a way up. All she needed was one little rock sticking out a couple of feet up, to give her the help she needed. Just as Sophie turned to walk away from the lake along the rock face, her back to Alex, he jumped down. As quickly as he did, he grabbed her waist and lifted her up.

'Hey, put me down!' Sophie snapped at him. Alex calmly said,

'Just grab the rock sticking out, you can do the rest.' Realising that Alex had lifted her up to a perfect sticking out rock, which meant she still had some work to do to get herself on to the ledge, she conceded. Having pulled herself up, she was now in front of Alex, which meant she would lead the way, in charge. She shuffled along the ledge out over the water. With Sophie now out of his way, Alex was clear to jump back up.

'Be careful, the ledge will be as slippery…' before he could finish his sentence, embarrassingly, one of his big feet slipped. He tried to grab the protruding rock Sophie had used which was at waist height, but it was too late, his weight and momentum were going the wrong way. Sophie couldn't help herself, she laughed out loud at his over confident misfortune.

'Yeh, yeh, ok,' was Alex's response to the laughter. His efforts at trying to take charge and impressing her having failed, for the third time, he climbed back up to the ledge and quickly caught up with Sophie, who, having got her technique sorted out, was flying along the ledge. It was about fifteen metres to the cave tunnel, so it didn't take long for them to get there. The tunnel, another five feet above the ledge, with no easy way up, meant that this time Sophie was happy to get a helping hand. She reached up and grabbed hold of the bottom edge of the tunnel opening. Alex, with his feet firmly on the ledge, his right hand holding on to a hole in the rock face and his other arm locked into his side, used his hand for Sophie to step onto and climb up.

'How are you getting up? Do you need some help?' Sophie asked with a smirk. Alex's response was a very careful and controlled jump, which took him just high enough to get his elbows to land on the tunnel's floor. Pausing for a second to make sure he wasn't going to slip back, he then pushed himself up, just as he would getting out of a swimming pool, in one quick, impressive movement.

'Show off!' Sophie said, whilst playfully hitting his shoulder.

'Looks kind of dark along there!' Alex said. Looking beyond the gem covered walls into the darkness, Sophie was well aware of how dark it was, and that she had been there before! In her nightmares! Where the beast haunted her, hunted her down and trapped her at a dead end, just before she would wake up. Just as the bright-eyed rescuer would appear. Sophie so much wanted to tell Alex to go first, but again she didn't want to seem weak. So, already in front, she made her way through the cave tunnel of gems, toward the dark.

Alex, too busy focusing on the darkness ahead, missed that he was getting very close to one of the tunnel walls. So close, he finally brushed his hand over a particularly sharp part.

'Well that was uncomfortable,' he said, whipping has hand away from the wall. Sophie turned round to look just in time to see a much brighter light being given off by the other gems, emanating from the one gem Alex had touched. As she walked over to get a closer look, it faded and returned to match the light of all the others.

'Did you see that?' she asked.

'See what?' Alex replied,

'The light on the wall.' Alex looked over to where she was pointing. 'It was seriously bright.' With no sign of what Sophie had seen, curious, Alex reached out and touched the gem he calculated was the one that had caught his hand. It lit up instantly. Leaving his hand on the bright gem, sparkles began dancing out from it, round his hand and up his arm.

'Does it hurt?' Sophie asked, concerned for Alex. To her, it looked he was holding a celebratory sparkler. The hot end!

'No, not at all,' Alex replied. He wondered if the other gems would have the same reaction. Slowly at first, he ran his hands over the wall, touching each gem in every colour of the rainbow as he passed them. Sophie stepped back to give him space, and to give herself a better view of the display. The effect was amazing. As his hand moved from gem to gem, it took with it a trail of sparkles, at the same time giving off an electrical crackling sound, like a shooting star was making its way across the tunnel wall. Apart from the occasional stab from a sharper gem, he felt no pain, just energy.

'Sophie, you have to try this!' Alex was filled with excitement, the energy revitalising him from the two days of stress, worry and pain he had lived through. 'It feels amazing. Come on try it.' Peer pressure was not something either of them had ever been swayed by, it would usually push them in completely the opposite direction, but on this occasion, seeing how happy Alex looked, Sophie wanted to try. Holding her breath, she slowly reached for a bright red gem that had caught her eye, one that hadn't yet been touched by Alex. The moment her dainty index finger made contact with it, the colours covering her body from her dragonfly bite began to swirl, light up and warm her entirely. Unlike the gems Alex touched which got brighter, hers was dimming! The thought that she was taking the life of the gem away made her instantly remove her hand.

'Alex, I can't,' Sophie said. He was dashing backwards and forwards, running his hands over the walls on both sides of the tunnel, over the low ceiling, enjoying the recharge he was experiencing.

'Can't what?' Alex said with an out of breath voice,

'Look.' Sophie pointed at the dull-looking gem. Alex, high on the energy, danced his way over to her to get a look. Without thinking, he touched the gem which instantly did as every other one did - it filled with brightness and spat out its sparkles.

'I don't understand!' a sad-looking Sophie said. She turned and walked away towards the dark tunnel. Alex sensed her change in mood and let go of the walls. He wanted so much for her to feel what he had.

'Hold my hand,' he said to the slow moving Sophie. 'Come on whenever we are connected things seem to happen. So hold my hand!' he said again. His positiveness washing over her, she stopped. Without turning to face him, she lifted her hand up behind her back for Alex to take hold of, which he did. Alex then placed his free hand back on the gem-filled wall and Sophie received what he hoped she would. The hairs on her freckle-covered arms stood up. Even the thick red hair on her head lifted slightly with the electricity that was passing between them. Feeling the same high as Alex was, Sophie realised exactly why she drained the gems, and why Alex seemed to bring them to life.

'It's the dragonfly. Its magic gives life,' she said. The realisation gave her confidence that their journey into the dark tunnel was not going to be quite as scary as she had first thought.

Turning round, Sophie looked up at Alex's smiling face. The eyes were back!

Her tunnel saviour's eyes were far from as bright as the gems he touched, but shone with the purple she had become obsessed with in her dreams. She joined Alex running up and down the tunnel, her hand holding his, her other hand touching whichever side Alex wasn't. With the two connected, she was having the same effect on the gems as he was. The sound of their laughter and the crackles from the sparkling gems echoed around the tunnel, into the dark tunnel and out into the cave with the lake at its base.

Intoxicated by the experience, a massive crash brought the experience to a sudden end. Snapped out of their bliss, something had fallen, crashed to the ground. The crashing sound was replaced with a whooshing sound, as the tunnel filled with dust.

'Alex!' Sophie yelled, 'I can't see anything!' The dust was so thick they didn't know if they were facing back towards the lake or into the dark tunnel.

'Don't let go of my hand!' Alex shouted back. Trying to escape the dust that was making it hard to breathe, he pulled her to the ground. Huddled together, their free hands covering their noses and mouths to protect their lungs from the dust, they waited for it to settle. It took some time, but finally it did. As the air cleared, they looked in the direction they had hoped was their way out, hoping that it still could be.

'Do you think that was our fault?' Alex asked. Sophie stood up as she continued to try to focus on what may have fallen.

'I guess it could have been.'

Alex shook his head. As he did, his curly hair bouncing produced a cloud of dust which puffed around him. He then wiped his face and patted down his arms, body and legs to remove as much dust as he could. Having done what he could, he turned his attention to Sophie who looked like she had been caught in a sandstorm. Brushing her shoulder clean, he couldn't help but laugh,

'Looks like you have aged a bit!' Her long, curly, thick red hair looked grey. Her face was covered in the same pale dust that covered him. It was so thick it hid her freckles, her eyebrows and her eyelashes, making her look like a ghost. Without invitation, Alex lifted her hair up and rubbed it, which created a much larger cloud of dust than had come off his own. Sophie joined in, happy to be patting him down, as he was her. Having completed the task as best they could and their eyes having gone through their natural reaction of filling up with tears to clear the scratchy dust, they both looked back along the tunnel. Whatever had fallen was further along the dark tunnel than they could see.

'I guess we should go and have a look then hey!' Sophie said.

'Yep!' Alex replied.

'You know what, I think you can go first!' Sophie instructed Alex. Still full of the revitalising energy he had received, he was happy to. With each step they took more dust fell from them, until, after about one hundred metres, their ghost-like appearances had completely fallen to the tunnel floor. Sophie's confidence restored, she moved from behind and joined him, side by side, equal partners in their adventure.

The light given off by the gems at the tunnel entrance was just about gone. Their eyes adjusted to the darkness as best they could. They were just about able to make out shapes.

'What was that?' Alex, who had been hit in the face by Sophie's long hair, asked in a panic.

'A gust of wind,' Sophie replied. She turned to look where it had come from. 'Do you see that?' Sophie asked. The gust of wind had come from a tunnel they had both missed in the dark, to the side of them. Stepping back to investigate, Sophie could just make out a green light far off into the distance. 'I am not imagining that am I?' Sophie questioned, as she pulled Alex to have a look.

'If you are talking about the green light, nope, you are not!' Alex replied. As they assessed whether or not they should head towards it, Sophie's heart stopped. She heard a familiar sound. The terrifying sound from her dreams. It came from behind them, from the dark tunnel they had been heading down. The growl was closely followed by the sound of heavy paws slipping over rubble,

'Well, what do you say to heading this way?' Alex asked, already pushing Sophie in the direction of the green light. More than happy with Alex's suggestion, she dodged another shove from him and stepped aside to let him go first.

Leaving the easy to walk in, possibly dangerous tunnel, they headed at speed towards the green light, hoping it would give them the exit they were looking for, and an escape from whatever was coming for them.

Getting closer to the light, the tunnel got smaller. Before they knew it, they were on their hands and knees, before finally having no choice but to lie flat and crawl. The sound of whatever was in the tunnel behind them, the sound from Sophie's nightmares, seemed to have stopped, which they were very pleased about. However, the ever reducing size of the tunnel they had chosen to escape down, was something they were not so pleased about,

'I am not liking this!' Alex said, his size making it harder for him to keep going than Sophie. With the walls pressing on his shoulders, he managed to get his arms out in front of him to help pull him along. He was finding it hard to breathe. Sophie, for the first time in her life, was happy to be as small as she was, plus she had an escape route behind her, well sort of.

Pitch black, other than the green light that didn't seem to be getting any closer, Alex could feel panic starting to set in. Stopping for a moment, he closed his eyes in an effort to calm himself down. Slow breathing, trying to think of anything other than where he was, he tried to bring his heart rate down.

'Alex you ok?' Sophie asked. Not getting a response from the motionless, meditating Alex, she pulled herself right up behind him and tapped on his ankle. 'Alex, can you hear me?' she asked. With one more deep breath Alex opened his eyes. As he did, he realised the green light they were heading towards, that he thought was still far away in the distance, was right in front of him. They had reached a dead end. The light they had been heading towards was actually coming from a tiny hole. Alex closed his eyes again and somehow, through the fast returning panic, he managed to speak calmly,

'It's a dead end. Sophie, I can't turn round. You need to go back, please, as quick as you can!' Sophie thought for a moment. It was easy enough for her to crawl back, but she was conscious that whatever the light was, was the only light they had seen, plus there was the growling to consider.

'Are you sure Alex? Is the wall solid rock?' she asked. Alex assumed it was, but with his eyes still closed he reached forward to touch it. His assumption was wrong. His hand was not met with a solid surface. Instead, his hand went straight through a thin wall of dust, loose mud and small broken rocks that fell away, opening up a hole big enough for Alex and Sophie to get through.

With the blockage gone, Alex could feel a different kind of air to that of the tunnel on his skin. Realising he may have an escape from the tunnel that felt like a coffin, Alex opened his eyes. Even though he couldn't see properly, his eyes having to adjust from the darkness to the light, his toes dug into the ground and he pushed himself forward, clearing his shoulders from being trapped. His arms were finally free from the tunnel and he stretched out into open air. With a mighty push on the outer walls, he pulled himself forward, breaking free from the claustrophobic tunnel.

'Oh crap!' Alex exclaimed. Unable to see clearly, what he hadn't realised was that yes, they had found another cave, but they were in fact ten feet up from the ground and he was about to fall head first to whatever was below. Somehow, he managed to jam his feet on to the roof of the small tunnel and wedge his knees on to the floor. The instinctive action created an anchor, saving him from what would have been a painful ending. His torso now floating in midair, he wasn't sure how he was going to get down.

'What can you see?' Sophie asked. It took a few moments, but his eyes finally adjusted to the light of the small cave.

'Sophie, can you hold on to my legs? I am going to try to shuffle back towards you a bit.' Doing as he asked, she braced herself as best she could to help him. With a couple of wiggles and jumps, and a bit of help from his hands he had braced on the cold rocky wall, Alex got himself into a less precarious position. Once getting himself as comfortable as he could be, he had a proper assessment of their situation, after which he said,

'Ok, so we have another cave. The floor I reckon is about ten foot down.' Looking up, he could see that the ceiling was different to that of the cave with the lake they had not long left. The ceiling was not covered in roots, it was covered in branches from fully grown trees. The green light that was bathing the cave, that had guided them, was coming from thousands of small pods hanging from every branch.

Continuing his visual search, Alex saw thick tree trunks equally spaced all the way round the cave walls. Between them were hanging vines covered in flowers. He reached up, grabbed hold of one of the vines, and gave it a firm yank. It appeared to be well fixed to wherever it had grown from. 'I think I have found a way for us to get down,' Alex said to Sophie. 'You aren't going to believe this place!'

Having wiggled his way free, again, with some help from an eager to see what Alex was seeing Sophie, Alex was quickly out of the tunnel and hanging on the vine.

'Come on, I will help you,' Alex instructed the very excited to be out of the darkness Sophie. He was right, Sophie was amazed at what she saw - it was a little forest deep in the earth. Full of colour and smells, a beautifulness that she could have never imagined.

Alex pulled another vine free from the wall and passed it to Sophie. 'Don't worry, I will make sure you're ok.' He held on to Sophie's arm as she climbed out of the tunnel and took hold of the vine. She didn't need any help at all - as quick as she was out, Sophie was down the vine and on the ground. As lush and new as the cave felt and looked, the ground was not what either of them had expected. It was soft, like an underground meadow.

'Wow, this is incredible,' Sophie said, feeling safe enough to allow herself to take it all in. The vines they had lowered themselves down on were swaying slowly, free from them and the wall. On closer inspection, Sophie noticed that they looked different to the rest. There was a vein of purple light that ran through them, up to the canopy of trees. Having pointed out her find, Alex reached for a vine that didn't have the purple light. As soon as he made contact with it, the lightless vine came to life. Alex followed the light with his eyes as it quickly rose up the vine, up into the trees, until it came to a stop. As the light's journey came to an end at one of the branches covered in pods, the first pod on the branch pulsed. Alex looked back to the two vines they had climbed down and followed the light to where they stopped, to see if the same thing had happened. It had.

'Sophie, you try it,' Alex ordered. She did. However, just as with the gems in the cave's tunnel, she did not have the same effect on the vine that Alex did.

'It's the dragonfly Alex, I told you,' Sophie said, a bit disappointed she didn't have whatever Alex did, and a little annoyed he kept finding ways to point it out to her. She got over it quickly as stepping back, she touched the trunk of the tree next to her, and it reacted. It rumbled, the roots that ran around the walls' edges that seemed to connect each of the trees to each other, rose slightly from the ground, and right in the centre of the room an image appeared! The image was of the inside of the Dragonfly island cottage.

'That has to be our way out!' Sophie exclaimed excitedly. Making their way over to the floating image, they were stopped in their tracks by a sudden shooting pain which they both felt. Alex's hand and Sophie's neck - their dragonfly bites. The pain caused Sophie to throw her head back. As she did, looking up, she exclaimed,

'Alex!' She pointed at the first pulsing pod. It was not giving off any green light or pulsing any more. It was dark. Empty. Open! 'If that is where that pain just came from, there are two more!' Sophie said in a panicked voice. They watched as the pulsing of the two remaining lit pods got more intense. With nowhere to hide, they braced themselves. The branch that was connected to the vine Sophie had climbed down on, passed to her by Alex, was the first to go.

The second pod burst open and they watched as a lightening bolt shot right at them, splitting into two as it got closer. Once again they felt the shooting pain, just as sharp, just as painful as the first, and there was one more to come. As the third one struck, Sophie couldn't help but let out a scream. Angrily she said to Alex,

'Do not touch another vine!' She wasn't going to get any argument from him. Having given out her warning, Sophie turned and walked away from Alex, towards the assumed exit - the floating image in the centre of the cave,

'Sophie! Your neck, the bite, it's moving!' Alex said, stepping closer for a better look. Right in the centre of the bite he saw the tiniest of movement. 'Sophie, it's dragonflies! They are coming out of you!'

'What!' Freaking out at the grossness of the thought of insects coming out of her, Sophie began running in circles, shaking her whole body as she did.

'Hey, calm down, calm down, it's fine,' Alex said, managing to grab one of her arms to stop her spinning. Holding her tight so she couldn't escape, he focused on the three newborns. Their tiny wings buzzed into life as they pulled their bodies from Sophie's. Freaking out inside, Sophie felt a breeze, which intensified as their wings sped up in preparation for flight. Finally taking off, heading straight for Alex, he let Sophie go and took a couple of steps back to get out of their way, then to the side, and then the other side. It didn't matter where he stepped, they carried on heading in his direction. Accepting that he was not going to escape the remarkably quick-moving babies, he stopped, then calmly lifted his hand to give them a place to land. As each one settled on him, he felt a slight sting and then their tiny feet walking. They were heading towards the site of his dragonfly bite.

As they got closer to the bite, Alex felt a flutter on his back, followed by a warmth which spread over his shoulder and made its way down his arm. The feeling seeped into his hand and Alex saw what had been his invisible veins hidden under his skin, fill up with an illuminous light. Sophie saw it also, and couldn't help her shocked intake of breath.

'Can you feel that?' she asked, her heart still racing, freaked out by their new friends just having crawled out of her. Curiosity got the better of her, as she pulled the sleeve of Alex's top up his arm as high as she could. His whole arm was the same, each vein visible with the bright light that filled them up.

'It just feels warm. It's actually nice when you get over the oddness of it,' Alex replied. Turning their focus back to his hand, they watched as the light that was travelling through his veins, reached his bite, exited and engulfed the tiny dragonflies, hiding them from sight for a moment. Alex could feel something was changing, they seemed heavier. With a blink of the eye the light was gone and the tiny dragonflies were visible again. But they weren't tiny any more. Each one had grown to about three inches in length and were disappearing, sinking into his hand. Just as the dragonfly back at grandmother's Dragonfly Manor, and the dragonfly he had on his back did, they settled under his skin. A free moving, living tattoo.

'Well, we were told "together, always together." Seems one way or another, that is going to be the way of it,' Alex said.

Turning his attention to the floating image, his desire to leave the cave took over as he continued, 'I think we should see if that floating image you created is a doorway back.'

'Don't you think we need a moment to acknowledge what has just happened here before we run away?' Sophie replied.

'Run away?' Alex said, unhappy at her assumption. 'I am not running away from anything!' Sensing she had said something wrong, and feeling uncomfortable at his tone of voice, Sophie turned away and awkwardly walked towards the tree she had touched to create the doorway. Alex knew how he had sounded. His defensive response was a new thing for him. After years of being bullied, years of people thinking he was something he wasn't, years of his only protector being his mum, Melissa, his newfound confidence to stand up and not allow people to push him down left him feeling awful. 'Sophie, I am sorry. I didn't mean for it to come out like that!' He made his way over to her and took her hand. 'It's not who I am, it's just…' Sophie interrupted,

'It's ok, I get it.'

The fact he had gone over to her and said what he had, was enough. Him taking her hand softly instantly brought tears to her eyes. Completely out of character for her, just like she was back at grandmother's Dragonfly Manor, she removed her hand from his, wrapped her arms round him and resting her head on his chest, squeezed him tight. She had feelings for him that made little sense to her, but in a very different way, made more sense than anything she had ever known. Alex returned the hug with one hand squeezing her back, the other getting caught in her matted, dusty, thick hair as he held the back of her head. 'Do you feel what I do?' Sophie asked. Alex wasn't really sure what she meant,

'Erm, do you mean like that we are still covered in dust?' was his awkward response. Sophie let him go and red-faced, playfully hit his arm. His response to her question that she was very unlikely to ask again, would normally have seen Sophie retreating into her loner shell, but not this time. In fact, she went further than she would have thought she would ever have, 'I know you do. We have something more than the sum of our experiences over the last couple of days.'

Alex looked into her still tear-filled eyes, 'It's more than what we are supposed to do according to grandmother, or that dragonfly on your back. I know you. I have this feeling inside that I want to tell you something I can't believe I am about to.'

Sophie walked past Alex, away from the trees and towards the middle of the room where the doorway was fading and said, 'The moment I really saw you, my heart melted. Whatever is to come, no matter what happens on this journey, my heart is yours.'

Alex was overwhelmed by her words. For years he had been closed off to the possibility of a real connection with anyone because of his continual changing, moving from place to place life, and the nastiness of the people he encountered. Although not happy about it, he had accepted his lot in life.

He didn't say a word, he couldn't! In a moment of certainty, he walked into the light shining from the doorway where Sophie stood. He could feel her bright green eyes looking right into his soul. The emotions unexplainably took his breath away, causing him to fall to his knees. On the floor in front of Sophie, Alex wrapped his arms around her. Lovingly placing her hands on his face, Sophie lifted his head from her abdomen and looked down into the eyes of the bright-eyed Alex, who, as much as he wanted to say how he felt, act on how he felt, couldn't. Sophie was the one who could. Sophie was the one with all the strength in that moment to bring together two people that had to be together. Bending forwards lifting his head up, she placed her lips on his and they shared the most delicate and perfect of first kisses.

'Together, always together. Your hearts are purer than any heart I have ever witnessed.'

The ancient dragonfly's voice echoed round the heads of both Alex and Sophie. The words brought an end to their kiss. Alex got to his feet, took hold of Sophie's hand and led her towards the fading floating doorway. Without hesitation he stepped in and through, pulling Sophie with him. It was no different to walking from one room to another. Stepping out of the tree that was in its centre, they were once again back in the home of Shuing - the Dragonfly island cottage.

The curved walls of the old cottage surrounding them were showing a live broadcast from the beautiful tree, flower and vine-filled cave they just left. The moving wobbly cobbles beneath their feet were settling down as Sophie made a dash for the front door, hoping to find her grandmother. As soon as she passed through the dancing with light and images doorframe and open door, out into the fresh morning air, the cottage's walls stopped moving. A frozen in time image remained.

'Interesting!' Alex said to himself as he followed Sophie and made his way out.

'They're not here!' Sophie exclaimed. Alex looked around,

'Maybe they are in the woods, or on the other side of them,' Alex said.

Even though they were able to see through the wooded area to the beach beyond it, they decided to investigate anyway. They weren't there.

'They wouldn't have left, I am sure of it,' Alex said as they made their way back to the cottage. Breaking free from the small forest, Sophie glanced across the loch,

'The van, it's gone, they've left us!'

Alex was sure they wouldn't have, that maybe she was just looking in the wrong place. It didn't take him long to realise that she wasn't, and that there was more than the van missing.

'So has the road. And look, the house we passed, it's gone too!' Alex said in a worried voice. Sophie looked for anything that was where it was supposed to be. For an explanation as to why the things that should be there weren't. Then it dawned on her,

'Alex. I think we're in Heart!'

Chapter 4

All six having squeezed back into the rickety old boat, the huge horse Troy led them across the loch, back towards the sandy beach. Alexandria, hoping the island had stayed hidden, looked back at the same time as Vicky, who said,

'I can't see it any more.'

'Thank goodness,' Alexandria replied.

'Does that mean they won't have seen it then? Oh hang on, why can't I see it? I did before!' Vicky said. Alexandria had no idea why that would be the case so didn't offer an answer, but Melissa did,

'Maybe it's because Alex has gone with the dragonfly.' Her suggestion got Alexandria's inquisitive mind thinking,

'That sort of makes sense. But if the island is still hidden, it means there is still magic there and if there is still magic, I would have thought you would still be able to see it Vicky. Odd!'

Stepping out of the loch's clear water, Troy shook his entire body. The shake started from his head, down his mane and through his muscular body. The droplets of water forced off him created a glistening fan that spread out from his steaming body. With a final flick of his tail, he was dry. The momentum of the boat as it arrived at the beach, meant its final resting place was well clear of the water, making it possible for its occupants to step out on to the beach without getting their feet wet.

'Do you want to hide the boat again?' Melissa asked. Not wanting to waste any time, she didn't wait for a response. Taking hold of the short piece of rope that hung from the boat's bow, being as strong as she was, she pulled the boat up the beach with ease by herself, back towards the same bush Alexandria had produced it from earlier that morning.

'Just leave it. I want to get back to the house,' Alexandria said assertively, as Melissa powered passed her with the boat which was creating a deep groove in the sand behind her. Having already dragged it halfway up the beach, she ignored her and carried on. Back in its hiding place, covered in the same branches that had hidden it before and tied to a tree, Melissa was happy it was well hidden, safe, in case they needed it again, which she figured was more than likely! Turning back round to see where the others were, she was just in time to see Alexandria and Troy disappearing off into the distance.

'I think that is rather rude!' grandmother said, referring to Alexandria's lack of goodbye or invitation to follow. She was feeling quite secondary to the morning's events, particularly by the way Alexandria had been avoiding her, as though she was being punished for her grandchildren's actions. Not that she felt she should be given any special treatment, but she had many decades of knowledge that could be helpful, and thoughts on why the island's magic remained with Alex and Sophie having left. She also knew with certainty that there was no way anything would have changed at Alexandria's Dragonfly home - her haste in returning was pointless. She had removed the tree that was the centre point to her home's magic. This along with her dragonfly being lost meant that all the ingredients that made her Dragonfly home an unexpectedly, splendidly, wonderfully perfect home were gone. But grandmother wasn't asked, or given the chance, to pass on her thoughts.

'Pretty sure we will catch up with her. And if we don't, it's not a problem seeing as we know where she lives!' Melissa said, opening the sliding side door of the old van for the soggy dogs to jump in. Grandmother joined Vicky, who had already climbed into the front both thankful for the long bench seat that fitted three, as neither were keen on being soaked by the back seat sitting, loving, canine duo. Not that it kept them safe, as, sitting comfortably, waiting for Melissa to climb into the driver's side, two dripping wet heads appeared between them!

The old van fired up instantly, as though it was excited to be heading off on another adventure. With a not so quick twenty point turn on the small single lane road, Melissa headed back towards the village. What felt like a very long fifteen minutes later, they were back at the entrance of the long tree-lined drive, the place they assumed was the location of Alexandria's Dragonfly home.

'Should we just go up?' Melissa asked her passengers.

'I feel that would be the best course of action,' grandmother replied. The van wasn't likely to spin its wheels as it wasn't the fastest of vehicles, but Melissa took it slow anyway, crawling down the drive which was covered in frozen moss and ice. Finally, leaving the trees that towered over them, the drive opened up and showed off a large, grassed garden leading up to the old, deserted, very grand looking house.

'That doesn't look very lived in!' Vicky said, wiping away the condensation from her window to get a better look. 'There's no sign of Alexandria or

Troy either,' she said. Melissa and grandmother didn't respond. They were both too busy figuring out if they had assumed incorrectly and it wasn't the Dragonfly house after all, and if it wasn't, where would it be? The silence was broken by a barking Anchor, who, looking out the opposite side of the van, had found life.

'Well done Anchor. But you can be quiet now!' grandmother ordered to a very proud looking German Shepherd. At the end of the drive which weaved past the grand old house, off to the side, was a small cottage surrounded and partially hidden by tall trees, with very dead looking plants, bushes and patchy grass leading up to it. The only visible parts were an iron gate, a short wobbly cobbly path and a slightly open, very dull looking red front door, which Troy appeared to be standing guard to the side of.

Melissa stopped the van, and they all piled out. Paying no attention to the big, old, creepy looking abandoned house, they headed straight for the cottage. Vicky's vision was back to its normal state and with no-one waiting to help her, Bart was happy to be back at her side in his role of guardian. Arriving at the cottage's front door, Troy nodded knowingly and took a step to the side.

'Helloooo!' grandmother said as she peeked her head inside the open door. There was no answer, so the group made their way in.

It really was a small cottage. Directly in front of them was a very steep, tiny staircase that made its way up the back wall. To the side of it was a large hole in the floor with some skirting board and a part of the wall above it missing, where the tree Alexandria said she had removed once lived. Only two doors were in the hallway, both of which were open. Through one they could see a broken down, smaller version of grandmother's kitchen, and through the other, what looked like a cross between a library and a sitting room, equally as old, messy and well used looking. Being winter, the cottage was cold. With the front door open and no sign of a fire being lit in either of the rooms, it was no surprise they could all see their breath as they looked about.

A bang came from the kitchen. The sound of a door being slammed shut. Anchor being his brave self, moved quickly to defend and protect… himself! Cowering behind grandmother, he watched as Vicky, although shaken by the bang, did the opposite. With Bart at her side, she walked in. Her confident walk nearly ended in a collision as a fast moving Alexandria appeared holding an axe. The offensive item put Bart into full protect mode, his bark so aggressive it even took Vicky by surprise. Anchor stayed hidden.

'It's ok,' Alexandria said. Quickly realising what the problem was, she dropped the axe. With her free hand Vicky patted Bart on his head and told him how good he had been, calm was restored. Although no longer barking, Bart continued a quiet, slightly threatening growl. 'What's the axe for?' Vicky asked.

'The tree,' was her reply. Stepping clear of the door so that all could see her, grandmother pointed out that the tree hadn't been there for some time. To which Alexandria responded,

'No, but I have parts of it out the back. I wanted to make sure it hadn't started growing again.' There were a few moments of awkward silence until Alexandria broke it with a worried look on her face. Directing questions at grandmother she asked, 'So what do we do now? Where have the kids gone?'

Hearing the concern in her voice, grandmother felt guilty for thinking bad thoughts after she felt ignored and abandoned at the loch's beach.

'I have every confidence the children will be fine, they are both stronger than they know. For whatever reason they have disappeared, I am sure they will return. By my calculations, their return has to be back at the island. With every dragonfly on earth being lost, that could be the only place they could return to.' Grandmother paused for a moment as she thought on before speaking. 'Having said that…! We should be prepared for something quite different. I know what should be, what had been, what I have been told, and learnt, but for the two to have been chosen, not just the one! Hmmmm… Anything could happen.'

'So should we stay here, go to the island or go back to your Dragonfly Manor?' Melissa asked.

'I think we should remain here. We cannot be seen at, or near the island, just in case my granddaughter is looking for us. But we must watch for them.' Grandmother walked over to and out of the small front door. Scurrying down the wobbly cobbly path, she made her way out of the gate to where she could see the big old house. 'Do you think we could see the loch and the island from the top floor of that house?' she asked Alexandria.

'Yes. Probably,' was her reply. Grandmother had made an assumption, as it turned out correctly, that Alexandria had something to do with the big old creepy place.

Alexandria's Dragonfly Cottage, and variations of it, had been there for many thousands of years. However, the big creepy house had only appeared one hundred and fifty years earlier, built by a nasty and incredibly arrogant man from a city many hundreds of miles away. He had been passing through the area but got trapped there because of a snowstorm. After a week of being trapped, the snow finally melted enough for him to leave, but he had become captivated by the area's beauty. There was also something else that attracted him to the place that he couldn't quite put his finger on! So, being the arrogant man he was, before leaving, he decided that where the Dragonfly cottage sat was going to be the place he would build a statement country home, grand enough to show off to his peers. With no one to challenge him, he claimed the land around the cottage as his own.

What he thought would be an easy thing to do, did not turn out to be! Nothing he did, no matter how many threats or how much money he threw at it, nothing, would get rid of the fabulously wonderful Dragonfly Cottage, so instead, refusing to be beaten, he built the big old creepy house that stood empty, the house grandmother pointed at.

Alexandria's mother had told her stories of the abuse her grandmother and great grandmother had received at his hands. Ultimately, if he couldn't demolish the cottage, he was going to try his best to get rid of its occupants. Of course being a Dragonfly home, that was never going to happen. Ten short years later he died in unexplained circumstances. Being as self-centred as he was, he had no family, no heirs to leave the house and its land to. It was left to rot. Decades later, a very particular attention to detail obsessed record keeper of land and property came visiting. With no true records ever having been lodged, this particular record keeper made a specific assumption that saw the big house owners recorded as Alexandria's family. Just happy to have peace, certainty of their surroundings, they never moved in. Why would they? They were the owners of the most splendidly wonderfully perfect of homes. One very odd thing happened the day that Alexandria's family took ownership of it, however - it also appeared in Heart! The perfect mirror of itself. It was something that had never happened in all the years of the dragonfly and Shuing. The house wasn't built round a tree; the house was too young for Shuing to have placed a dragonfly in it, so the only explanation that could be found was its proximity to their Dragonfly Cottage. In the years that followed, they were simply respectful caretakers of the big old house.

'If you are serious about going in there, you don't want to be in there after dark!' Alexandria warned. There was one other reason they and no other cared to move in - the regular ghostly happenings!

'Why?' Vicky asked,

'It's a long story and for another day. But things happen, not fun things!' Alexandria answered. Having listened to the story and the warning, grandmother was in no way put off. She headed straight for the front door. A bouncing Anchor had taken off down the garden and was darting in and out of the trees. Bart watched, trying very hard not to let his desire to join him take over from his responsibility of staying with Vicky.

Before following the group, Alexandria went back to her Dragonfly Cottage to check for the last time that there was absolutely no sign of the tree growing back. There wasn't. Happy that the awakened dragonfly and the magic that had been witnessed had not returned, she closed the old red front door and joined the others.

'It's open!' Alexandria shouted to the group patiently waiting at the creepy front door. Melissa turned the handle, and the door creaked open. A cold air, colder than the winter's air they were standing in, fell out of the door, followed by the smell of burning wood.

'Is it safe to go in? It smells like the place is on fire!' Melissa shouted to the just arriving Alexandria.

'It always smells like that in the mornings. There hasn't been a log fire lit in there for as long as I remember,' Alexandria replied. Not interested in ghost stories, grandmother pushed past the hesitant Melissa and went straight to the stairs. The barely lived in house's wooden floors showed no sign of wear, and the stairs were no different. They did however creak, as the old rusty nails holding the boards in place, moved with every step she took.

'I guess we are going in then?' Melissa said to Vicky, whose usual up for anything attitude, wasn't quite what it usually was as she looked into the dark hallway. Bart was very happy to remain outside and watch the "without a care in the world" Anchor. With so much space to run free in, his legs were unable to keep up with his momentum. On more than one occasion he narrowly missed face-planting into the frozen grass. This amused Bart greatly. It was a far cry from the small garden back at grandmother's Dragonfly Manor, or the leashed walks Sophie would occasionally take him on.

'Oh, this is silly! What am I worried about?' Vicky announced, and with a pull that broke Bart's focus on Anchor, she dragged the not-so-keen to follow dog, up the creaky stairs and out of sight.

Melissa and Alexandria left standing at the front door, heard the echoing footsteps of Vicky and Bart,

'A Legend Remembered' 63

who, having caught up with grandmother, made their way to a room directly above the front door vestibule. The room gave them the perfect viewing point to see over the trees, fields and hill towards the loch.

'Why me?' Melissa asked. Alexandria, not knowing what she was referring to, but also not wanting to be rude by saying nothing, replied,

'I have no idea.'

'Alex. Why me, why did you leave him with me?' Melissa said, clarifying the question she was looking for an answer to. Alexandria knew the question would come at some point, but wasn't as ready to answer it as she would have liked.

'Maybe we could talk about that when we know what has happened to him,' Alexandria said, hoping that reminding her why they were where they were, would be enough to distract her from the question. It wasn't. Looking away from the view of the playing by himself dog, Melissa turned to Alexandria and said, in a firm voice,

'At this moment in time, there is nothing to do but wait. I would say this is the perfect time to ask the question.'

With no other excuses coming to mind, Alexandria accepted that she didn't really have any other choice other than to open up more than she wanted. She sat herself down on the front door's single step and hoped that what she was about to say did not cause awkwardness. Or for her to be judged in a negative way. It was a delicate subject for her on more than one level. What she felt towards Melissa and the reasons for leaving her son with her, were complicated, intertwined, and would leave her more vulnerable than she would like.

'I don't know where to start,' Alexandria said,

'Well, how did you know it would be me that would find him outside the hospital? Also, the hospital is so far away from here, how did you find it, and me?' Melissa asked. Alexandria was glad to have more specific questions that she could respond to.

'I had to get him as far away from here as I possibly could. The hospital you worked at was the farthest I could bear to go. I wanted to keep him on the island we live on, even though my brother had told me to take him to the other side of the world. As much as we may fight it, what is meant to be is quite often what just is!' Melissa interrupted,

'What was meant to be?' her intense eyes looking right into Alexandria's as she said it.

'You! You were meant to be.'

Melissa didn't understand,

'So you didn't choose me. It was just coincidence! No, that's not right, as the letter you left with him, it was to me!' Melissa was answering her own question, which left her wanting still more answers.

'He was newborn. I had got in my car and driven as far south as I could and...' Melissa interrupted again,

'He was not newborn when I found him. He was at least a month old!'

'Give me a minute please!' the tone of Alexandria's voice changing to that of frustration. 'Just sit there and listen.' The frustration had the effect of clearing her mind and giving her the strength to tell Melissa her story.

Alexandria's life changed within minutes of giving birth to Alex. After asking the midwife,

'Where is the other one?' and getting the response,

'There is no other one!' Alexandria knew something was different. She had assumed she would be the same as all dragonfly key-keepers and would have twins.

She spent the first night of Alex's life in a state of joy for her new baby boy, but also confusion as to the lack of a twin sister. Going over and over the reasons why it could have happened, she began to blame herself - had the circumstances in which he had been conceived been the reason for there being only one? Having spent the nine months of her pregnancy blocking from her mind the reality of what she did - were they the reasons why?!

Having not slept a wink, the morning's revitalising sun shining in through her bedroom window was a relief to her. She looked down into the eyes of her baby boy and everything changed. A burst of adrenalin ran through her veins as what she saw was not the blue of a newborn's eyes, she saw purple!

Alexandria screamed for her brother who had spent an equally restless night sitting outside her bedroom door, and he arrived within seconds. The brightness, the purple in the baby's eyes was unmissable. Alexandria's brother picked up his new nephew to get a closer look. With her son being held high above her, she carefully moved to the edge of the bed, surprised at the lack of pain she was in having given birth only twelve hours earlier. She then noticed something else! On her baby's hand was a mark that the legends forgotten had once talked about. Being the keeper of not only her own Dragonfly home, but also the Dragonfly island, Alexandria and her brother were the last ones on Earth who had insight and understanding into what had been. Who remembered the legends forgot by all others on Earth, and what could be with the evil twins trapped in Heart. She knew that the mark she was looking at had only been on one other - Shuing! She knew in that moment her newborn son was different, and potentially as dangerous as much as he could be a light in the darkness. He had to be kept hidden until such time came that Leilani and Lanny were no more.

Alexandria spent one day in her Dragonfly home with her baby and her brother. A day that was filled with discussion of what could be, what they should do and much more. A decision was made to hide all traces of them from Leilani and Lanny, including the destruction of their wonderfully magical tree. Although it was the only Dragonfly home that had never been seen by the evil twins, thanks to their families' connection with the Dragonfly island, Alexandria did not want to take any chances. Any connection to Heart had to be covered up. That included her own brother! Neither must know where the other would end up. It was a separation that was going to be as hard for Alexandria as abandoning her own child, but it had to be done.

Two days old, Alex was wrapped up and safely hidden in their old car. With one long tight hug, tears running down their faces they said their goodbyes, not knowing if they would ever see each other again.

As she told the story to Melissa, Alexandria's usually hidden emotions were about to take over. She stopped for a moment, took a couple of deep breaths and carried on.

'That was the last time I saw my brother. I felt him like I always did when we were apart, for several days after I left. But when I arrived at the town you lived and worked, that day it changed. Our connection was lost, as much as I tried I couldn't feel him...' She stopped again, this time closing her eyes for a moment before speaking out the words she had never spoken before, 'That was the day my brother died.' Melissa moved closer and put her arm round her to comfort her. 'No, don't!' Alexandria said sternly, wiggling free from Melissa's arm and creating distance between them. Somehow she brought herself back from the emotional cliff's edge and continued with her story.

The day she lost her connection with her brother, was the day her journey found her in the Cornish town of Truro. Alexandria knew that the heartbreaking action of leaving her son, could only be made slightly better by finding someone who would care for him as she would. Someone who had a love for children. With many hours on the road trying to figure out who and where that place may be, she had a moment of inspiration. There could be no better place to find such a person than in the British Isles southernmost maternity hospital. Although not as far as the other side of the world which was suggested by her brother, Alexandria felt its nearly eight hundred mile distance from her home was enough to keep him safe.

At just one week old, the newly named Alex was her perfect cover to enter the hospital without any awkward questions. It was something she did every day over a two-week period. Listening, watching the doctors and nurses, trying to get any kind of insight or inspiration as to who could be the one. No one gave her the comfort she was looking for.

As week three began and Alexandria was questioning whether it was the perfect place to find the perfect person, she literally bumped into Melissa as she came hurtling through one of the large swinging doors, clearly on a mission. As they brushed shoulders, Alexandria felt something she had not felt before. It was a warmth inside that made her feel as though she could have handed her son over there and then. However, the cautious, mistrusting side of her personality kept her from doing so. Two more weeks followed with Alexandria watching and learning all should could about Melissa. Not only did she watch her at work, she also followed her home, to the shops, everywhere she could to figure out who she was and if her initial instincts were correct.

Eventually, she concluded that Melissa was a hard worker; she had no family nearby and her friends appeared to be acquaintances more than good friends. Her life was her job. She seemed to be strong, confident and respectful to whoever she conversed with. She appeared to have no love interest and no children, a fact that led Alexandria to wonder if maybe Melissa couldn't have children.

During the time spent secretly watching Melissa, Alexandria couldn't help herself. Unexpected feelings began to grow towards her, more than just seeing her as the perfect mother for her son! There was no question it was Melissa, and the time had finally come. All that was left to do was to pick the perfect moment, and place, to leave her precious baby boy, Alex, for her to find.

'The day I wrote the note for you, the day I left Alex with you, do you remember it?' Alexandria asked,

'I will never forget it. It was a warm sunny day, with a peace in the air. It was strange, because when I went into work it was like the place was on holiday, everyone seemed so happy. The few mums, the patients admitted, they were all healthy and happy. And of course then finding Alex. So yes, I remember the day well,' Melissa replied.

'I remember it like it was yesterday. Not only for being the last day I would be able to hold my baby boy, but for also being the day I would fall in love for the first time. I watched you as you left for work. I felt your soul, your beauty, pass through me as you walked past me on the footpath outside your flat. I had fallen in love with you! I didn't just lose my son that day, I lost my heart to the one person I thought, until this morning, I could never be with.'

Alexandria's story and declaration left Melissa speechless. Shivers ran up her spine and up into the back of Melissa's head. She stood up and walked away, down the footpath towards Anchor, who, having got bored chasing himself and the leaves around the large garden, was sitting just outside the gate, looking up at grandmother and Vicky in one of the upstairs windows.

'I am sorry! Maybe. Oh I don't know. Have I made you uncomfortable?' Alexandria asked, not moving from the seated position at the front door of the creepy old house. Her elbows resting on her knees, she dropped her head into her hands to hide her face, she was so embarrassed. Unlike Melissa's shivers, Alexandria was burning up. Physically hiding her eyes, her subconscious closing off all her other senses, she got the fright of her life when she felt two hands lifting her up under her arms. In a fraction of a second she was suddenly on her feet. Opening her eyes, her heart racing, she found herself facing the shadowy face of Melissa, her face in shadow due to the low winter's sun crawling across the crisp blue sky behind her. The then embarrassed heat of one, and the cold reality of the other, became the warmth of a loving embrace and the warmth of a loving kiss.

'Oh my goodness! Look down there!' a surprised grandmother said to Vicky, who was squinting her eyes, trying to get them to make out any kind of detail in the distance. She quietly hoped her clear sight of the island would return. Doing as requested, Vicky looked down. She could see the shape of a very excited Anchor jumping, running around the shape of what she assumed was Melissa and Alexandria. What she could not make out, was what had got grandmother so excited.

'So you do remember that I can't see clearly that far, right!' Vicky said with a scowl.

'Oh my dear, I am sorry. These last two days have been so confusing. Well, standing below us are two wonderful ladies in a loving embrace. Kissing!' grandmother said. Vicky was slightly taken aback and wanted to see for herself, but didn't want to make the two ladies feel uncomfortable. With very heavy feet, to make sure that Melissa and Alexandria were aware of her heading back to see them, Vicky stomped her way back across the upstairs room, through across the landing and down the stairs.

As she stepped off the bottom step of the staircase, she let go of Bart's harness. Having glanced up and got a nod of permission, he took off to join Anchor in his excited dance around Melissa and Alexandria, who appeared completely oblivious to anything other than each other.

'Guys, there are children present you know!' Vicky said from inside the hallway.

'You're no child Vicky,' came the voice of Melissa, 'Far from it. You are possibly older and wiser in mind than the rest of us.'

'Why thank you. Glad to have some purpose here. Vicky the wise, I like it.' Vicky laughed whilst making her way up to Melissa, who had let go of Alexandria. 'I don't know, I go out of sight for just a short time and miss all the important stuff. Come on girls, what is going on here? Well, I can kind of see what was going on, but you know what I mean!'

Grandmother took a few more moments to arrive. Finally, appearing from the darkness of the hallway, she joined the group on the steps and said,

'I feel I may have just witnessed a most important and special moment in your lives.'

Walking right up to them and taking a hand from each of them, she continued. 'Love in every form is the most beautiful of things to experience, and to be part of. I have lived for more years than I should have, and in that time I have not seen enough love on this Earth. To witness two people come together the way I felt you two do, brings me hope. As frightening as initially I thought the consequences of us all meeting could be, these last couple of days have shown me that no matter what is to come, there is love, even in the starkest of times.' Letting go of their hands, grandmother raised herself as high as she could. Up on the tips of her toes, she gave them both a kiss on the cheek.

'I may be jumping the gun here, but how amazing is that? Alex's two mums becoming Alex's two in love mums. Pretty sure he will be happy with that, well, it will make things easier on his birthday!' Vicky said. As she was giving them a small celebratory hug, she noticed something. 'Hey what's that?' For the tiniest of moments, her eyesight was as clear as it was at grandmother's Dragonfly Manor and Dragonfly island.

'What?' Melissa asked.

'There. The other side of the staircase on the floor by the wall. I am sure I saw something sparkle,' Vicky replied.

Alexandria knew the house very well. As scary as it was, she had spent many hours in the place since returning sixteen years earlier, after leaving her baby boy. Oddly, something kept pulling her in. She had never experienced anything but dull, dark, damp, smoke smelling and the occasional ghostly happening, certainly nothing sparkle. On closer inspection to where Vicky was pointing, Alexandria found something.

'A leaf! I mean a tiny tree. I don't understand! How have I not seen that before?' she asked.

'To be fair, I don't know how anyone would have seen that,' Melissa replied. Although the tree was only an inch tall, on closer inspection its detail was that of a fully grown tree. 'Yeh, that is kind of odd!' Melissa, on her hands and knees, getting as close a look as she could said. 'Can't see any sparkles though!' Having spent time with Vicky, grandmother knew she had seen what she said she had, and how. Enlightening Alexandria and reminding Melissa she said,

'Her eyes are clear when she sees anything to do with Heart!'

'No, that can't be!' Alexandria said, and in a panic ripped the tiny tree from the ground. 'Quickly, we must burn it.' Running into one of the rooms that led off the hallway, she went straight to an old, dusty fireplace. On the mantle were matches she had left on one of her visits, many years earlier, to light a candle on a particularly dark day. The old, dry remains of the last fire, lit tens of years earlier, exploded into life with the first strike of the match. Not even giving the flames a chance to develop into a strong heat, desperate to destroy what they had found, she threw the tiny tree straight into the flickering flames,

'Oh my goodness!' grandmother exclaimed. As soon as the tree made contact with the fire, sparks filled the room. The onlookers couldn't avoid the sparks. They felt like tiny insect bites as they landed on any exposed skin. Thankfully, it didn't last for long, as the loud crackling sounds and sparks came to an end with a small, anticlimactic popping sound, followed by a skinny swirl of smoke. The fire was out, the tiny tree was gone.

'How was that possible?' Alexandria said loudly.

'Not sure if it's relevant but look!' Vicky, who had been standing in the doorway whilst the poor little tree was unceremoniously burnt, with the excitement over, had turned to walk back upstairs, and this time she was seeing a bright light on the doorframe that was lighting up the dark hallway. As she got closer, it faded. The rest of the group made it out the room just in time to see the light go completely. In its place was a mark, a carving, a rather familiar and specific carving.

'That's my brother!' A shocked Alexandria said under her breath. Grandmother was the only one to hear what she said.

'It looks like a waterfall to me!' Vicky said, her nose almost on the motionless image.

'It is, it's my brother. That's his symbol. His physical self has never appeared in any carving on our Dragonfly door's frame, or any we visited. When he has been part of a story, we discovered it was always a waterfall,' Alexandria said. Pushing Vicky out of the way she touched it. It was warm, but cooling, just as the light it gave off had faded. 'I don't understand! This is no Dragonfly home.'

'I have never heard of such a thing. I have never seen a Dragonfly home whose doorframe wasn't filled with all kinds of memories, and apart from that I have never seen a doorframe with any sign of magic on it that didn't have a...' grandmother stopped mid-sentence. She was about to make a statement that she realised with Vicky's discovery, was not going to be correct. Instead she asked, 'how did that tiny tree get here?'

'Well, if you don't know, we sure as heck don't!' Vicky said. No more sparkles, no more lights and realising that she could see clearly in the right circumstances, she headed back up the stairs to her viewing spot, where she hoped she would once again be able to see the island, closely followed by Bart and Anchor.

Ignoring grandmother's question, mainly as she also didn't have any idea how it got there, Alexandria changed the subject,

'Let's not analyse what we don't understand. We should get comfortable and wait for Alex and Sophie to turn up.' Then a thought entered her mind that took her down a dark road. The magic appearing in the big old house meant that there was a chance Leilani and her brother could become aware of its existence. If that happened, what would have been the point in all the time she spent away from her son.

Sensing the change in Alexandria's mood and seeing the sparkle in her eyes dulling, also confident that Vicky would alert them to any change on the island, or if Alex and Sophie appeared, Melissa took Alexandria's hand and led her out of the house, through the garden and into a wooded area that ran

'A Legend Remembered'

along the side of the property. Finding a small open area, she stopped and turned to Alexandria and said,

'We were interrupted before!'

Feeling the power and energy from the winter's forest, the pine trees giving off their distinctive sweet and beautiful scent, Melissa, hoping to bring that sparkle back, pulled Alexandria in close. 'Wherever your mind is going don't let it. Those three words you said to me, that was the first time, apart from Alex of course, that I felt them to be true. I have searched for so many years for an answer to why I was content to be alone. Why, even as a child, I felt uncomfortable around girls, why I felt things towards them I thought were not right. Why boys were only friends, I mean, there was plenty who wanted to be more, but the thought of it wasn't right. My upbringing, my family, although they never knew it, they left me feeling like there was something wrong with me. You giving me your son, it gave me purpose, a love that I thought I did not deserve. And now, what you said, you have given me something just as special. You have given me, me!'

Releasing Alexandria slightly from her tight hug, she looked into her bright blue eyes and said, 'You have shown me who I am!'

As she spoke, Melissa's own beautiful dark eyes had filled up. The tears broke free, running over her cheeks and off her jaw. Just managing to hold it together she went on, 'it's a gift that will be with me always. Whatever happens today, tomorrow, if we make it to tomorrow! Thank you.'

Alexandria gave Melissa an uncharacteristically vulnerable smile. Unable to find words of her own, she moved back in close to Melissa and hugged her so tight she found it difficult to breathe. Their special moment together was short lived as they heard a loud bang! It was an upstairs window being flung open by an excited Vicky, who shouted,

'Did you feel that? It came from the island!'

'No, it can't be!' Alexandria exclaimed, as she turned and ran back towards the house, 'Describe what you saw!'

'Nothing, there was nothing,' grandmother replied.

'It was like an invisible wave. It came from the island. As it came towards us everything was distorted, like I was looking through melted glass.'

'Could you see any movement on the island Vicky?' Alexandria asked.

'Even good eyes would not see that much detail, and my eyes are bad, so no!' Vicky replied,

'Yes, but you see clearly whatever the dragonfly magic touches,' Alexandria stated, frustrated. After a moment of consideration Vicky said,

'Well, there was movement on the water now I think about it. It was just before the energy wave.' Alexandria turned to Melissa, her heart racing, her breath in a state of stress, her mind full of consequences and awful possible realities and said,

'Now it's time to worry. There is no sign of our son, no sign of Sophie. There was a dragonfly tree in that old house which I have no idea how long had been there. And now the energy wave which from what I know, only ever happens when someone has used the cottage on Dragonfly island, to pass between Heart and here! Melissa, this could be the end!'

Chapter 5

'Look, someone's coming!' Sophie said, pointing towards the loch's shoreline where a small wooden boat was being pushed into the water, by what looked like a man covered in trees.

'Should we hide, run, or swim for it?' Alex asked, his mind running a hundred miles an hour with the reality that they could be on Heart.

'I don't think it would be a bad idea to make ourselves a little less visible!' Sophie replied. Whoever was in the boat was making fast progress towards the island.

'Wait a minute! I thought no one could see the island, unless you're Vicky, or on it,' Alex said. Sophie couldn't help herself and responded with a valid point, in a slightly sarcastic tone,

'Pretty sure if Vicky could see it, there will be others who can as well. Also, if we are in Heart, maybe everyone can see it.'

Alex didn't respond. As he looked around for a good place to hide, Sophie kept an eye on the fast approaching boat.

'There really is nowhere to hide, well, apart from inside the house,' Alex said. The wooded area was not dense, the bushes and flowers not large enough to provide anything other than slight cover, 'Maybe we should just wait here! We have the high ground so could just push the boat back out!' With the boat only twenty metres from the island's small sandy beach and still unable to make out who or what was approaching, Alex's nerve gave way. He grabbed

Sophie's hand and pulled her into the woods behind the Dragonfly island's cottage. They were going to be found of course, but he figured at least it would give them the opportunity to see who, or what, climbed out of the boat.

Finally, with a gritty crunch, the boat hit the sand. In one swift and seamless movement, its captain pulled the old wooden rotting oars out of the water and lay them on the damp floor of the boat. Slowly standing up and turning, in the beached wobbling boat, pieces of the camouflage cape falling away, the concealed Alex and Sophie saw the bright blue eyes of the hidden figure piercing out from the shadows of a hood.

'I know you are here. It's ok it's me, we need to get you off the island!' The voice was deep, but had a kindness to it. Stepping away from the damp sand on to the grass, hands appeared at chest height and pushed off what had hidden the person beneath. The branches and leaves falling to the floor stood in a pile three feet high. Alex wondered how the person could have moved with so much weight, let alone row a boat with the ease in which they had appeared to. Confident that it was a human they were being approached by, Alex went to step out from their temporary hiding place. Sophie stopped him. Catching his arm, she whispered,

'Wait a few more moments.' Doing as he was told, he sat back on his heels. Together they watched as the man got closer. Having clear sight of him, Alex's question as to how he was able to row the boat under all the weight of his camouflage was answered. He was well over six foot in height, with broad shoulders and thick arms and legs that looked like they were going to burst out of the trousers he wore. Making his way towards the Dragonfly Cottage, his intense blue eyes, now in shadow from his blonde shoulder length hair draped over his face, darted from side to side. Alex was convinced they had been seen.

'There is something familiar about him,' Alex whispered. With every step the man took towards them, Alex felt the heat within him building up, the heat he had come to know well. One way or another, they were going to be discovered! Not wanting the return of the same uncontrollable explosion that had come from him outside grandmother's Dragonfly Manor that had hurt his mum, Alex stood up and walked calmly out from where they had been crouched. The intimidating looking man having seen the movement, laid eyes on Alex said,

'Well, you aren't who I was expecting to find! But no matter. I have to assume you have something to do with what has been going on this morning! Whoever you are, we need to get you as far from the island as we can, as they aren't far away!'

'Who are you?' Alex asked.

'I am sorry,' the man dropped and shook his head, annoyed at himself for his lack of politeness. He then continued, 'My name is Jason Hugins, and you are?' In his entire life, Alex had never heard of anyone with the same surname as his, and now in two days he had met two.

'Hugins, you are a Hugins?' Alex asked.

'Well yes, has been my family name for generations. Nothing special really, I didn't earn it or anything, it's just my name,' was Jason's reply. Before either of them could say another word, happy that the man seemed not to be a threat, Sophie appeared from the shadows and said,

'You two must be related then!'

'Related?' Jason asked,

'I am Alex, Alex Hugins. Although I have recently found out that I am actually a Shuing!' Jason ran up to him and grabbed his shoulders,

'Alex, you are Alex! My sister's boy! And you know about Shuing!' Alex had never seen a grown man cry, let alone one that looked like he did, so he was a little surprised to see the tears pour from Jason's eyes. The emotions from years of loss, fear and loneliness, in that moment, were set free. He pulled Alex into a hug. Holding his head to his chest, he kissed the top of his head. With the heat build up subsiding, although Alex was feeling a little uncomfortable in the stranger's embrace, remarkably he was able to think clearly.

'So your sister is Alexandria then?' Alex asked.

'Is she alive, is she well?' Jason nervously asked, he had no idea.

'She is fine, I think, well she was when we left her,' Alex replied.

'You said we need to get Alex off the island, and you said they are not far away. Who aren't far away?' Sophie asked, interrupting the family reunion. Jason replied in a slightly annoyed tone,

'Young lady....' this time Alex interrupted, his instincts to protect Sophie producing extra confidence,

'Her name is Sophie, and she is as much part of this as I am!'

'Sorry. Sophie, you are right I did say those things and with good reason. The two that are here, the two I have managed to avoid my entire life are here, just a few miles away. They are brother and sister, siblings, that have been terrorising this place for hundreds of years!'

'A Legend Remembered' 81

'You mean Heart and you mean Leilani and Lanny, my ancestors who are strangely still alive, don't you!' Sophie said. Jason stepped away from them,

'How do you know that? In fact, how did you get here?' Jason had stayed hidden for the sixteen years he found himself trapped on Heart. For as long as he could remember, and as far as he knew from the time before his birth, no one but his family, the direct descendants of Shuing, had ever been on the island. Alex made sense, if his story was true, but Sophie's arrival had changed that. His family's true purpose of protecting the Dragonfly island had been kept secret from all, before and after the legend had been forgot. With this revelation, the arrival of two, one allegedly from the bloodline that had brought such peace and balance to Earth, and the other from the bloodline that had almost taken it all away, Jason needed a moment.

His mind conflicted, he considered that his discovery was not his at all. Maybe it was a twisted trap set by Leilani and her brother? The reality that was being shown to him - his sister's son's miraculous appearance, it simply could not be... a trap made far more sense.

Jason turned his back to Alex and Sophie and made his way back towards his boat. His mind raced through as many scenarios as he could come up with as he did. Should he run from them, leave the island as quick as he arrived? Should he also leave the small highland village, the place that had been his home his entire life, twenty years on Earth and now sixteen years trapped on Heart? He was there on the island for one reason - the explosion he had witnessed.

Having spent sixteen years trying and failing to find a way back to his twin sister, Alexandria, when he saw the explosion of water and light earlier that morning he thought she had found a way to him. That was his reason for breaking cover and heading for the island, his reason for risking everything, knowing the evil twins were so close. His usual rational self lost, the flight of the fight-or-flight instinct taking over and having not giving them a chance to answer his "how did you get here?" question, he said,

'This is a trap! You two, you know too much.' Jason's slow walk turned into a run for his boat. Arriving at it, his speed and strength pushed it off the sand and out into the loch's cold, still waters with ease. Holding on to its bow as it drifted away from the shoreline, he jumped and spun himself in and on to the thin wooden seat that the oars rested below. Having lifted up the oars and crashed them into the water, he began pulling hard to create speed and distance from the two young ones he left standing on the lush, green grass of Dragonfly island.

'Do you want to swim?' Alex asked Sophie, surprisingly calm,

'No, not really!' was her reply.

'I think the boat was probably the only way to have avoided that, so maybe we should get it back.' Alex took hold of Sophie's hand and walked over to the water, stepped in and instructed Sophie not to let go.

'What are you doing?' Sophie asked.

Whilst they had been watching Jason leave, the dragonfly had spoken to Alex. Going against his own rules of not helping he had said, 'Go to the water, he will return.' Alex, having no reason to doubt what had become part of him, did as he suggested.

'Join him!' Sophie's hand in Alex's, the voice of the dragonfly this time was also heard by her. As soon as they joined, Alex felt a tingle in his arm which made its way down into his hand. At the same time, the rainbow of colours began to swirl around Sophie's back, moving up her neck and spreading down her arm to join Alex's hand. With a burst of colourful light, one of the small dragonflies that had found their home in Alex, left his hand. The dragonfly dove into the water with a trail of its own colourful light streaming off its back and headed straight for the bobbing boat. Jason, having seen what had just happened, instantly stopped rowing. His strong body was able to hold the oars stationary under the water, meaning that they had a braking effect that caused the boat to come to a full stop. He watched as the light got closer and closer and finally, with a larger than expected explosion of water, the dragonfly appeared at the back of his boat. Hovering right in front of him, its big eyes looking right into his, Jason quietly said,

'I could be wrong of course.'

Pulling the oars from the water, not losing eye contact with the dragonfly, he secured them so as not to lose them. With his hands now free, he reached forward. As soon as he did, the dragonfly returned along its trail of colours under the water, back up to Alex and Sophie. Looking down at the hovering insect, Alex instinctively said,

'Welcome back!' at which point the dragonfly flew straight at Alex's hand, and with the sharp pain he was getting used to, disappeared into his scar. 'No swimming for us then,' Alex said.

'Thank goodness. Also, should we be more surprised at what just happened?' Sophie asked.

'You would think so wouldn't you!' was Alex's response, as they watched the returning Jason.

'Ok, so I may have got things a bit wrong in my head! Can we start again, please?' Jason said as he climbed out of the boat once again. 'So I can safely assume you haven't come from Leilani or her brother. If they were able to control dragonflies like that, they wouldn't be interested in me or this island. I feel I need to go back to my last question. How did you get here?'

Alex was nervous to give too much information away to a stranger, related or not. So, missing out the part of how they came from the incredible cave, he said,

'Through the cottage.'

'But that doorway has never been used, well certainly since I have been alive. Actually, as far as I know since Shuing passed away. I was told his dragonfly left when he did,' Jason said.

'Did you say something about grandmother's grandchildren nearby?' Sophie asked, changing the subject.

'Oh, damn, yes. Ok, come on. I will take you back to my place, you should be safe there,' Jason replied. They all climbed into the boat, not the biggest, but they managed to squeeze in.

'Jason. Now you know how we got here, well sort of! Maybe you can tell us how you got here? Grandmother said that all the doors have been lost for years, no way back and forth between Earth and Heart?' Sophie asked.

'Soon, let's get you away from here first,' Jason replied. It didn't take them long to get back to the loch side, a very different looking loch side to the one they had first arrived on. 'We need to stay undercover as much as we can. My house is about five miles if we go straight over that hill,' Jason said, pointing in the direction of the small highland village, which both Alex and Sophie were curious to see in relation to how different it would look.

'No car then?' Alex asked. Jason laughed and shook his head.

'Hurry, hurry, they are in the valley.' The voice came from above them. Looking up, Sophie and Alex saw what looked like an owl circling them.

'Did you hear that? I think that owl just spoke!' Sophie said to Alex. Not giving him a chance to reply, Jason said,

'You're in Heart now, every living thing has a voice understood by every other living thing. And actually that is a Tawny Frogmouth, guess he looks a bit like a small owl. He's not native to these parts, back on Earth his kind would usually be found living in Australia. His name is Renga.'

Sophie recalled the stories grandmother had told them and felt a little silly for asking the question.

'Excuse me, but I can introduce myself!' Renga said, landing on a rock a few feet in front of them. 'My name is Renga. I am most happy to make your acquaintance Alex, Sophie and whoever it is hiding under your skin.'

The stocky, compact bird with its big head, strong beak, silvery feathers and little legs sat looking up at the group with its large, yellowy orange eyes.

'Which is the best way to head back do you think?' Jason asked his feathery companion. Renga described the route that Leilani and Lanny were taking. It was clear they had seen what Jason had and were heading for the loch as well. The one saving grace, as far as Jason was concerned, was that they may have seen the explosion of water and light, but they would not be able to see the island. Renga took off in the direction that Jason, Alex and Sophie were to follow. The land was not as lush as the island, but although cold, it was not as winter dead as back in the village of Lairg they had arrived in and left. Dashing across open stretches of land, they stopped in small clumps of trees, not big enough to be called a wood, but enough for them to stay hidden, to check that they had not been seen and to get their breath back.

The route took them about thirty minutes, time which they were sure meant the evil siblings would have got to the loch. Having not passed a single person or property on their run, they found themselves standing on top of a small hill hiding between rocks, looking down to where the loch came to an end and the village shop should have been. It was nothing like the village back on Earth, here there was just a scattering of cottages.

'That looks like the house where we first saw your mum Alex,' Sophie said. Alex looked to where she was pointing. It was. Hiding amongst massively tall pine trees it was different to the one back on Earth, most obviously there was no driveway. If it hadn't been for a strong gust of wind separating the pines trees, the house may not have even been seen by Sophie from where they stood. 'That's where we are heading,' Jason said.

'You are safe to go,' Renga informed them, swooping down from a height where he could not be seen by anyone.

'Fire's still lit, good,' Jason said as he ran into the big old house. Alex and Sophie were a little behind so the front door had closed before they got there.

'Do we just go in?' Sophie, out of breath, asked the not so out of breath Alex. He didn't respond, instead took hold of Sophie's hand and made his way up the couple of steps where he knocked on the door.

'Come in, it's unlocked!' The muffled voice came from Jason, who was heading back out of the room where he had been warming his hands on the open fire.

'Damn it, not again!' Alex exclaimed, as he threw the front door open far wider and harder than he had intended. The sound of splintering wood echoed round the empty hallway as the hinges holding it in place were taken beyond where they could hold. The dramatic entrance was a symptom of the adrenalin running through his veins from the their long run, and the annoyance at a pain that was becoming too common. The sharp, electric shock like pain he experienced when entering grandmother's Dragonfly Manor, in the cave, on the island, just now…

'Well, that's new!' a surprised Jason said. Instantly feeling embarrassed about his pain induced tantrum and that he had probably broken the door, Alex, assuming Jason's words were directed at him said,

'I am sorry, that wasn't right. I'll try and fix it if it's broken!'

'Yeh, no, that's fine, don't worry about the door, it complains at the best of times. I mean that,' Jason said as he pointed at a part of the skirting board that was full of light.

'What is it?' Sophie asked.

'It was a tiny piece, a twig, from a tree I found in my pocket a long time ago. It's never done that before.' Squinting, Jason noticed something else. 'Actually, it doesn't look like a twig anymore, it looks more like a tree!' Alex and Sophie walked over to get a closer look, and as they did, Sophie felt a breeze go past her. It was gentle, but strong enough to move her heavy, curly hair.

'Alex, check your arm,' she said sternly,

'My arm?' Alex asked. Sophie grabbed at his sleeve, pulled it up to his elbow and seeing what she had expected, said,

'There are only two dragonflies.'

'The other one will just be further up,' Alex said as he stretched the cuff as wide as it would go and pulled his sleeve further up. 'Where is it?'

'It's on the doorframe!' a surprised Jason said. It was hovering over an image. A waterfall. 'That can't be!' he said, walking over to a very familiar picture. 'How is this possible? You two need to tell me what is going on here.' Then the image outlined in light went dark, becoming a single carving on a large and ornate doorframe. Jason looked back towards where the sparkles had been coming from on the skirting board. They had gone, replaced by a swirling, skinny, single line of smoke and what had a once been a tiny twig, most recently a tiny tree, was now a singed tiny tree. Its leaves all shrivelled up, dropping off one by one with the vibrations from each footstep made by the three as they walked closer.

'I guess you two are the reason for this!' Jason said as he bent down and pulled up the dead tree. Its roots slipped out from between the floorboard and skirting board with ease. A single tear ran down his cheek. 'This was from somewhere very special to me.' His mind went back to the day he found it, 'I sense you aren't in a place of trusting me yet, so I will tell you where it came from. When I have finished, I hope that you will start to trust me and will share with me what you two are together, and how you came to be here.'

Jason walked off in the direction of the room that had its fire lit. The smoke smell filled the whole house. There was no magic involved in that, it was simply the chimney that should take it away, was not clean enough to be effective. The room had no comfortable furniture in it, just a handmade, chunky looking table that sat in its middle, surrounded by five chairs. The table was covered in wood shavings that also covered most of the floor. Larger piles than anywhere else were round the chair that Jason pulled out and sat down on. 'Grab a seat,' Jason said, gesturing to the four available ones. Sophie and Alex, as comfortable as they were going to get on the crooked, cold, wooden chairs, sat and waited for his story to begin. 'As I said before, I am Jason Hugins. I am part of the bloodline that have been the protectors of the Dragonfly island since its beginning, the only family who have ever known of its location. The stories that have been written about the first dragonfly told of the place, but never of its location. I, my family and you are direct descendants of Shuing, but you know that, so I shall go back to the day I found the twig.'

The day in question was the day Jason last set eyes on Alex. It was the day his sister, Alexandria, left their Dragonfly Cottage in fear of what would happen if Alex was ever discovered. He described how together they had cut down and then ripped up the roots of the dragonfly tree that had given them so many happy memories as children. Days sitting round it in the small hallway, looking up at the doorframe, reading all the carved picture stories, learning about the cottage's history. Climbing its branches and giving their own parents frights when they jumped down from them as they passed by.

The day Alexandria left him behind to find Alex a new home, he had gone to find comfort on the Dragonfly island. Unable to pass through to Heart all their lives, both his sister and he would visit the island's house to watch life on Heart through its walls. Unfortunately for Jason, on that day the images were motionless, just a snapshot in time. Although never having her own key, Alexandria still had the magic inside her of the Key Keeper. She was born the girl of twins; it was inherited, learnt, just never completed.

'I was angry. I shouldn't have been, it was selfish, I know that. But that day I had lost our tree, I had lost my sister, and I had lost you.' In his anger, Jason had gone to the tree in the centre of the Dragonfly island's cottage and punched its old and wise trunk. He did not stop punching, not even when his skin could take no more. His blood splashed with every strike, his screams would have been heard for miles around if not for the hidden protection the island maintained. Exhausted, he fell onto the tree. Throwing his arms around it to keep himself upright, he closed his eyes, clenched his teeth, breathed deeply through his nose and tried to compose himself. As he relaxed, he could feel the pain coming from his hands, his bones, that had taken impact after impact on the tree trunk's uneven, solid surface.

'It was in that moment, somewhere between reality and despair, I felt a stab in my side. It was the twig that just turned into a tree, it was in my pocket. I took it out. It must have got in there when we pulled up our tree back at our Dragonfly Cottage. It had a tiny bud on it, just one. I touched it and as soon as I did I went dizzy, my eyesight blurry, I would have fallen over if the tree hadn't been there. The feeling passed eventually. But I wasn't where I started. The air was different, the images on the walls were different.'

Jason was in Heart. Not only had he lost all he had, he had now lost the only home he had known. Over the years, he tried everything to get back. He replicated the moment as best he could - punching the tree, cutting his own hands, holding the twig, but nothing worked. The window in the cottage stayed stuck on one image. He had no way of knowing if his sister and her baby were alive and well. What he did know was, with every day that ended, Leilani and Lanny had not appeared, so as heartbreaking and as lonely as the situation he found himself in was, he knew that his role in keeping the island safe was done, and he could sleep comfortably in that knowledge.

Having found himself in Heart, he headed straight for the place he knew his family's Dragonfly Cottage would be. The land was very different - no roads, cars, houses, nature fully in control. Jason used the landscape as his guide. Arriving on top of the same hill Alex and Sophie had, he looked down to his family's Dragonfly Cottage, hidden in the shadows of the big old house. However, he did not understand how that was there! As far as he knew, all the houses, homes, cottages and mansions in Heart, were either those of the dragonfly, the doorways between Heart and Earth, or they were built by those who chose to stay. To see a house that was not created many thousands of years earlier as a Dragonfly home, duplicated in Heart, or built by new visitors to Heart, as far as Jason was concerned, had never been heard of. He spent many of his years of trying to stay hidden, trying to understand how and why the creepy old house was there. He never found an answer.

After some time he chose to see it as an opportunity to stay hidden, so with his paranoia of being found intensifying, he took apart his Dragonfly Cottage tile by tile, stone by stone, so that it no longer existed on Heart. Despite knowing the history of its original builder and how cold and uninviting it was, he chose to live in the big old house. He placed the twig he had found in his pocket, that had taken him to Heart, where he imagined a dragonfly tree would have been if the house had been built around it, as it would have been when Shuing lived.

'Honestly, I had forgotten it was even there. I had given up on ever being able to get back to Earth, I had given up on ever seeing Alexandria or you. And then today happens. I have made friends since I have been here, carefully. Friends like Renga have kept me informed of what has been going on across Heart. Oh, Renga told me something about a strange sky... hang on, did we shut him out!' Looking out of a dirty window, Jason saw the unamused face of the bird peering in. He stood up from his seat, which almost toppled backwards as it got caught on one of the piles of sawdust and wood chippings that surrounded it, went over to the window, lifted it open with a loud and lengthy squeak and said, 'Come on in fella.'

'About time young man. It's not easy hearing what's being said from out here!' Renga said as he flew in and perched himself on the mantlepiece, the warmest part of the room. He gave his body a good shake which puffed up his feathers, creating space for the warm air to get under and heat up his cold body. 'Don't let me stop your stories. You were telling them about how I keep you informed about all things, and about the strange sky that was seen by some acquaintances of mine in a town hundreds of miles to the south of here, above the home of Leilani and Lanny.'

'That's my home,' Sophie said, 'but I didn't see anything strange in the sky!'

'Nor did I, but then we probably weren't looking,' Alex interrupted.

'You haven't told anyone about these two arriving have you?' Jason asked Renga, a very curious bird, who often said more than he should to anyone who would listen. This trait was helpful to Jason to stay informed, but not so good to those who wished something to remain secret.

'Of course not, they are quite safe,' Renga replied.

'What was strange about the sky?' Alex asked. Happy to be part of the story-telling process, Renga didn't give Jason a chance to respond.

'Well, they told me it was a swirl of colours with a centre to it. Quite spectacular by all accounts. But that wasn't the best part! They also told me that a dragonfly, bigger than they had ever seen, flew out of the house and up into the sky.' Sophie interrupted,

'That must have been when my dragonfly went through the door and disappeared. What happened to it, is it ok?'

'I think it's fine, it flew back into the house. But the ones watching left, as they were warned off by, of all creatures, Leilani's right hand step polecat, Earl! That was odd I have to say.' Jason had heard these stories already. He wanted to get back to finding out how Alex and Sophie had got to Heart, and anything else that would give him insight as to what had been, and what was possibly to come. During their run back to the old house, he had already started to make assumptions and wanted to know if they were correct.

'We came here through the cottage on the island,' Alex started,

'Clearly you did. You said that before back on the island, but how?' Jason's words were snapped at Alex, his impatience getting the better of him. Alex decided if they were going to get help from Jason and Renga, he would be just as well to tell them all that had happened. So he did. Starting from the first visit into grandmother's, Sophie's, Dragonfly Manor, darting further back in time to his moving from place to place, his experience in the canteen, their journey to the Highlands and the odd experience they had with the deer. To finding his birth mother, the island and the cave which brought the first dragonfly to him, to join with him and the connection between himself and Sophie, which ultimately took them to the cave where the pods holding dragonflies for whatever reason were found and the window, doorway, opened up, bringing them to the Dragonfly island on Heart.

Jason had been perched on the edge of his seat, leaning forward, his elbows on the table, as he intensely listened to every word. Alex's story done, Jason sat back in his chair, crossed his arms, raised his eyebrows, shook his head and said,

'Well, that is quite the story. At least that answers the tree in the hallway and the carving on the door. You are who we were born to protect.' Jason looked over to Renga, 'You can't say a word to anyone!' he said in a tone that left Renga in no doubt that he was being serious. 'So what do we do with you now then?' Although he asked the question out loud, Jason was asking himself rather than Alex and Sophie. 'I am inclined to ask you to try to bring this house to life, like you nearly did when you came in and wrecked my door! I do miss our fabulously wonderful old kitchen!' Alex and Sophie, having experienced together what magic was inside grandmother's kitchen, agreed.

'I would try again, but why did the tree burst into flames?' Alex asked. Sophie, the clever woman she was, quickly developed a theory.

'Alex, if we had created a new Dragonfly home, even if it is this creepy old house, would it also be seen back on Earth? Could someone there have seen it and burnt the tree? Remember, we saw this house at the end of the drive where your birth mother was, could she be there and have done it?'

'Yes,' Jason said. Happy to think of his sister alive and well, he stood up from his chair and made his way out of the room. Renga was happy where he was, the warmth from the fire not quite that of the Australian outback, but it was sufficient. Sophie took Alex's hand which was resting on the table, an action that Renga did not miss, who said,

'You two are more than you have said aren't you! I feel that there is a connection you may not fully understand yet, which is beyond the dragonfly. Two opposites who have found love together, that is where your real power comes from, why the power you seem to have is more intense than the stories and legends told of Shuing. You two, you are here for more than reopening Dragonfly homes.' Renga left his perch of warmth and flew down to the table, landing on their joined hands. 'Love is more powerful than any kind of hate, however not all love is good. Love can be the most magical creator, but love can also be twisted into the worst pain. Search deep inside, do not lie to yourselves with what you find, there is a darkness in all of us. With the power you have, if that darkness takes hold of your love, then that is when what once was, what has almost been lost, will be lost forever. Today the legend of the dragonfly, never completely forgotten on Heart, just never spoken about, has been brought back into our reality. Jason has asked me not to tell another. Jason is wrong.'

Renga's speech concluded, he left the still clasped hands of Alex and Sophie. Not giving notice to the danger of the flames flickering in the fireplace, he flew straight at them and up the hot chimney. Their dragonfly connection, their connection with Shuing, their arrival on Heart, none of it was going to be a secret for long.

Chapter 6

'The loss of your antlers will not slow you down I assume?' Leilani's question to the injured and trapped stag being more of a statement than a question. Having released the vines wrapped round his legs, Lanny helped his sister up on to the stag's broad back and they began the slow trek down the hillside, over the coarse heather and rocks, on to the winter's frosty grass. Occasionally rustles could be heard in the distance, beyond trees and bushes, created by those who were too curious to see why she was there to run away, but scared enough to stay hidden. Well aware of the watching eyes, Leilani wasn't interested in the cowering creatures, she was more interested in the fact her brother and his bears were disappearing out of sight. Despite Leilani making it quite clear that he was not capable of taking any kind of control, Lanny, in his arrogance, still believed that if there was any chance of the dragonfly returning, the magic returning, he would find a way to use it against her. With that in his mind, he knew he had to be the first to arrive at the loch.

Finally Lanny found himself standing at the very spot Sophie, Alex and Jason had landed. The boat was abandoned on the beach, forgotten about as they ran to keep their presence hidden from anyone who may be watching. Their fresh footsteps still imprinted in the sand, Lanny was convinced and excited that he was in the right place. He had other reasons for his happy state - although it remained a mystery to him as to how Leilani was able to control what grew on land; it appeared over the years that the same abilities were not present in water. This meant that with the distance she was from him, she was not going to be able to stop him from doing what he was going to do. The final and biggest reason for his heightened state of joy, was that although he was the male of the siblings, fully aware he could never have control of a dragonfly that already resided within any Dragonfly home, he was convinced that the island, if he could find it, would be different. The first dragonfly had chosen Shuing, a man.

'Time to find what she has been looking for boys,' Lanny said as he shoved the boat off the sand and into the water. George and Gregg, nasty and viscous in the right circumstances, were cowards when it came to water, especially cold water. Pretending to join him, they pushed the boat as Lanny got himself comfortable and, oh dear, the boat was now too far out for them to jump into. Having only just got their paws wet, they stepped back on to the sand. Lanny, struggling to get the big old oars in place, hadn't even noticed his companions' lack of presence. By the time he was settled and noticed he was alone, he was twenty metres out from shore.

'You pathetic excuse for generals!' he yelled back at the very happy with themselves bears. Happy not to be in the water, but also happy at the fact that if Lanny did find any kind of power or doorway out there, they would not be the ones he would be experimenting on.

Oars in place, roughly where he wanted to go pinpointed, he began rowing. He couldn't see any island, but what he did see was an area of mist which he assumed was hiding it. The air was cold and silent, there was not a breeze, not a ripple on the surface of the loch's water. The only sound was the water being pushed aside by the slow moving oars. It was eerie.

His back to the direction he was travelling, Lanny frequently looked over his shoulder to make sure he was still heading in the right direction.

The eerie silence didn't last for long. When Leilani arrived at the place her brother had cast the boat from, she began screaming across the loch at him. He watched as she got off the stag's back and proceeded to kick George and Gregg in frustration. Her bony legs, almost void of muscle, caused the bears no real discomfort. Lanny could hear the screams coming from his mad sister, but couldn't make out her words, not that it would have made any difference to him - as far as he was concerned, he was about to take back control.

Suddenly the screaming stopped, as did the gentle sound of water rolling over the oars. His actions hadn't changed, he was still pulling them through the water, but they weren't making any sound. The mist Lanny thought he was some distance from had engulfed him.

'I don't like this!' he said out loud. Well, he thought he said it out loud, he did hear his own words, but in his head. The dullness of the sound was like it would be if he was under the water, not in a boat above it. Then he felt a pressure squeezing his body, again as though he was underwater - deep, deep underwater. The pressure caused his head to throb and his ears to hurt in a way he had never experienced. He went to cover his ears with his hands and hold his head, and in doing so, he dropped the oars, which floated off into the thickening mist. He was stranded, lost, in the bright, white, silent world he found himself in. Just at the point Lanny thought he was about to be completely crushed by the invisible pressure, the boat began to spin. Slowly at first, then it got faster and faster. Fearful that he was going to be thrown over the edge, he had no choice but to let go of his head and hold on tight to the sharp seat he had been thrown to one side of.

Faster and faster he and the boat spun. The pain from the pressure his body and head were feeling was added to, as the feeling of dizziness and sickness arrived. Lanny closed his eyes, hoping for it to end, but instead he felt and heard a pop that came from inside his ears, which was followed by the feeling of wetness! The liquid pouring from his ears ran across his face and round his head, taken there by the continual, seemingly never-ending spinning. His body slowly adjusted to the motion as his ears were able to hear again. What he heard was a high-pitched noise which made the pain his head was feeling even worse. It caused his eyes to pop wide open! As soon as they did, the boat stopped spinning and with great force it was thrown from the mist, back out across the loch towards the beach. Back to where his sister stood. Although the boat had stopped spinning, his insides had not. It felt as though his brain was spinning in his head, so he closed his eyes once again, hoping for it to stop. It did not. He couldn't feel any part of his body anymore, he had no control over it. So when he fell backwards off his seat, he was unable to stop himself. Before making contact with the damp floor of the boat, Lanny lost consciousness.

The boat drifted to the shore where Leilani, George, Gregg and the enslaved stag had been waiting. They had seen the boat vanish for what had been a relatively short time for Lanny, but for Leilani, it had been a frustrating two hours. Helpless, unable to catch up with her brother, all she had been able to do was wait. Leilani shouted at the boat as it approached. There was no answer. She had seen that Lanny was in it as he and the boat were spat out from the mist. She had seen him fall from his seat. She was certain he had not found what they were looking for, as he would most certainly be making it known, and she would most probably already have been the subject of his wrath. The boat, having lost some of its initial momentum, gently landed on the sand.

'George, Gregg, go and see what has happened to your master.' Leilani did not want to be the subject of a surprise attack. Together, they tentatively peeked over the side of the beached boat. Lanny was lying backwards, bent over the seat, his head and feet the only parts of him making contact with the boat's damp floor. Mixed in with the water that had found its way into the boat, was the liquid that Lanny had felt across his face - blood that had been forced out from not only his ears, but also his eyes.

'He isn't moving!' George shouted back to Leilani.

'What do you mean, is he alive?' Leilani screeched back. Neither George nor Gregg were too keen on getting in, but knowing it was either that or Leilani forcing them to, they thrust their claws into the old wood, climbed up the side of the boat and got in. With the back of his paw Gregg pushed the leg of the motionless Lanny. He did not respond. So George placed his paw on Lanny's chest,

'He is breathing, but he doesn't look so well,' he shouted back to Leilani.

'Well get him out of there. Bring him to me,' she ordered back. George took hold of Lanny's shoulders and Gregg took hold of his legs as they lifted him up and unceremoniously dropped him over the side, his upper body's landing cushioned by the soft sand, his legs splashing into the water. Leilani let out a gasp as she approached her brother. What she saw was not what she had seen before he left her side at the top of the hill. Lanny's youth had been taken from him. It was as though the last dragonfly he consumed, the one that had left him many years younger than her, had never been. He was old, skinny, wrinkled, almost unrecognisable. It was the first time in her life she had seen her brother old! The surprise passing, in true Leilani style, she burst out laughing.

'Ha, ha, ha, ha... you stupid old man. I told you you would never be in control.' Revelling in the moment, she left her brother laying on the cold, wet ground and walked back up the beach to where she had seen a rock she could sit on. She was not interested in helping her brother. If he survived, he survived. If he didn't, oh well. What she was interested in, was figuring out if she went out in the boat, would she return the same way? After a short while of contemplation, she decided that she had two courses of action to choose from. Firstly, she could send one of the bears into the mist, or secondly, she had to wake her brother, if he could be woken! to ask what had happened in the two hours he had gone missing... what he had seen. Not one hundred percent sure she was ready to hear from her brother, she decided that as much information as possible before he woke would be the better option, just in case, as would be the norm, he tried to tell her things other than the truth.

'One of you is going for a cruise, you can choose!' Leilani said to George and Gregg who were still in the boat. George was the fastest of the two and had already anticipated that may have been the outcome, so he was the first to react. Out of the boat in a flash, he pushed it back into the loch before Gregg had a chance to react or protest.

'There are no oars!' Gregg shouted back to a smug-looking George.

'Use your ugly paws, they're big enough!' George's insult and advice were not appreciated, but Gregg didn't have much choice. Leaning over the front of the boat, his weight lifting the rear of it out of the water, his paws just reached as he began his first ever swim with the biggest, most disproportionate float ever. Thankfully, George's push had got him out quite far and drifting in the right direction. It didn't take long for him to feel the change in temperature as the mist got closer. Gregg lifted himself up from the water and stood up on all fours as the mist wrapped itself round him.

'Bang!' The thud on the boat's hull gave him a fright. He went to the side to see what he had hit. It was the oars, contently floating where they had been lost. He reached over the side and jamming the first one into the side of the boat, he harpooned it with his claws and pulled it in. He repeated the process with the other oar, happy to have a way of getting back out of the place he found himself in, if something went wrong. He listened to the quiet relaxing sound of the water bouncing off the boat, occasionally broken by the not so relaxing sounds of Leilani screeching from the shore. After finding nothing remarkable in the thick mist, and unlike Lanny, being able to hear clearly, Gregg and the boat slowly appeared from the mist again, although this time out the other side of it. Looking down at his body, arms and legs nervously, Gregg smiled a toothy smile as he saw no sign of aging at all, anywhere. He was as young as he was when he drifted into the mist. His joy getting the better of him, he began jumping up and down, causing the boat to rock violently side to side, almost throwing him into the loch. Realising how close he was to getting wet, he got control of himself and sat back down.

Having come out the opposite side of the mist unchanged, safe, he decided not to chance his luck a second time, so after popping the oars back into their rusted mounts, he rowed his way round it, rather than going through it.

Arriving back at the beach, Gregg saw Lanny resting up against a rock. He had been pulled from the water by George. Although he had been placed in an upright position, he was still unconscious. He also saw Leilani who, having no interest in her brother's wellbeing, had been staring out, waiting for his return. Climbing out of the boat, he couldn't help but think there was something missing. It took him a moment to figure it out, but eventually he realised that the something missing was a someone - the stag had gone! With Leilani and George preoccupied, he had taken the opportunity to escape, bouncing as quietly as he could over the open countryside to the closest wooded area to hide.

'So what have you to report? Was there an island in there?' Leilani enquired as the returning bear finished his climb out of the boat, 'What are you smirking about you matted mess of a bear?!' Gregg couldn't hide his joy at returning to dry land, and that he was unchanged. As hard as he tried, he couldn't get the smile off his face. Leilani was happy to help - she threw a jagged-edged stone that she had picked up whilst waiting for his return, with incredible accuracy. Rubbing his furry head at the site of the impact, Gregg finally answered, without a smile!

'There was nothing, just mist!'

'Nothing, nothing! How is that possible? George come here. You can go out and see what your useless comrade could not.' Leilani was not amused. George, doing as instructed, arrived at Leilani's side and said,

'Mistress, with all loyal and devoted respect, could I suggest we look for whoever those footprints belong to.' George pointed to the deep prints that were still visible in the sand, set by Sophie, Alex and Jason. 'Whatever caused the explosion of water and light, could it be that they were responsible? Maybe there is no island!' Leilani heard his words, but rage was taking over.

'Footprints, you stupid creature!' she screamed as loud as they had ever heard her, 'Get in the boat!' There was a pause before George very nervously said,

'Erm, what boat?'

During the debate, the boat had drifted away from shore. Not only that, but with its age getting the better of it, and thanks to the jumping, celebrating Gregg, whose claws had punctured holes in its floor, it was sinking! George and Gregg, anticipating some sort of a blow, scurried up the beach, back to the side of Lanny.

'Where is the stag?!' Leilani's screeching this time slightly quieter, although her tone was still as viciously angry. Gregg looked at George, his eyes wide open, and whispered,

'Should we do as the stag, you know, disappear?'

'Do you really think we would get far, and what about master Lanny?' George replied. As scared of both Lanny and Leilani as they were, Lanny would occasionally show them kindness. They stayed. George tried again with his suggestion, 'Mistress Leilani. We should look for who those footprints belong to.'

'You expect me to walk? And what about my brother?' was Leilani's reply.

'We can carry master Lanny, and we are sure to find another stag or other four legged creature not too far away to help with your transport.'

Blunt instruments in the dragonfly searches, tearing apart whoever did not comply, both George and Gregg had been around Lanny long enough to learn tactics, and how to deal with Leilani. They always tried to have as little communication with Leilani as possible, but with Lanny in the state he was, this time they had no choice. Leilani was surprised at their intelligence, quite different to their usual cowardice towards her and aggression to all others. She dug her toes deep into the sand as she took a moment to contemplate. Feeling the energies of all the living creatures around her, she felt a spooked nesting eagle take off with her two young ones. As with the water and those that lived in it, as long as they didn't touch the bed of the loch, Leilani had no control of birds in flight. However before they had taken off, she sensed something.

'We shall head towards that big house I saw from the hill. They are there,' Leilani said knowingly. She removed her feet from the cold, wet sand and with her old bones creaking, she began walking in its direction.

'How are we going to lift him? He looks much lighter than he was before, but he is still bigger than we are,' Gregg said to George. George didn't answer, he was already looking around for something that would help them.

'The oars, they will work!' George said excitedly. Having not been secured by Gregg as he left the boat, they had fallen into and got stuck in the sand below the shallow water, protruding out just enough for George to grab them without getting his paws too wet. 'These will work quite well.' He took off his leather shoulder armour and wrapped the two oars together. Instructing Gregg to remove his as well, attaching the two together he created a harness for the two bears to pull their master. It took them ten minutes to construct their masterpiece of ingenuity, as they saw it, and get Lanny safely on it before heading off in the direction Leilani had gone. It didn't take long for them to catch up with her, her old legs tiring fast.

'Who do you think was at the loch boys? Who do you think we are going to find in that house?' Leilani asked. Having had ten minutes away from her brother and his bears, plus having got the information she had from the fleeing eagle, meant her anger had subsided. The bears showing intelligence Leilani was unaware they had, not that she respected them any more than she did any other creature, meant that to the bears surprise, she was talking to them like she would her lost Earl. The two bears sent a secret glance each other's way, eyes wide, eyebrows raised, shocked! Nervous to be the one who may say the wrong thing, they gestured with their heads in each other's direction for the other to answer. 'BOYS!' Her patience was gone already.

'Mistress Leilani, I do not know. But be assured whoever is there will give us answers,' was George's response. With Leilani's old legs and the bears tiring as they dragged Lanny, it was a slow walk across the flat section of land passing through the same clumps of trees that Alex, Sophie and Jason had used as cover, before dashing across the next open section of land. Eventually they came to the bottom of the small hill, beyond which was the house. The hill itself, on the side they were about to climb, was covered in tall pine trees. The tops were thick with deep green needles, whereas the majority of the lower sections were sparse, which made it easy for them to see far up the hillside, but not to its top. Considering Leilani's age and frail state, she was incredibly hardy. Not stopping for a rest, she carried on, determined to get to the house in as quick a time as she could. Just as they were about to enter the trees, Gregg shouted,

'Mistress Leilani, wait!' He had heard snapping twigs. Focusing hard on the area he thought the sound came from, he saw movement. He dropped the part of the makeshift harness he was using to pull Lanny and shot off into the woods at great speed. The creature who had stepped on the twigs was a fox. He didn't stand a chance. By the time he knew what was happening, Gregg had him pinned to the floor, standing over him with his huge, razor-sharp teeth on full show. George wasn't far behind. Once he arrived, Gregg stepped to the side of the fox and together they pulled him up and led the shaking creature back out of the woods, back to Leilani.

'Well he is no good for transport,' Leilani sarcastically said. 'Stop your shaking and tell me who passed through here earlier today. I know they went to the big house over the hill, are they still there?' The petrified fox couldn't help himself. He had heard all the stories about the siblings and their evil doings, how they tortured and maimed anyone who stood in their way. So the fox, scared of what would happen to him, told them all he knew. Sadly for those in the big house, he knew quite a lot, thanks to the big-mouthed Renga.

'There are three. One has lived there for many years, but two have just arrived. They have the magic of the dragonfly with them, a boy and a girl. But I don't know if they are still there.'

'How do you know this?' Leilani asked.

'Word is spreading fast. Spread by a bird who witnessed it,' the fox replied.

'So you have not seen them. You do not know for fact what you are saying is the truth. You do not know if what you are saying is a stupid bird's exaggeration of nothing!' Leilani said. As cynical as she was, she always believed that the truth was somewhere between the lines of what anyone said to her. On this occasion, on the one hand the words he said seemed too good to be true, and on the other, was a truth she did not want to hear as she wanted to be the one with the magic of the dragonfly.

'There is only one way we are going to find out. Cut his throat, we will see for ourselves!' Leilani gave her order to the two bears, who carried it out with more pleasure than any creature should whilst taking the life of another. 'Come on,' Leilani said to the bears as she walked away from the lifeless fox. About to follow, Gregg saw more movement from where he had seen the fox informant. Two small baby foxes and their mother had broken cover, their eyes filled with horror at what they had just witnessed.

Knowing they had been seen, they turned and vanished out of sight, beyond some fallen trees.

'Leave them! They are of no use to us.' Going against their instincts, George and Gregg did as instructed and turned back to collect Lanny, before following Leilani into the trees.

With the sun unable to break through the thick pine needles high above them, the air in the trees was cold enough for Leilani to see her breath. Not that she felt cold. With her unusual exertion of physical energy, she was quite warm. Climbing over fallen trees, brush, the skeletons of heather that no longer flowered, and with no one talking, Leilani found herself going over the past couple of days in her mind. Analysing every moment just in case she had missed something. The torso on her doorstep, the first sight of the dragonfly, losing the dragonfly, discovering the location, the very existence of the island and what she believed was on it. Through all her mind's searching of the past, the fox's recent words kept coming back to her - "they have the magic of the dragonfly with them, a boy and a girl." Could it be the boy and girl he referred to were the two she had seen through her window to Earth? But how could it be, how could they be on Heart?

'Gregg, you saw nothing in the mist?' Leilani asked.

'No mistress Leilani,' he replied.

'Stop!' Leilani ordered. Interest in her brother's care had not developed, but interest in waking him to find out what he had seen, what had happened to him, had. Before they got to the house she wanted more information. She slapped his grey looking bony cheek, which went red. 'I am sure you can hear me you ridiculous man. Open your eyes!' He didn't.

'A Legend Remembered' 111

Leilani had an idea. 'Lay him on the ground.' The bears did as she asked. They then undid Lanny's belt, the strap that was holding him in place, and rolled him off the oars.

Leilani walked up beside him and pushed her feet, with their gold and diamond jewellery, into the earth. As soon as she did, Lanny was catapulted above the height of Leilani's head. She had used nature's energy, found deep in the ground, to shoot a surge of electricity into him. George and Gregg instinctively ran to catch him before he landed back on the harsh, sharp, twig and dead plant-covered ground. With incredible precision, they caught him and lowered him back down.

'He doesn't deserve your help! Stupid man brought whatever is wrong with him on himself,' Leilani snapped at the bears.

'What have I brought on myself?!' The hoarse voice came from Lanny. Sitting himself up and looking around the unfamiliar surroundings he found himself in, he then asked, 'how did I get here?' Then it all came rushing back - the boat trip, the pain in his head from the crushing pressure, his age! He looked down at his hands. He hadn't imagined it. They were skinny and bony, the skin patchy and pale. 'Sister...' she didn't give him a chance to finish his question.

'What did you see in the mist?'

'Nothing, just mist!' Lanny replied, still looking at his old hands,

'Don't talk such rubbish, you were gone for hours.' Lanny snapped his cracking neck round to look at his sister,

'Hours?!' he said.

'Yes hours. You found something in there, how else could you be the old man you are? Tell me or I will find the most painful way to put you back in your coma!' she replied. Lanny, with the help of his generals, got himself to his feet.

'You can do as you wish, but what happened to me happened in moments, not hours. As quick as I was in it, I was spat out of that strange mist. Wait! Why did you leave? Why did you take me away from the loch? We have to go back,' he said. As nervous as he was that returning to the mist could age him to his death, he was convinced that what had happened to him was proof there was magic there, magic that, if it could take his youth, could return it. George interrupted the conversation and informed Lanny of what had happened to Gregg when he entered in, and through the mist. He brought him up to date with the reason for them heading to where they were, and what the dead fox had told them.

'Interesting. The dragonfly lives,' Lanny said.

'Any particular dragonfly, or are you just being dramatic?' Leilani said, belittling her brother as she always did since becoming the dominant one of the two.

'Sister, do you not understand? If we were going to the island where it all began, the likelihood is that the dragonfly that started it all, is why the boy and girl the fox referred to hold some sort of magic.' Lanny's head was no longer in pain, he was old but his strength was returning. He could feel a tingle of excitement spreading through his body. The magic of the dragonfly had left the place that had spat him out, it had not been claimed by Leilani, a fact that to him meant he still had a chance to take the power for himself. His youth would return, the doors to Earth would open for him, his gold would bring him back the power on Earth he craved, he would have control of all humankind, animal-kind and all of nature. All he had to do was find them, and from what George and Gregg had told him, his search would end just over the hill.

'We will have the dragonfly magic by the end of today!' He turned and winked one of his wrinkled eyes at his generals and whispered,

'Well I will anyway.'

Chapter 7

'What's that noise?' Sophie asked.

'Sounds like it's coming from the hallway!' Alex replied as he quickly got up and disappeared out of the room to investigate. Jason, who had been in another part of the house and having also heard the sound, arrived at the same time as Sophie, to see Alex with a worried look on his face, staring at the front door as a frantic scratching noise echoed around the hallway.

'Would appear someone would like to come in,' Jason said calmly as he walked past Alex and opened the door. Just slightly open, two fluffy foxes scrambled their way in, forcing the door open faster than Jason had planned. The two fluff balls were closely followed by their mother, who was more controlled in her entrance. Once inside, the door closed behind her. Out of breath, she said,

'They are coming... my partner told them... it's them!' Jason was just able to decipher her frantically spoken words, but they were totally missed by Alex, who was still getting used to animals talking, and by Sophie, who had instantly fallen in love with the two small foxes running towards her. Jason, trying to calm her down said,

'It's ok, slow down and take a breath.'

'The evil woman, the sister, she is here, she is coming! She killed him!' Her head dropped. Heartbroken, she couldn't say another word. The bodies of the small foxes, who had jumped into Sophie's arms as she bent down to say hello, were shaking uncontrollably. In a tiny voice, the one snuggling into her left shoulder looked up and said,

'The bear made my dad's throat bleed! Then he didn't move, like he was sleeping!' The fox's words brought tears to Sophie's eyes.

Having pieced together what he could from the broken sentences of the cubs' mother, Jason quickly came to a conclusion. Before acting on it, he wanted to clarify something. He ran out the front door and into the trees in the opposite direction of the trees they had all arrived through, the ones Leilani and her brother were not far from. Once he was through them and across a field of grass, having climbed over a pile of rocks taller than he was, he arrived at a hidden door on the ground. It was not as well hidden as the occupier would have liked. The grass that covered it, which was supposed to be there so that only those who knew of the door's existence could find it, was a different shade to the surrounding grass. Jason pulled at a small, innocuous looking dead tree - a handle, and the not-so-well hidden door opened.

'Gracie, you in here?' Jason shouted, as he ran down a short flight of stairs cut into the stony soil. Gracie had lived in Heart for a little over fifty years. Never having known anything different from Heart, after her parents passed she spent ten years of her life without any human contact at all, until one day, a confused Jason appeared at the big old house and its Dragonfly cottage. She kept herself hidden from him for quite some time, worried that he was connected to Leilani and Lanny, especially after he completely demolished the Dragonfly cottage! That was until one dark and extremely wet night, when her underground home flooded. As she escaped out of her, at that time, very well hidden door, she found herself standing right in front of Jason. Eight years on, after a rocky and untrusting start, they had become very good friends.

'Yes my dear, as always, I am here,' a rough voice replied from a rocking chair which faced a small fireplace on the opposite side of the room. 'Quite the noisy entrance I have to say! And from the draught wrapping round my legs, I assume the door is still open!' She peeked round from her chair and smiled. Seeing the look on his face, her smile was quickly replaced with a concerned frown. 'What's wrong?' she asked.

'Have you seen Zachariah today?' Jason asked,

'No, actually I haven't. Unusual now I think about it,' Gracie replied. Zachariah was a stag who always seemed to be very well informed about all things, both nearby and far away. 'What's wrong Jason?'

'Give me a minute to think,' he said. 'Where do you think I could find him?' Jason then asked.

'He is usually in the forest over the hill, that is if he isn't visiting me. Jason, you are beginning to worry me. I've never seen you like this!' Gracie said, getting up from her very old, but very comfortable chair.

'Leilani and Lanny, I think they are here. Close by. I think they know about my new friends,' Jason replied.

'New friends?' Gracie's curious tone asked as she grabbed his arm in an effort to stop him pacing round her room's already well-worn floor.

'You really haven't heard anything have you? I assumed with Renga leaving so suddenly everyone would know by now! Did you not see, or at least hear the explosion this morning?' Jason asked, adding to his first question.

'No, I've been here all day. You know what it's like in my little hole, once that door you have left open! Is closed, I am in my own little world. But that doesn't matter, everyone would know what?' she asked.

'Strange things have been happening today. Back in my house are two people with a dragonfly! They are special Gracie, they have come from Earth's realm and Leilani and Lanny, I think they know,' Jason replied.

'What, on Heart! Is there anything I can do? What do you need Zachariah for?' Gracie asked,

'Confirmation, he usually knows everything that happens. And no, no, not really, I think the fewer involved the better. I think we need somewhere to hide, I need to get them away from here in a hurry,' Jason said. Not getting the answers he was hoping for, he turned, and as quickly as he had descended, he climbed back up the well-used stairs, back out into the cold day.

'Wait for me, I am coming with you,' Gracie shouted, her voice muffled by the coat she was frantically trying to get on. By the time Gracie had closed her grassy door, Jason was already halfway across the field. She shouted his name hoping he would stop and wait for her. She knew how quick he could move and with the trees not too far ahead, she was going to lose sight of him. Not stopping or slowing, Jason was too focused on getting back to Alex and Sophie. Having left them without explanation and in such a hurry, he was worried that they may have left, or been discovered by the evil siblings.

Through the trees and out the other side, much to his relief he saw Alex standing at the front door. The light hit him in such a way that Jason couldn't help but see the resemblance to his sister, Alex's mother. The sight of him standing where he was caused Jason to stop, as it brought back memories of the times Alexandria would be standing in that very same place back on Earth, her mind wandering, looking out over the land. His pause was momentary, as a rustle from the trees pulled him out of his happy memories. Darting sideways, back into the trees and away from where the sound had come from, he hid himself.

'Jason you silly boy, it's me!' Gracie had caught him up. Not saying a word, just giving Gracie a little smile he carried on back towards the house, with an out of breath Gracie following.

'Sophie, he's back!' Alex shouted. Sophie was sitting on the bottom step of the staircase playing with the two fox cubs - a very welcome distraction. Getting up to join Alex, she almost fell over the excited foxes as they ran round her ankles.

'Who is that?' Sophie asked, looking across to see a woman walking alongside Jason. Her extremely long, below her waist, thick, straight hair bounced, just as her long, flower-covered coat did with every step she took. They figured if she was returning with Jason, she was no-one to be afraid of.

'Gracie, this is my nephew Alex and his friend Sophie,' Jason said, introducing everyone as they arrived at the steps of the big old house. The enormity of who Gracie was being introduced to hit her.

'But how can this be? He is on Earth!' She stepped closer, 'he does have your eyes.' As she said it, the sun popped out from behind a low-lying cloud and shone across Alex's face. 'I take that back!' She had seen the hint of purple that only those who looked closely were lucky enough to see. 'His eyes are like nothing I have seen before! Can I assume these two are the reason for the state you are in Jason?' she asked. His response was,

'Come inside, we need to figure out what to do.'

'Oh, hello Averie. Aah, look how big your babies have got,' Gracie said, as she bent down to say a loving hello to Ryley and Hanne, the two fox cubs. The happy greeting was short lived as Averie, the cubs' mother, told Gracie about what had happened to her partner, her cubs father.

'Oh my goodness! I am so sorry. Is there anything I can do for you?' Gracie asked the heartbroken Averie. Before she had time to answer, Gracie took a sudden intake of breath and said, 'Please tell me the cubs didn't see?!' Sadly, Averie confirmed that they had seen every second of the horrific ten minutes. Jason felt bad for interrupting, but he was concerned, and said,

'The same may happen to all of us if we don't figure out where they are and how much they know.' Alex and Sophie, bystanders, had been quietly listening and watching, still not quite believing where they were and what they were seeing.

'I think we should go. If it's us that this crazy woman is after, it's not fair to bring these innocents into it,' Sophie whispered to Alex. Having been a loner all his life, having to fight every battle himself, becoming one with the dragonfly meant that his mind and heart were being opened to bigger possibilities, bigger realities. He replied,

'No. That is the problem in today's reality. Too many working on their own rather than together for the good of all. No, we should involve as many as we can, the minority should not speak for the majority any more.' Alex recalled all the times he had suffered at the hands of one or two bullies whilst many watched, either too nervous to help or so self-involved they didn't care. From the stories he had heard from grandmother, he so wanted Heart to be the place of escape and healing that it had once been, for all. To do that there was only one way forward. 'Together, remember, always together.'

Sophie knew he was right, and feeling slightly embarrassed she looked away from him. As she dropped her head, her hair fell forward and exposed the colours on her neck. They were changing from bright, vibrant colours to dull versions of themselves. Alex could see in her, feel from her, how he himself had felt on far too many occasions in his life. He pulled her close and took her in his arms. 'You have no reason to feel the way you are. Believe in yourself. What you said came from a place of love and protection of others. You weren't wrong in what you said, it's just a different point of view.'

Sophie, as loved as she was by her grandmother and given all kinds of positive in her life, had actually never heard anything like the words Alex said to her. It was like a lightbulb had been turned on in her head. The bright colours returning to her swirls, she squeezed Alex tight. Her usual self would have retreated and found a place to hide from the world, but with Alex she felt she could take it on.

'What was that?'

Gracie had seen the colours on Sophie fade and return. 'Jason, can you fill me in here please?' she requested. With a quick and short rundown of what Sophie and Alex had told him, she was up to speed. 'We have to get them away from here!' Gracie said,

'That's what I have been saying!' was Jason's reply.

'A Legend Remembered'

'Don't mean to be rude, but you two are aware we are standing right here! I appreciate what you are saying, but I have spent my life running away, not that I knew that was what we were doing right enough. Less than two days ago I was told to leave a house because of fear of what may be. For one of the first times I chose not to run, a choice that meant that I am standing here today. This is not the time for running away, we can run forward but not away!'

Alex's words surprised the older ones in their maturity. For them, having lived in Heart in fear because of what Leilani and Lanny had done to all they came across, they had a different perspective, a more informed perspective. But maybe Alex was right.

'You have not seen firsthand what they are capable of!' Averie said with a lump in her throat. Her two cubs ran over to her and rubbed their noses on her face. 'It's alright you two, I am ok,' she said, composing herself. Alex was suddenly finding it hard to breathe. He didn't want anyone to notice, so he stepped away from Sophie and the group who were focused on Averie, back into the warm room with the old wooden table surrounded by sawdust.

'What's wrong with me?' he said quietly.

'You know what's wrong with you. You have felt it many times before. Remember, you are a descendant of Shuing. You, as he did, will feel all emotion around you. I have been protecting you since we joined, but you needed to feel what Averie and her cubs were feeling. Your words were wise, but do not underestimate the horrors that could be.'

The dragonfly's words filled his head. Like an injury that had healed, forgotten as quickly as it arrived, he had completely missed the fact that he was not feeling what he had many times back on Earth, ever since that day in the school canteen. Thinking back, he realised the only emotions he had felt since their visit to the cave had been Sophie's.

The pain in his heart subsiding and his breath returning to normal, he straightened himself up and stepped back out into the hallway.

'You must open your heart to all around you Alex. Embrace the love, the fear, the loss, the hope, the memories, and when you are ready, I will allow you to feel them once more. Be the part of nature that brings all things together, that heals those who need it. To do that first you must survive.' Alex had taken Sophie's hand as the dragonfly's speech was coming to an end. She heard the last sentence.

'Surviving seems like a very good idea to me,' Sophie said, reminding Alex what happens when they touch. With the front door still open and Sophie and Alex being the only ones looking towards it, they were suddenly greeted by a frightening sight. Both instinctively stepped back, crashing into the door Alex had just come out of. What they saw was a creature with its face covered in blood! A stag, the very stag that had escaped from Leilani, her brother and the bears on the loch's beach.

'Zachariah!' Gracie exclaimed, having turned to see what Sophie and Alex were backing away from. She ran over to him, took his face in her hands and with the sleeve of her coat, tried to wipe away some of the dry blood. The blood that had run down his face after his first failed attempt at an escape, when Leilani caused him to somersault and crash into the ground which resulted in his impressive antlers being ripped from his head.

'Give no mind to me. You all need to leave. Now! Leilani and her brother will be in sight of here within minutes.' Zachariah's deep booming voice echoed through the hallway. Unlike the usual gentleman he was, he shook his head to free it from Gracie's hands and barged past her. 'You two cannot be found by them, they know you are here and what you have with you.'

'I knew it! That bird can't keep his mouth shut!' a frustrated Jason said.

'Do not hold any ill thoughts towards him. He is right to tell all who will listen. Too much time hiding in the shadows has been spent by all of us. At this time all that is important is to get away from here,' Zachariah reiterated. The direction in which Leilani, Lanny and his generals would come from was known, so the choice of direction in which they should make their escape was a simple one. Zachariah took them north from the big old house to avoid the westerly arrival of the twins, and to avoid the direction Averie thought they were likely to head when they didn't find Alex and Sophie there - the direction of the run-down Dragonfly cottage the siblings had arrived to the area through.

It was quickly apparent that the cubs little legs were not going to be able to keep up with the group. Having been helped up they were enjoying a ride on the back of Zachariah, squeaking with every jump or quick change of direction he made. Through the trees, across the field and past Gracie's hidden home, they arrived at a much larger grouping of trees as a sea of eyes greeted the group, unseen by all but Zachariah. The news of Alex, Sophie and the dragonfly had the same effect as the swirling colours above Leilani's Dragonfly Manor the morning before. Every kind of living creature was curious to see what it meant, curious to see those who may return peace, calm, healing and balance to Heart, and in turn, Earth.

Zachariah, having crashed through several metres of thick, sharp gorse bushes at the forest's entrance, cleared a way for the rest to follow and led them deep into the forest whilst the eyes watched. They finally arrived at the small clearing he was heading for, a place he knew Leilani and Lanny would not find without help. The perfect place with its soft ground for the group to take a seat and catch their breath.

'We should be safe here for the time being. The birds will soon tell us if there is any reason for us to leave,' Zachariah said.

Standing in silence and looking around at the magnificent trees that towered over them, their breathing quietened. The group could hear movement coming from all around them. The many creatures that had been following them, the ones Zachariah was well aware of, were jostling for positions to get a look at the forest's visitors.

'Don't worry, there is nothing here that will hurt you,' Zachariah said.

True to his word, the ancient dragonfly slowly let Alex feel those responsible for the rustling. To begin with, it was a mixture of love and fear. As the heat built up inside him, Sophie noticed a change in Alex. His eyes wide open, the hint of purple in their usual blue was changing, just as it did back at grandmother's Dragonfly Manor. The blue was being replaced with purple and the whites of his eyes were shining with a supernatural light. Sophie stepped towards him. Aware of the movement, he lifted his arm and gestured for her not to come any closer. The intensity rising he did not want her to be hurt, for her to be broken as the tray had been those four years earlier, or thrown like his mother back at the square when he lost control of what he was feeling, experiencing. Seeing what was happening, although not really understanding it, Jason grabbed hold of Sophie's arm and tried to pull her back. As soon as he did he was met with an electric shock! Sophie could feel the sensation of the unseen colours on her back swirling, a wave of colourful energy that made its way up her neck and over her shoulders.

'Together!'

The single word spoken by the dragonfly pierced the fog of emotions that were filling Alex's mind. He reached out his arm, this time beckoning Sophie to come closer. Just a foot from him, the colours that were wrapped around her body spread out from her like an angel spreading its wings and surrounded Alex. The intense colours encapsulating them had the effect of hiding them from the secret onlookers. As soon as they touched, Sophie felt exactly what Alex was feeling.

'Together you can see everything,' the dragonfly said, removing all the barriers he had put in place when he joined with Alex on the Dragonfly island. Barriers to protect him from the intense emotions he would not have understood or coped with at the time. Holding each other tight, Alex and Sophie were witnessing similar images to those Alex had experienced at the age of twelve. The experience that had put him into an unconscious state in the grounds of his school. They could see the happy memories and feel the feelings, the emotions, of all that were around them. Thankfully for Alex, the heat that had been building inside him dissipated as soon as Sophie and her swirling colours wrapped him up. However, the intensity and pressure in his head and heart had not.

'This is beautiful!' Sophie exclaimed. She wasn't feeling the pressure Alex was, she was just seeing. Just as he was relaxing, letting himself go and allowing himself to feel what he was feeling, the visions changed! Darker, frightening. He was hit with the reality of living life on Heart with Leilani and her brother, as was Sophie. The loss, the suffering, the pain that every living thing around them had experienced. Sophie, not liking it one bit, pulled away from Alex. As soon as she did, the images shared between them came to an end, for her.

Although she was free, she was not back in the real world. Still inside her swirling colours Sophie let out a scream! The calm silence she had been experiencing was broken by the horrifying, familiar sound of pounding feet, growls and the heavy breathing of the huge, unseen animal that had stalked her in the cave's tunnels in her dreams. The same cave she and Alex had experienced in real life earlier that day, back on Dragonfly island. Trapped in her waking dream, the sounds getting closer and closer, she screamed 'Alex!' As soon as she did, the familiar silhouette of her protector and his bright eyes appeared.

'It's ok,' Alex's voice calmly said. With a blink of Sophie's eyes, the silhouette became Alex. Still in the tunnel with the growls and pounding paws as close as they had ever been, for the first time he was there with her. Alex was in her mind and heart, as though a doorway had been opened and he was not only seeing her memories, he was feeling them! Everything - her childhood, being abandoned by her parents, her life with her grandmother and her life outside the protective door of her grandmother's Dragonfly Manor, her home back on Earth.

With the journey through Sophie's life coming to an end, together they started another journey - Alex's. They travelled through his life and some memories he didn't even know he had, from the day he was born, through the pain he suffered living a life of not belonging, right up to the day of their meeting. Suddenly, with a bolt of lightening that ripped them apart throwing them to the ground several metres from one another, the journey through each other's lives ended.

'What happened?' a concerned Jason said, running over to the discarded Alex, as Gracie did to Sophie. Sitting on the damp, pine needle-covered ground being comforted and questioned by Gracie, Sophie suddenly whipped her head round and with a worried look on her face, caught Alex's eye. Somehow she just knew something, the same something that Alex knew in the very same moment. He confirmed this in a much calmer tone than Sophie expected considering what it was, as he said,

'She's in the house.' His calm tone didn't last however. In a panic he exclaimed, 'Oh no!' whilst scrambling to his feet and pulling the sleeve of his jumper up. He searched his arm for what his head knew he wouldn't find, but his heart hoped he would. The search over, his eyes wide and unblinking, he looked up at the group - 'The dragonflies, I only have two!'

Chapter 8

'And there it is,' Leilani said, as she and her brother arrived at the top of the hill overlooking the line of trees, beyond which was the big old house. Lanny was not enjoying his first ever experience of being physically very old. It certainly hadn't been a particularly gentle introduction with the long walk he had just completed. His knees were creaking as much as Leilani's, his hunched back was providing him with all kinds of shooting pains. But the potential of what could soon be, kept him going. He had to concentrate hard on putting one foot carefully in front of the other so he didn't fall, as the group made their way down the hill.

'George, Gregg, you two run ahead. Quietly! Once you get to the tree line, wait there and start on a plan for getting into the house!' Lanny coughed as he finished barking his orders. His old lungs were not as clear as they had been prior to his boat trip into the loch's mist. In a flash of greasy fur they shot down the hill, not as quietly as Lanny had wanted! As expected, their careless dash resulted in birds that were hidden in the winter heather, to fly away, calling out a warning as they did.

'Good grief, they are stupid!' Leilani said. Too busy watching the birds, she caught her foot in the undergrowth and started to fall. In an effort to stop herself she grabbed hold of her brother. Not having as much control of his limbs as he did earlier in the day, he threw his arms out to keep his balance. This had the unfortunate result of slapping his sister across her face! It was an accident that he regretted instantly. A burning sensation spread across the back of his neck as the angry Leilani's talon-like nails tore open his wrinkled skin.

'You're lucky you're my brother!' Leilani said, inferring he got off lightly for the slap she received. Convinced he would soon be in charge, Lanny gritted his teeth and stayed silent.

Having made it down the hill, Leilani and Lanny were happy to receive the bears report that no-one had left the house whilst they had been there watching. However, the bears hadn't come up with any kind of plan to gain entry. So with an assumption that the ones they were looking for were still inside, a kick from Leilani and instructions from Lanny, George was sent off round the front of the house and Gregg round the back to get an idea of where the occupants were. And to find a way to sneak in.

'What's with all this covertness Lanny? You usually just kick down the door!' she laughed, knowing fine well why this time it was different, 'feeling your age by any chance!' Lanny paid no attention to her, his focus was on the house and what was inside. George, having checked out the front, met up with Gregg who had been round the back. After a quick conversation confirming it was safe to do so, they gestured Lanny to join them.

Instructing Leilani to stay where she was, he slowly made his way over to join the bears. His body may have felt old, but his mind was sharp. His hundreds of years of life had taught him well when it came to the likely behaviour of people in confrontational situations. With his physical capabilities being different to the day before, and not having an army of bears with him, he knew his ability to take control of the situation, if there were more than a couple of living beings inside, would be a challenge.

'There doesn't seem to be anyone downstairs. It could be they are all upstairs,' George reported as Lanny arrived. He was pleased as it meant their entrance could be made via a door, rather than having to try to climb in through one of the large, but high off the ground windows. Lanny stood to one side of the front door and Gregg the other, as George slowly tried the door handle. With a scratching sound as the latch came away from the door frame, the door opened. George looked up at Lanny for his next instruction.

'Slowly, quietly.' The only guidance he gave was enough for George to know what to do. The door, although slightly broken, was surprisingly quiet - the hinges did not squeak as loud as expected. With the door open just enough for Lanny to see that the coast was clear, he reached out and grabbed a handful of George's fur and pulled him back. Having stepped into the hall, his arms at his side, he turned his hands so the palms were facing back towards his bears, a gesture that meant they were to stay behind him. He wanted a moment to take in his surroundings, and to listen for any sounds.

Having heard no movement or voices, and not having seen any sign of life, Lanny concluded that if there was any living thing in the house they were hiding, scared. With no need to be quiet anymore, and not interested in expending any energy in searching himself, he let his bears loose to tear the big old house apart, until they found whoever or whatever was hiding. They were off like a shot, happy to be back doing what they love - creating destruction. It took them some time to go through all the rooms, ripping up floorboards, tearing off cupboard doors, their huge claws puncturing holes into any wall that could have had a hidden room behind it. Lanny stayed in the hallway choosing a central point, a place that gave him a good view into every downstairs room. No one was going to be able to escape without being seen by him. He enjoyed the sounds of destruction his generals were making as they made their way around the house. To him, it was as relaxing as sitting on a summer's day with nothing but nature's sounds might be to others. The chaos brought him calm.

As he soaked up the sounds, the anticipation of who he would find hiding inside, he noticed something. A carving on the frame surrounding the front door. The waterfall - the carving that had appeared after Sophie and Alex's arrival. He left his perfect vantage point to get a closer look. It was just above his eye level on the hinge side of the door. Cut deep into the wood frame, he could see the incredible detail of the carving, each droplet of water, the rocks and plants that surrounded it.

'This has not been carved by hand,' he said to himself. Reaching up, he touched it. As his wrinkled fingers followed the grooves of the carving, he felt a warmth. 'Leilani!' he screamed at the top of his hoarse voice. She was right outside the door, her patience in waiting in the trees had been short lived, plus she could hear that the bears had been set loose on the poor house.

'Where are they?' Leilani said, scanning the area for signs of life other than her brother.

'There's no one! But look.' He pointed up at the waterfall. 'It's warm!' Leilani knew exactly what that meant, as Lanny did, and said,

'Either this is a Dragonfly house that we have missed, or we were correct in our thoughts. Something very special has happened here. A dragonfly!' She spun round looking back into the hallway, 'but there is no tree!' Lanny had missed that fact,

'Wait, look!' Having joined Leilani looking around the hall, he saw what was the burnt remains of Jason's Dragonfly Cottage's stick, once a tiny tree. 'It's warm as well.' Lanny ripped it up, an action that earned him a blow to the head.

'You idiot! If that was a dragonfly tree, if there was any life in it, there won't be now!' Leilani said, snatching the trees remains from his hand. Distracted by their discovery, they had not noticed that the house had fallen silent. George and Gregg, no longer in destruction mode, were standing at the top of the stairs, quietly arguing over who would give Lanny and his sister the bad news that they had found nothing.

'George, Gregg, get down here!' Lanny shouted, having caught sight of them skulking in the shadows. 'There is no one here is there?' His question was answered with a shake of the head from both of the bears. 'I don't understand. The fox said they were here!'

'Well, clearly whoever was here was warned. You two, get out and find me someone who will give me answers!' Happy to be given a job away from the siblings, whose frustration was growing and would inevitably be taken out on them, they bounded down the stairs and off out the front door, out of sight.

'They'll be back quick enough. In the meantime I think it would be worth our while to look round the house.' As was often the way, Leilani acknowledged

Lanny's thoughts by just walking off. Placing the dead tree into one of her ragged pockets, she headed into a room where she found a discarded table, its crooked chairs on their sides, surrounded by sawdust and Jason's carefully carved animals in bits, destroyed by the rampaging George and Gregg. Leilani picked up one of the chairs and dragged it over to the fireplace, where she was quite pleased to feel a warmth pulsing out from the ashes in the dully lit room. It emanated from its just alight embers. Glad to have her tiny weight off her skinny legs and sitting comfortably, Leilani looked around for a hint as to who lived in the very unloved looking house. There was nothing that gave her a clue, not a picture to be seen and anyone could have made the carvings.

Hearing squeaking floorboards telling Leilani where her brother was, she reflected on what had happened to him in the mist where the island should have been. She was very glad he had done what he did - if she had entered she may not have come out. As old as she was, the next step was death! Lost in her mind, she was unaware of a most unusual thing happening. One side of her long coat that had been carefully placed to cover her legs, was rising up. Finally reaching the point that was as high as it could go, the material unable to stretch any further, it fell back down onto Leilani's leg. She felt the impact and looked down to see what it was. Seeing nothing out of the ordinary, she put it down to her old legs' nerve endings sending incorrect messages to her brain.

Having not lifted her head back up from its downward searching position, she went back to thinking about the lost island and out of the corner of her eye, a small movement got her attention. The smallest of movements came from the pocket of her coat. The same pocket the burnt tiny tree had been placed in. Watching closely, the outer part of the pocket looked like it was vibrating. The experience would have most concerned, frightened, maybe even cause them to rip the coat off and throw it across the room. Leilani did not move. Instead, seated quite comfortably, she said out loud to herself 'Well that is strange!' Then once again, the lower part of the coat lifted off her leg. This time, a smirk growing on her face, she whispered 'The tree!'

Leilani slowly reached into her pocket, being careful not to make a gap so that whatever was in there could not escape. Passing the tiny tree's burnt branches, she got a prick on her forefinger. Not reacting to the jab, her hand continued in until she felt the vibrations she could see.

'There you are!' she said in a menacing voice, as the vibration was replaced by the feeling of a flutter on her hand. She knew exactly what she had trapped in her pocket - a dragonfly! The dragonfly that had been brought to the old house by Alex and Sophie, that had settled as all dragonflies do in a new or old Dragonfly home, on a magical tree. On this occasion a magical tree, a tiny burnt tree, that after snatching it from her brother, Leilani had placed in her pocket.

She had dealt with many dragonflies over the years and had no hesitation in gripping the smaller than usual version in her bony hands. Before removing it from her pocket she squeezed it tightly, so tight that all signs of life were taken from its young body. Its wings and wiggling legs motionless, Leilani took her hand from her pocket. Loosening her grip slightly, just enough that she could peer in, like looking through the iron bars of a prison cell, she confirmed the bug was no more. Her smirk became the largest of smiles just as Lanny entered the room, returning from his unsuccessful search.

'What is it?' He wasn't used to seeing his sister's face with such a smile. Leilani didn't respond. Instead, with the forefinger and thumb from her free hand, she plucked a wing from her discovery and placed it into her mouth. The effect was instant. With a sound like walking on crunchy, dead grass, hair that had not grown for many years appeared from unused follicles, not grey like the hair she had, but a deep red. Removing another wing, she repeated the process. Just as instantly as the change of her hair, the nails on her hands fell off and young fresh nails replaced what were previously cracked, dry, claw-like nails. In the same moment her eyes widened, the heavy lids lifted and her dull green eyes became emerald bright. The crow's feet surrounding them tightened, not completely gone, but enough to make her look many years younger.

'Sister, what about me?' Lanny shouted across the room. He was nervous to approach and take his share now she was younger and getting stronger. His question was not ignored. She took a moment to think about the situation they found themselves in and what could be ahead. Torn between being happy to have him old and of little threat, to liking the idea of him being younger once more as their combined strength would be far more effective in any confrontation. Leilani really didn't know which way to go. She knew from experience that there was plenty of magic, even in such a small dragonfly, for the two of them to return to their much younger selves, even younger than Lanny was before he had become old in the mist.

Her calculations at an end, still not saying a word, Leilani pulled off the last two wings and presented them to her brother. Lanny's knees cracked as he moved at speed across the dusty floor. He grabbed them like he hadn't eaten in months and shoved them in his mouth. Taking a deep breath he could feel his old lungs expanding, able to take in more oxygen than they could seconds before, and with no uncomfortable pain spreading across his old back.

'And the rest?' Lanny asked, as his grey hairs began falling out and were replaced with long, thick, black as black can be hair, his green eyes bright and skin tightening. Although there was magic in all parts of the dragonfly, the magic that came from its head was more. Leilani put the dragonfly in her mouth and bit down hard on its back. She felt the familiar warm juices spill out over her lips, as she pulled the lower half away and passed it to her brother. 'Well, I guess I should not have expected anything better!' Lanny said, throwing the bottom half of the dragonfly in the air whilst tilting his head back, opening his mouth and catching it as gravity pulled it down towards him. 'Still as bitter as ever!' he said, waiting for the renewal of the rest of him to begin.

Leilani rose from her seat, her body feeling warmer than it had in more years than she cared to remember. She could feel every strand of muscle that ran through her thicken, the warming fat trapped between her muscles and skin returning. Her size and weight increased as her protruding bones disappeared. The body that was so skinny it was painful to sit on anything but something soft, was gone. She rolled her shoulders and dropped her head from side to side, her joints moved freely without creaking or pain. Standing tall, she was perfectly straight, perfectly curvy. Her long graceful neck lifted her head high, her long red hair fell around her rounded shoulders, her clothes no longer fitted as they did. Her dress was tight, so much so it was actually uncomfortable around her shoulders, arms and chest, not that she cared. The old rotten coat she had worn for so many years was no longer dragging on the floor, it looked out of place as it hung off the intense, almost regal looking young woman it covered.

Lanny was enjoying each second of his transformation. His muscular self returning, he was throwing anything he could get his hands on and smashing chairs off the walls, adding to the gaping holes left by his bears. He ripped the mantelpiece from its old mountings. Crashing to the floor, it sent a plume of sawdust and decades of dust clouds into the air. Walking up to the door he punched a hole in it, for no other reason than he wanted to. He thoroughly enjoyed the feeling of his young skin tearing and seeing his bright, fresh blood dripping from the wound, knowing it would heal in a day rather than what would have been weeks if he had remained his old self.

'Sister, how good does this feel?' he yelled across the noise of the smashing and crashing he was creating. Leilani was being reflective in the moment. Raising the hand that had discovered the dragonfly, she looked at spots of its blood that had been left on one of her fingers. She wasn't sure if the sadness came from a place she had closed off at the time of her parents' death, or if it came from the dragonfly itself. Either way, it was something she felt and Lanny did not. She was more refined than Lanny and his blunt instrument approach to all things. This became his approach when Leilani had become the more twisted one. The one more capable of manipulation than he was during their younger years, the years he had patiently spent turning her against their parents, for his own gain.

'Lanny, come on!' Leilani said, walking at speed out of the room and out of the house. 'Whoever was here has clearly found the island that we were looking for. More than that, it would appear they have the ability to bring dragonflies back to where they had once been.' She had no idea the house had not been a Dragonfly house, the true power that Sophie and Alex had been given, or who Sophie and Alex really were. 'Fate is on our side brother. Whatever is happening we are here at the right time, young, strong and we have the upper hand.'

'Upper hand?' Lanny questioned, knowing that they had only had one dragonfly, and whoever had brought it to the house would be sure to have more power than they did at this point.

'Yes brother. My golden window back at Dragonfly Manor, I can see here as much as I can there,' Leilani replied. Lanny was shocked,

'You have always said it was only Earth you saw!' All the things he had done and said about his sister came flooding back to him. The colour drained from his face as he realised what she could potentially know. He had been careful knowing her missing companion Earl was never far away, but this was horrifying to him. Trying to act as calmly as he could in the circumstance of the revelation, he quickly filled the momentary silence, 'Well, we shall get you back there then.'

'I shall get myself back there. No need for transport, these stocky legs of mine are working just fine,' Leilani replied.

'What about this door?' Lanny pointed at the front door they had just left. Leilani was annoyed at missing such an obvious opportunity. Refusing to show any sign of weakness and happy to risk the loss of time, she confidently replied,

'There was one carving, the tree has gone, there is not a chance the doorway will work!' She took a gamble that he wouldn't check. It was a good gamble as he did not. Unknowingly, she had in fact made the right choice, seeing as the door and its frame had not been exposed to the dragonfly for long enough to absorb all of its magic. This meant that the words 'Unnatural light from the eyes of one, chosen by the healer to become one, now Delivered Received A Gift Of Nature's Freeing Love Yours,' found above every Dragonfly home's front door and the pin prick map of Heart's Dragonfly homes, that was also found on ever Dragonfly door, were not there. So with a purposeful stride, Leilani headed for the tree line which would take her back towards the hills, beyond which she would find the broken down cottage that had brought her, Lanny and the bears to where they found themselves.

Due to her excitement and focus on returning to her home, Leilani had missed something! Stepping into the trees, she realised her feet were sore,

'Damn and blast. My young feet are not used to walking without protection!' she exclaimed. The bottoms of her feet had been rough, like old rubber, which meant she had felt nothing as she walked. With her younger self having soft, unused pads to the underside of her feet, it meant she felt everything. One good thing however was that the loose fitting gold and diamond chains that wrapped round her old, skinny ankles and toes, were no longer giving her a rubbing discomfort. A healthy volume had returned to them so the chains fitted well, a fact she acknowledged as her initial annoyance passed. Leilani was good at shutting away pain, and her feet were to be subject to the same strength of mind. With every hard, crunching, sharp, step she took, the acknowledgement of the pain each nerve was sending to her brain lessened.

Just about to leave the trees for the field beyond, Lanny heard a rustle coming from high above them. Looking up, he saw the silhouette of two animals he knew well, not hiding as well as they thought they were.

'Come on you two, we're leaving!' Lanny shouted to his generals. At first they were not sure what to do. They recognised Lanny although they were surprised to see him young again, much younger even than before he had turned old, but the young woman he had with him, they did not recognise her at all. However, they did as commanded and shot down the thick tree trunk. Arriving at his side, the familiar old smell from torn, well-worn clothes made their way to the two bears' noses. George should have known better but he couldn't help himself, and in a far too familiar tone he said,

'Miss Leilani! Is that you?' The response from Leilani was a glare which George knew very well. It would usually be followed by some sort of object being thrown at him, a fist or some strange supernatural energy throwing him some distance. On this occasion however there was no violence, just the glare. Leilani was far more interested in getting back to her home. Gregg kicked George and whispered to him,

'Yep, that's her alright! But how?' George shrugged his furry shoulders and stepped in line with his master, unsure where they were leaving to, but happy just to follow.

Even though both were young once more, the walk back to the cottage still took some time. The route took them past many hidden eyes of humans and animals. The rumours, spreading fast from the gossiping Renga, had all watching curiously from the shadows, hoping to see something wonderful - a change that would bring heart back to Heart. Leilani was well aware of being the focus of all the living things' attention, but she did not care. She did not send the bears after them or use her own abilities to cause them pain; she was focused.

'Brother, I want that tree destroyed!' Leilani ordered as they arrived back in the torn apart cottage. She did not want who she knew was out there, with the abilities she assumed they had, to bring a dragonfly back to the cottage and use it. She also calculated that if she took the tree and destroyed it, the pinpricks of light would disappear, making the task of finding a way to travel around Heart or return to Earth a lot harder, if not impossible, for whoever came to the cottage.

'But, how do we get through if the tree is destroyed?' said Lanny, asking what he thought was a reasonable question.

'Burn this place around us, burn it to the ground. That will give us time to leave,' Leilani said, with a certainty in her eyes that unnerved Lanny.

The map alive, the location of their destination selected, she turned the handle of the door and opened it to see the familiar dead garden that was beyond her own Dragonfly Manor. Keeping hold of the door, she waved the bears and her brother through. Leilani wanted to be the last to leave, to stay until the last minute, to watch the cottage burn. Even with the heat of the fire beginning to burn her skin as she stood happily watching, she did not leave. The flickering flames danced around, up and all over the tree that had been given the magic of the dragonfly so many years before. Magic, not enough to open its door to Earth, but just enough, even without the dragonfly living within it, to open the doorways throughout Heart.

Finally Leilani took a step back. The step took her through the doorway, out on to the top step of her Dragonfly Manor, as the fire had grown to a heat and height that she could no longer bear, and she slammed the door closed.

Taking in a deeper breath than she had been capable of in some time, Leilani sighed and smiled as she looked at the reflection of her younger self in the door that was her own. The activities of the day before and the magic returning to her Dragonfly Manor, had returned to it its youth, as the dragonfly she'd consumed had to her. The door that had been old and flaking was shining bright red, new. She was happy. With a youthful, excited smile, she turned to Lanny and said,

'My dear brother, get me your gold and plenty of it. We have a window to open!'

Chapter 9

'We have to get back!' Sophie said in a raised voice, to a concerned-looking Alex.

'But if they are there, what can we do?' Alex replied. He had mixed feelings about returning. On the one hand, he was nervous, as he would potentially come face to face with the ones who wanted to take what he had and most probably take his life. On the other hand, part of him was curious to see what they looked like, to see if they were as bad as those he had met said they were, and if the stories told were actually true.

The eyes that had been watching them from the bushes and trees were turning into faces - furry ones, feathered ones and human ones, as they made their way out from the shadows. Having watched and heard what was going on, all were confident that the group they were watching were the ones they had very recently heard about from Renga's news, also known as gossip spreading. The rustling of leaves and cracking of sticks being walked over startled both Alex and Sophie, their heightened state of alert keeping their adrenalin high.

'It's fine. There's no need for concern, they are all friends and they will probably, no, they will, be more scared than you are,' Jason said, as he gestured the man to come and say hello. Even though they all lived so close to each other and he had knowledge of many, he had only met a few. All living things had become very adept at staying hidden after the decades of rampaging aggression that Leilani and her brother had brought to Heart. The clearing in the trees was soon full with life, with Alex and Sophie, the strangers to the area, being the focus. Jason stepped in front of them, and the clearing fell silent,

'I have no doubt you have already heard rumours by my gossiping friend Renga. I also have no doubt you will have seen some strange things today - some from the loch, maybe some from the sky. I know that you are all aware that Leilani and her brother have been closer to all of us today than they have been for some time.' Pausing for a moment, he turned to the two young strangers and gestured, 'these two, Alex and Sophie, are the reason for it all.' The smallest of voices came from somewhere inside the gathering,

'Does it mean we will have visitors again?' Jason looked for who asked the question, 'my mum told me that people used to come and it was always nice to make new friends.' A confident little creature appeared from between the many legs, chased by a larger version of the same kind of creature,

'It's a hedgehog,' Sophie exclaimed with delight, 'he's so cute!'

'If you would excuse me, the he is a she - my daughter, Pixie. My apologies, she is not so good at staying quiet!' The words came from the larger, out of breath hedgehog.

'It's quite alright,' Sophie replied, as she walked over to the young hedgehog. Her tiny black eyes shone brightly, protruding from her white face, her little nose hiding her excited smile. Sophie loved animals as much as she did her books. She had never seen a hedgehog in real life and was very excited at the meeting. It occurred to her for a passing moment that it was slightly odd that the hedgehog was speaking to her, but she moved on quickly. Bending down, Sophie said,

'Well, aren't you the cutest. In answer to your question, I don't know. But I am here, so maybe I can be a new friend to you.' Pixie, the tiny hedgehog, stood up as tall as she could on her tiny legs and starting running in circles whilst chanting,

'I have a new friend, I have a new friend, I have a new friend!' Sophie laughed and hoping to catch her, she put her hand down on the ground,

'I told you, I can't keep her quiet,' the tiny hedgehog's mum said as Pixie found herself faced with Sophie's hand. Running as fast as she was, she crashed into with her nose, causing her to roll up into her protective ball of spikes, confirming Sophie's thoughts,

'She is soooo cute, my goodness, sooo cute.' Looking over to Pixie's mum she asked, 'Is it ok if I pick her up?' The response was a smile and a nod. Carefully, she pushed her hands underneath the body of spikes, scooped Pixie up and stood up. Pixie, feeling the touch, movement and pull of gravity as she was suddenly higher from the ground than she had ever been, unrolled herself just enough to peek out. Held in Sophie's hands at head height, Pixie's peeking eye met with Sophie's smiling face. So excited, she unrolled herself from her protective ball and stood up in Sophie's hands and said,

'You are so pretty.' The words would have embarrassed Sophie if they were alone, let alone surrounded by nearly thirty other sets of eyes, so she couldn't help but come over all awkward and didn't know what to say. Thankfully, the awkward moment came to an end as Ryley and Hanne, the two fox cubs, arrived and ran round Sophie's ankles, occasionally jumping up trying to get a better look at Pixie.

'The house Sophie, what are we going to do?' Alex was as uncomfortable as Sophie at being the centre of attention. As pleased as he was not to have been attacked by the faces in the trees and bushes, to find out they were friendly faces, he did not enjoy being in a crowd. His life experience of groups had not been good, being alone with a select one or two was his comfort zone. With all that had happened to him, physically and emotionally over the last couple of days, the fact there had only been a couple of people at any one time, meant that he was able to keep his impulse to run away under control. That control was disappearing. He didn't want to appear rude, but his way of dealing with the situation was to pretend the eyes and faces in front of him just weren't there, 'We need to make sure the dragonfly is ok, come on let's get going!'

'Dragonfly, there is a dragonfly!' Pixie said excitedly, remembering the bedtime stories her mum had told her about the magical dragonflies.

'Yes there is. Would you like to see one?' Sophie replied. She wasn't intentionally ignoring Alex, she was lost in a world of her own, loving the chance to hold such a beautiful animal in her hands, to have the fox cubs running around her and to be surrounded by so many species she had read about and seen pictures of. Alex had turned away from the gathering and was walking back towards the light he could see through the trees and bushes Zachariah had crashed through to make a path. All eyes on Sophie, no one noticed as he disappeared.

The further Alex got away from the clearing, the calmer he got. Although he was calming down, the panic and fear of so many around him fading, he was experiencing a strong feeling of loneliness. With every step he took away from Sophie, he could feel a darkness growing inside him, as though something was missing, not that it stopped his direction of travel.

Out of the trees and having run across the fields, he was back at the tree line surrounding the big old house. Quietly and carefully, he found a place that gave him the perfect vantage point to see what he was both curious and fearful to see. The ancient dragonfly had remained silent as Alex left Sophie. The choices and direction of their journey was theirs to make. However, as Alex sat watching the house for any sign of movement, the dragonfly couldn't help himself. Breaking the rules, breaking his silence, he said one simple word,

'Together!' The word echoed round Alex's head. He was the one who had told Sophie they should move forward, not back. He was the one who had said they should work together with all. He was so conflicted. He felt and believed that together was the way forward, but his default setting of being more comfortable alone had taken over. Analysing himself and the feelings he was having, he thought maybe it was something else other than the crowds in the clearing that had made him uncomfortable. He wondered if it was something more selfish. Could he have been jealous of Sophie's attention being taken by the hedgehog and all the other animals? Was it that she ignored him when he spoke? Or was it just he needed to escape - a symptom of his life experiences, his automatic way of protecting himself from bullies and disappointment in the people he met.

Ten minutes passed, and Alex was getting annoyed at his over-analysing. Added to that, being crouched motionless in the trees, he was really feeling the cold. So, as he had seen no sign of movement in the house, in an effort to take back control of himself and get warm, he plotted a route that would get him to the house without being seen. In his head, he counted down from three and took off like a startled rabbit, his speed almost tripping him up. At the side of the big old house, crouched under a window, he slowly stood up. Tilting his head, he peered in through the dirty glass to a room that was not how they had left it. 'What on earth!' he said to himself out loud. It was a room that, like all the others, was old and worn, but Alex's reaction was because he saw a cupboard door only just hanging on with one screw, the walls ripped open, and the floorboards splintered, torn up.

With what he saw, his curiosity to see Leilani and Lanny was gone. Clearly the stories he had been told were true, and he needed to get away as quick as he could without being seen. He could feel the familiar heat growing inside. It had an affect on the two remaining young dragonflies who began dashing up and down his arm, which was yet another new feeling for Alex, one he didn't like.

'There is no need for fear!' The voice of the ancient dragonfly once again filled Alex's head. He was losing control. With the heat continuing to build, Alex knew what would come next, and if it did, if they were inside the house, he would no longer be hidden. On his feet to the side of the window he faced the wall, placed his hands on it, dropped his head and tried with all his strength to stop what he had not been able to before. He could see the purple light from his eyes shining on the stony path he was standing on, reflecting off the dampness that covered it. His breath was getting faster, heavier. Not only was he feeling the two young ones in his arm, he was now feeling the ancient dragonfly on his back move, its wings wrapping round his torso and shoulders causing his muscles to tense in reaction to the movement. Alex took an unnaturally long intake of breath and held it, closed his eyes, and took himself back to the cave with the underground lake, where the ancient dragonfly had joined with him. In his mind he was there, breathing in the cold damp air, standing at the water's edge, staring into the clear water, looking for who he had left behind in the clearing with the friendly animals and humans he needed to escape from. Fully lost in his mind, he was not aware of his physical self. Not seeing who he wanted to, he looked up towards the opening they took to find the dragonfly cave. He could see the sparkly gem-covered walls.

'Alex!' A loud voice and hard shake brought him back out from his mind. It was Jason. 'Are you alright my friend? You seemed a bit lost there.' Alex lifted his head and stood up, happy to have got control of himself again.

'I am fine. But your house is not looking so good I am afraid,' Alex said, looking in through the window, forgetting the fact that Leilani and her brother could still be inside. Jason, overcome with rage at what he saw, stormed off towards the front of the house. With the front door wide open on his arrival, he went in, only stopping when he caught his foot on a floorboard that was sticking up,

'What have they done to my home?' Jason shouted as he bent down, grabbed the floorboard and threw it across the hallway. Alex, having followed behind, was equally shocked at the destruction that had been done to the old house. Quickly seeing past all the mess, Alex began looking for what he had returned for,

'The tree, it's gone,' Alex said to Jason, who was not calming down.

'The tree! Seriously, you think I care about that stupid little thing! I wish they were still here, I wish they had the nerve to stand and face me right now, rather than coming in when we weren't even here and doing what they have!' Jason's words hid his true feelings, as he did care about the tree, he cared about it very much. It was one of the last things he had to remind him of his sister and his home back on Earth. Alex let him rant on. He was focused on finding the main reason for his return. With the tree gone, there was only one other place he thought the baby dragonfly might be. He spun round to look at the doorframe,

'They found it. They ate it!' The voice came from a familiar beak. Renga was back. The words snapped Jason from his rage.

'They have eaten it?' he said, looking for confirmation.

'Yes, they are no longer as old as they were when I flew over them in the woods towards the loch.' Renga confirmed Jason's fears.

'Where are they?' Jason asked,

'That's the reason I came back. I was near the old Dragonfly Cottage over the hills to the east and I saw them. Well, I assumed it was them as those horrible bears were running not far behind them. I heard them talking about finding the dragonfly in the house and how they were going to find whoever brought it, find as many as they needed and have all the power they needed. I knew they hadn't found you. So I came

'A Legend Remembered' 151

back here,' Renga said, as he landed on the splintered banister.

'They must be going to the cottage to use its doorway. But what for?' Jason threw the question out, hoping that somehow the answer would come to him. He pondered. What and who they were looking for was here, so why would they be going somewhere else. 'Maybe they just thought that's where we had gone. Maybe they thought we were heading to the cottage to escape.' Jason, happy with the conclusion he came to, stepped out the front door and looked off towards the hills the cottage was situated beyond.

'Smoke!' Jason shouted back at Alex and Renga, who were still inside. He could see thick, black smoke rising into the sky, joining with the white, low-lying clouds, turning them a sinister grey. Jason knew in an instant what it meant.

'Alex, I have seen you move quickly, you need to move quicker than you ever have. That's the closest dragonfly doorway that we can use, it's the only one I know of. If they destroy it, I don't know what use you will be here, or how you could possibly get home.' Jason's warning was taken in and assessed by Alex. He still had little understanding of what his true abilities were with his ancient dragonfly, but he was sure that the loss of one dragonfly and one dragonfly home would not be the end of the journey, so he did not feel Jason's urgency to race towards the fire. Before Alex had a chance to suggest that there may be an alternative, such as, surely he could bring another Dragonfly home and its magical doorway to life with his two other dragonflies, Jason was out of sight, having made it across the garden and through the trees in the smoke's direction.

Renga let out a squeak as he left the banister perch and flew out the front door. Flapping his wings hard so he could hover at Alex's head height, he said,

'Jason didn't give me a chance to respond to his question before answering it for himself. You should know that the twins left through the Dragonfly Cottage. I don't know where they went, but I watched as they went in. I watched as the handle turned the way it always did when used to travel between Dragonfly homes. Then the door opened, and they were gone. But they left fire!' Renga, then disappeared high into the sky and in Jason's direction.

Alex stood watching the smoke, which seemed to be lessoning in its thickness and quantity - a sure sign that Jason, as quick as he may be, would not get to the cottage in time to save any part of it. With nothing left to burn, the fire was going out. Alone again, Alex asked his companion a question,

'Am I best to be alone as I always have been, or should I do as I said to Sophie and join with others?' The ancient dragonfly responded,

'You are not alone. You never have been. You have been joined with all since the day of your birth.'

'You are saying I have no choice?' Alex asked,

'You have every choice. You chose to close down what has always been inside you. You chose to be alone in your life. You chose to help the girl in distress in her garden. You chose to go back to the house to help her once you had been asked to leave, even after you had experienced pain. You chose to come to the island. You chose to be here where you stand. The ability to choose is not the issue here, it is what you choose to do. Do not look to others, fate or influence as excuses to act or not to act. Where you go, what you do and who you do it with are completely your choice. Choice is a freedom you are privileged to have. Own your choices, as painful as they may be.' The ancient dragonfly fell silent, his words carefully chosen not to influence, but to point out fact.

'I choose to be with Sophie.' Confident in his words, Alex left the old house and headed back to where he had left her and the others. He didn't have to go far, as a fast-moving Zachariah came bounding through the trees, skidding to a halt on the wet grass in front of him,

'My family is where that smoke is coming from. The others are on their way already. Please, will you come with me?' Alex didn't hesitate, he turned and ran at full speed in his effort to catch up with everyone. 'We will be quicker if you get on,' Zachariah said, barely reaching a canter as he came up beside Alex. He didn't need to receive the offer twice. With a jump as though he was back at an athletic event clearing the highest pole of the high jump, Alex was on the great stag's back. Having never been on the back of any animal, Alex had no idea what he should do, so he just grabbed Zachariah's thick neck and held on as tight as he could. The flat fields were easy. Passing through the woods was more of a challenge, but the steep, rocky hillsides really took all of Alex's strength not to fall from the stag's back. He could feel the worry that drove Zachariah's never slowing pace. He could see the images of family that flashed through his head, as well as being able to hear and feel his fast-beating heart, as though he was becoming part of the one who carried him.

'Allow yourself to feel, but do not lose who you are.' The cautionary, always slightly cryptic words came from the ancient dragonfly, just as they passed Jason, who, incredibly, after such a distance, was powering his way up the hillside at great speed.

'Wait! You don't know what you are running into,' Jason managed to yell between his fast breaths, as Alex and Zachariah went ahead of him. Alex, with the knowledge that the twins were not there, thanks to Renga, was not scared about what they were heading into. He also knew that nothing would stop the great stag from finding his family. Having got used to the motion and with the words of the dragonfly helping to pull him back to the moment, Alex realised that the stag's family could well be the silhouettes standing at the top of the hill, to one side of the burning Dragonfly Cottage that was just coming into sight.

In no time, Alex was face to face with more than just Zachariah's family. The wooded area Alex had left Sophie in being much closer to the Dragonfly cottage than the old house he had just left, meant that Sophie, Gracie, Averie, Ryley and Hanne were already there. Standing helpless, there was nothing they could do to save the Dragonfly cottage and, more importantly, its tree and doorway.

Renga, who had been circling the smoke high in the sky, spiralled his way down to the group, arriving just as Jason did. All were silent because of a mixture of catching their breath after the frantic dash, and being transfixed by the flickering of the flames. Flames that were lessoning, turning into pulsing glows of orange, yellow and red that spread across the charcoal-singed wood of the floors, stairs, doorways, windows and roof, all finding themselves in a pile where the three rooms downstairs and upstairs had become just one. Sweating from the journey, the fire's heat was drying all present - their clothes, hair, fur and feathers. It was a strange experience being comforted and warmed by the aftermath of the destruction of a loving home. It didn't sit right with Alex, who stepped away from it, taking Sophie's arm as he did. Pulling her with him, he asked,

'Where are all the others?'

'Why did you leave me?' was her response, said with a hurt tone. She couldn't look at him. As much as Alex had needed to leave, she needed him to be with her. 'I don't understand why you would do that to me. I didn't see you leave, I didn't know where you would have gone, I didn't know what to do, and then Jason left.'

'You didn't see me leave! If you wanted me there, if you needed me there, how could you not see me leave?' Alex was surprised at his own defensive reaction. 'You noticed Jason leave!' He couldn't help himself, he wanted to stop, but he couldn't.

'Yes, because he told me he was going to find you,' Sophie replied, her tone beginning to change to one of frustration, joining Alex's. Alex could see the colours on Sophie's neck changing. They were swirling into dark reds and blacks.

'That does put you at a disadvantage, doesn't it!' Alex said, as he flicked Sophie's hair aside to show her. Embarrassed and with a quick movement of her neck, Sophie flicked her hair back, smacking Alex across the face as she did.

'I have spent my whole life hiding my feelings, but actually you know what, I am quite pleased they can be seen now without me even saying a word.' Sophie pulled her arm out of Alex's hand and started back towards the cottage and the others. Alex stayed, looking in the other direction, cross with himself for being unable to keep control of his emotions.

Something he had always done with ease. Being around Sophie was different. He was feeling things he didn't know were possible.

'I am sorry. Please understand, I had to get away from all those animals and people, I found it..' Sophie interrupted, ending his sentence for him,

'Uncomfortable!'

'It's more than that. I have spent my entire life trying to avoid people, to avoid being the centre of attention like that. I had to go.' Alex said,

'I understand, I truly do. But we are not in our world here. Animals are always pure of heart here or back home, but here so are the humans. Could you not feel the love there? Could you not feel the lack of judgement? Could you not feel that we were welcome?' Sophie had stepped back to Alex and made her way around him so she could look into his eyes.

'No, I didn't,' Alex said, dropping his head to avoid eye contact. 'Is there something wrong with me?' he asked.

'Wrong with you! Are you seriously asking that question? I know I am young, but in all my years I have never met someone like you. You are everything you were in my dreams and nightmares. The only problem you have, Alex, is the life you have had to survive through. But even with that life, the two days I have known you, you have shown more kindness to strangers than I have ever experienced. No Alex, there is nothing wrong with you.' She stepped in to him. Nervous to invade his space, she stopped close enough to be inviting him to invade hers, if he wanted to. He did. He wrapped his arms around her shoulders and pulled her mass of red hair into his chest. As he did, he felt the flutter of all three of his dragonflies where they sat under his skin, and a spark that travelled from his stomach into his heart. Sophie reached up, took hold of the arms wrapped around her and allowed herself to melt into the moment. They forgot where they were and what they were facing so far from their own homes, far from their own families. "CRASH!"

Their moment ended - with the crash came a scream from those still enjoying the warmth of the fire. The four walls, the only things left standing, fell to the ground like dominos - one wall, followed by the next, by the next and finally the last. The Dragonfly cottage becoming a pile of smoking, smouldering rubble.

'So what now then?' Jason asked. The anger that had driven him there at great speed was turning into concern. Alex and Sophie were still a little way from the rest of the group. Alex wanted to know how Sophie and the others got to the cottage.

'Well, when you disappeared everyone got scared, they thought Leilani had somehow taken you and they all ran away. I guess they are used to taking no chances!' Sophie started. She then went on to explain how with everyone gone, including Alex and Jason, she couldn't help but panic. She was left with Zachariah, Gracie, Averie and her cubs, all lovely, but no one she had known for any time. She wanted to head back to the big old house, but didn't know if that was clever in case Leilani and her brother would be there, so when Zachariah said that he had to leave to make sure his family were safe, 'I decided to go with him,' she said. The trip took her out of the trees and up a hillside just as the smoke rose from over the hill. 'Zachariah took off. He didn't say a word, he just left us, it looked like he was heading back towards the big old house. We stayed waiting on the hillside for a little while, but for some reason I just had to go and see what was on fire. We arrived here and then you appeared on the back of Zachariah.' She was going to go on, but Alex interrupted.

'The dragonfly at the house, it's gone!'

'What do you mean gone?' Sophie asked.

'I mean, the twins, they found it! They have done whatever they do to them and according to Renga they are young again!' Alex responded.

'What does that mean?' Sophie asked,

'It means we need to be more careful,' Alex answered. He stepped away from Sophie and walked over to the Dragonfly cottage, now burnt to the ground. Sophie followed behind.

'Was this an accident?' Alex asked as he arrived at the group,

'No! We saw them. It was the evil twins, younger looking, but it was them!' The stressed voice came from a beautiful roe deer who was standing guard of two babies. It was the voice of Zachariah's partner. 'We heard them arriving through the woods. I am sure they saw us, but they carried on, so we followed. They weren't inside for too long before I saw the handle turn that particular way. The door opened and those awful bears, her brother and finally Leilani disappeared as they stepped through. It was just like it used to be when people visited. That's when we saw the flames. I am so sorry there was nothing we could do.' Zachariah stepped beside her and put his head over her neck and pulled hers into him,

'You are safe and that is all that matters,' he said.

'So you two young ones, what is it you're actually here for?' Gracie asked. Neither of them really knew how to answer. Not having had a chance to gather their thoughts, Renga said,

'They have the first dragonfly. So they are either here to bring back the Dragonfly homes or provide the twins with everlasting youth. So far the latter seems to be winning!' His words did not help Alex, who was already feeling guilty at losing the dragonfly, and concerned that he and Sophie would be facing a revitalised Leilani and Lanny if they ever came face to face. He said,

'If I could go back home, leave you all safe in this world, I would. I don't want to cause you any pain, I certainly don't want to help Sophie's ancestors in any way.' he was interrupted,

'Her ancestors! You are related to Leilani and Lanny?' Jason questioned, picking up on a reality that worried him. Stepping away from her he went on, 'That's information you should have given us before now Alex! Why did you bring her?' he continued. Alex moved over to Sophie and took her hand,

'We did tell you, back at the beach, and apart from that you should not assume to know me. You should not assume to know Sophie. You and your sister chose to abandon me. Has that made you a bad person, someone not to be trusted? No, I don't think so. Sophie should not be judged by relatives separated by hundreds of years. I was recently told I have chosen the path I am on, well so has she. She could have chosen not to be kind to me, not to follow me to a place that is in her nightmares and full of pain, but she did. Don't ever assume to know us.' Alex finished his rant, his strong words coming from his experiences in life. 'Together we brought life to that house you lived in. Without Sophie, the young dragonflies that live in me would not be there.

Together we will do what has to be done. I don't know what that is yet, but be assured it will be done despite judgement from anyone watching.' He pulled Sophie, whose eyes were filling up at his defence of her, away from the silenced group and took her to the cottage's smouldering ruins.

'There is something still there! The house may be gone, but something, I feel something familiar,' Alex said. They walked side-by-side, right up to where the front door had been. Looking down to where the wobbly cobbles stopped, Sophie noticed that the doorway, although full of rubble, still existed. To the left was about half a foot of doorframe, charred and blackened at its top sticking up from the ground. To the right was two feet of doorframe. Attached to it was one hinge and remnants of the door itself, still open, smoking, the remaining triangle shape hidden in the rubble.

'So that's the entrance then,' Sophie said, pointing to what Alex had missed. The flames completely gone and the intense heat subsiding, Alex said,

'Let's climb in.' Letting go of Sophie's hand, he wanted to make sure it was safe enough for her and her tiny feet to climb in with him. Moving his right leg through what remained of the doorway, he felt a pleasant warming energy make its way up his leg. Finding a firm piece of rubble, he put his weight fully on the leg inside and pulled the other leg in to join it. The same feeling greeted his entire body, just for a moment. The heat of the smouldering embers dancing along the blackened wood scattered through the stone of the cottage had completely gone. Looking down, the firm piece of rubble he had carefully placed his feet on was new, no rubble, instead, fresh looking floorboards.

He spun his head round to hear Sophie screaming his name. As he looked at her, confused by her scream and the floorboards beneath his feet, she began to fade. Sophie's vanishing body was becoming mixed up with a completely different view, a sort of familiar view, a similar one to one he had seen before - grandmother's Dragonfly Manor front garden.

'The door, it wasn't closed! The fire stopped the door being closed from this side. Alex, if you can hear me, come back, you need to come back here, NOW!' Jason's shout came from behind the disappearing Sophie. Alex reached his hand back out through the doorway and as soon as he did, it was visible to Sophie. Just a floating hand and part of an arm. She knew it was Alex's and didn't hesitate in taking hold of it. She tried to pull it, to pull Alex back, but his hand did not move from its position. Alex watched as Jason stepped round her and grabbed his wrist to help. His hand went straight through, just as Alex's mum, Melissa's had, back at Dragonfly Manor. Alex could feel Sophie's hand on his, but did not feel the strength she was putting into pulling him. As much as she couldn't move him, he seemed to be unable to move her. It was a strange experience. Sophie readjusted her footing to get a better angle to pull Alex. As she did, there was a split second where he was able to pull her. She had no defence, Sophie was pulled in through the doorframe! Just as Alex had, she disappeared from the sight of Jason, Zachariah, Gracie and the others who were all left not knowing what to do, or precisely where they had gone. Although they had a very good idea.

'Together Sophie, always together,' Alex said,

'Where are we?' Sophie asked. Still in a state of panic from Alex disappearing, she had not realised how familiar the place she found herself standing in was.

'We are in your Dragonfly Manor. Well sort of, I don't think it's the one you grew up in!' Alex said. Looking around, enjoying the familiarity of the hallway, a smile grew on Sophie's face. She loved the old, cold, slightly broken down Dragonfly Manor she grew up in, but she had forgotten about the newer one that replaced it, just before they left on their journey to the highland village in search of the island, and it was magically exciting. Her new hallway was identical to the one they were standing in - the same floorboards, raised where the roots of the dragonfly tree ran under them and through them, the red rug, the dull wall lights, the new-looking staircase that disappeared off up to the beautifully colourful stained glass window. But it was a different house. The open doors to each side of them showed a sparsely furnished living room and a library, with very few books compared to the one she had grown up in. The desk sitting at its far end was clear of the book towers blocking the view she knew well.

Alex, paying no attention to the house, was looking at the ever-fading view of Jason and the others, with the view out to the Dragonfly Manor garden getting clearer as they faded.

'Lanny, will you hurry with the gold!' A screeching voice came from down the corridor beyond the kitchen. Alex snapped his head round and looked in the voice's direction. Motionless, as though they were in a nightmare where they couldn't scream for help or run to escape, Sophie and Alex waited for whoever was going to arrive. Hearing the creaking of a door opening and the sound of footsteps going from a stony floor to a wooden one, the screech came again, 'Lanny!' just as both Alex and Sophie saw the one who was screeching. The rainbow of colours living inside Sophie began swirling around her. The dragonflies in Alex's arm began fluttering and the ancient dragonfly on Alex's back squeezed him, forcing the breath he was holding out. Then the owner of the voice looked round at them. For a moment, Leilani did not recognise who was standing in her home, she just saw uninvited humans who had to be dealt with. Alex unfrozen, able to move again, spun round looking for the best escape route. The picture of the place they had left was now the faintest of ghostly images. The more in focus view of the Dragonfly Manor's garden would not be a good option as an escape route,

'Leilani, it's them, it's the two!' Lanny was outside the house, coming up the path with his two generals who were carrying the gold Leilani had ordered them to get. Angry with herself for not realising instantly who the two intruders were, no soil beneath her feet to use nature's energies, she had no other option than to run at them. As she did, she shouted out orders for George and Gregg to block their escape. They unceremoniously dropped the gold, which poured away, falling between the edges of the wobbly cobbles. Breaking free from the stare of the eyes that looked so familiar, bright green, surrounded by the longest of eyelashes, she could have been looking in a mirror, Sophie looked up at Alex and said,

'Can you still see the land outside the cottage, like me?' Alex didn't reply. She felt his intentions with their hands still clasped together.

'Together, you must move together!' Both heard the voice of the ancient dragonfly, although they already instinctively knew what to do. Looking back at Leilani, slowly they changed the hands that each of them were holding to make as smooth a turn as possible, when the moment was right.

'Now!' Alex shouted. They ran at the doorway, right towards the two bears with their teeth glistening, drool falling from their mouths, ready to take control of Alex and Sophie by whatever means necessary. The doorway was only several feet from Alex and Sophie but the bears were covering ground fast and were already at the bottom step. As Alex and Sophie were just close enough to step through, George leapt at them, clearing the steps, his claws on his paws leading the way, diving to take out his prey. He was not going to miss, he was not going to be the one to fail the young Leilani.

Chapter 10

'Oh, thank goodness!' a very happy to see them Gracie said. She was the only one still at the cottage as Jason, Zachariah and the other animals had all left, made their escape, in fear that something not so friendly would come back through the remnants of the doorway Alex and Sophie had disappeared through. 'Are you two ok?' she asked the slightly shell-shocked looking duo, Alex and Sophie. They didn't respond. Instead, Alex asked Sophie,

'Are you ok?' as he visually checked her over for any sign of injury,

'How on earth did we manage that? I was sure those two terrifying creatures were going to get us!' Sophie replied. Then they both burst out laughing from a mixture of adrenalin and relief, having somehow escaped untouched. The sound of their laughter echoed down the hill and into the valley full of trees, causing the escapees to stop in their tracks when they heard the happy sound. Looking back, they could see three figures. Assuming one was Gracie, they were too far away to make out exactly who the other two were. But seeing as it was laughter and Gracie didn't seem to be running away, they assumed whoever it was, was no threat, so they headed back up the hill.

'What happened to you, what did you see?' Gracie asked, having not got a response to her first question.

'We were in the twins' home! I saw her, Leilani, and she definitely saw us. I genuinely have no idea how we made it out. It was petrifying!' Sophie replied,

'How did you make it out? I mean, how did you get back here? Oh! If she saw you, how come she isn't here?' Gracie asked. Jason, arriving back at the cottage ruins was overjoyed to see that it was Sophie and Alex. He answered Gracie's question,

'The first dragonfly, now I remember. The stories passed down to me told that it, along with Shuing, created the dragonfly homes, doors and trees, not just Shuing! I am beginning to think the dragonfly does a lot more than any legend forgot or remembered. That's how they got back!' He was partially right. But the truth was more coincidence than the power of the dragonfly. Leilani opened the doorway of the cottage for her, her brother and the bears to pass through to her Dragonfly Manor. Once through, as always, she would have closed it. However, on this occasion, at the very moment she thought she had closed the door, parts of the collapsing cottage she had left burning, fell into the cottage's doorway, so the door did not close, something she missed. Left open, unseen, the doorway to the burnt cottage over time would have faded as the magic faded, but with Alex being there when he was, walking into the house when he did, because of the ancient dragonfly inhabiting him, holding Sophie's hand meant that they were able to pass through to Leilani's Dragonfly Manor.

Unaware of the sequence of coincidental events, not knowing how it all happened, they decided to just accept that it did. Jason couldn't help himself, so happy to see him back, he grabbed Alex and gave him a hug. Not something he was used to, it made Alex feel a little uncomfortable. Once finished, Jason turned his attention to Sophie. He didn't hug her, instead he tapped her on the shoulder and said, 'I am sorry if I questioned your reasons for being here Sophie! Hope I didn't cause offence.'

'It's fine. I understand that things are changing in odd ways for you. Believe me, they are for us as well. But we need to do as Alex said earlier, we need to stay together and keep moving forward.' Sophie confidently replied. Having seen the stories about Leilani and her brother were not exaggerated in any way, she had an overwhelming feeling of urgency to find a way back to her grandmother. 'Alex, do you think there is a way home?' she asked.

'I'm not one hundred percent sure. But I know someone that might know.' Pausing for a moment and looking around the group he said, 'I could do with a bit of space if that's ok with you all.' The energies of those around him were affecting his ability to see things clearly, to be able to listen and learn from the ancient dragonfly.

'You want me to leave you alone as well?' Sophie asked. Alex let out a small chuckle and replied,

'No Sophie, together remember.'

'Come on, we can all go back to mine for some warmth and sustenance,' Gracie announced.

'Again! I have been up and down this hill, over that hill, through the forest, woods and across fields far too many times today already! If you don't mind, I think I would like to go home and make sure the rest of our families are ok. And make sure they know what has happened, what could be coming,' Zachariah said as he flicked his neck, gesturing for his partner and babies to yet again head back down the hillside with its rocks, dead grass and fallen trees.

'Thank you for all you have done today, I hope we see you again,' Alex said. Zachariah nodded and replied,

'You will.' As he turned and walked away with his family, in his deep voice he gave one last piece of wise advice, 'Have your space, but don't let them get too far away from you young man,' gesturing towards Jason and the leading Gracie, who looked as though she was floating with no sign of her feet, just her long flowing dress which hid them.

Alex sat down on the grey, moss-covered stone garden wall, and despite the advice given by the stag, was happy to have distance from everyone, except Sophie of course!

'I don't want to be left here Alex. You saw what was on the other side of that door!' Sophie said. Having only just got comfortable and allowing himself to enjoy the weight being taken from his legs, Alex stood back up. Without saying a word, he walked over to the cottage and threw aside the rubble that blocked the door from closing.

'I know which way to go to get back to the big old house, so if we lose sight of them don't worry,' Alex said.

'Why are you doing that?' Sophie asked,

'Well, you're right. Our visit to the other side of the door was not going to end well if we hadn't escaped. They haven't come through, which makes me think they can't. But it's probably a good idea to make sure they definitely can't. My understanding is that if the door is shut, that should do the job,' Alex replied. It wasn't long before he cleared the rubble and could close what remained of the door. As he did, there was a thud, followed by a click sound. It was as though a full-sized door had just closed into its tight-fitting doorframe, catching its latch in its lock.

'Well, that was strange!' Sophie said. Alex nodded in agreement, although he was getting less and less surprised at experiencing things that were not what was expected. 'Thank you for doing that,' Sophie said to a visibly tired looking Alex.

'That's ok. I guess we should really make a move then hey.' The time it took to close the door meant Jason and the others were just heading out of sight. Alex, as confident as he was that he knew which way to go, thought it probably best to keep them in view. No time for a rest, he wrapped his arm around Sophie's shoulders and guided her down the hidden remains of the wobbly cobbly path, out the gap where the iron gate once sat and off in the direction of the soon to be setting sun.

'So why did you want to be alone?' Sophie asked.

'I don't like people watching. I think I probably look slightly crazy responding to a voice no one else hears,' Alex replied. Sophie was struggling to understand the very complicated Alex. On the one hand he was confident, strong, and on the other, vulnerable and self-conscious. He was like two different people. 'Also, we don't know those people or animals,' Alex continued, which made Sophie add to her list of Alex traits, untrusting. She completely understood that side of him, after all, that was her default setting. Although she felt different towards the people of Heart, who she felt empathy with. She sensed the goodness hidden away behind their fears of living in a place that had been full of so much pain and suffering, the total opposite to what Heart was supposed to be. What it once was.

Walking in silence, Alex took his arm from around Sophie's shoulders and took her hand. She hoped, just like she did at the clearing in the trees, that she would hear Alex's thoughts. She wasn't so interested in the ancient dragonfly; she wanted to know more about Alex. Unusually for him, his mind was clear of thoughts, so Sophie learnt nothing.

Not having the back of Zachariah to ride on, it was quite some time before the familiar large open field, which at its far end, sat the trees hiding the big old house they were returning towards, appeared. As they stepped into the field, something lit up in Alex. It wasn't a thought; it was a feeling. Sophie, pleased to be sensing something from him, at last also felt it and said,

'I don't know what you are thinking right at this moment, but I feel conflict.' Alex didn't stop walking or respond to her. He could feel his temperature rising as could Sophie. She wanted to calm him down, to help to focus his mind. 'Remember why this all started, what we have found out, the reason for us being here. Our home, our planet Earth, its people, animals, nature, being in a place of spiralling sadness, loss, selfishness, destruction, that's why we are here. From grandmother's stories and library of papers and books, I know Heart was the balance to counteract humanity's successful efforts of driving our Earth to a hopeless reality. Sadness, loss, selfishness and destruction has come here to Heart not because of nature, not because of its native species, but once again because of humans. My relatives. We have a responsibility to help here which will in turn help our home. Alex, please don't get lost in your mind, we know what we have to do!' Sophie's heartfelt words came to an end as they saw Jason disappear into the ground, followed by the others. Into the home of Gracie. Alex dropped Sophie's hand and took off running, shouting as he did,

'Something isn't right!' He was so fast, even at full sprint Sophie's short legs couldn't keep up. The result of her chosen pastime of sitting in libraries or hiding in corners reading her books, had left her with a fitness level unable to carry her any distance at speed. It wasn't long before she was a long way behind,

'Alex, wait!' she shouted. He didn't respond or slow down. Out of breath, she managed one more frustrated shout before stopping and sitting down in the middle of the field. The ground was softer than she had expected on that frosty day. Her out of breath state progressed to the point she couldn't catch her breath at all. She started to panic. There wasn't enough air in her lungs to shout out for help. Her head was going fuzzy, her eyesight out of focus. Gripping the grass each side of her, her fingers passing through their thawed blades, sinking through the roots and into the soil they grew from, a most unexpected thing happened. Sophie could feel currents of energy. She had somehow connected to nature itself. Suddenly she was no longer in control of her body. Her back straightened up, her shoulders pulled back, her head raised, her lungs filling up with the air she couldn't find. Colours swirled from the centre of her bite and spread out over her back as her hands were pulled deeper into the ground, from which shot a colourful stream of light just under the ground's surface to the fast moving feet of Alex. It exploded out from the ground and wrapped itself round his legs, stopping him instantly. So strong was its hold, he didn't fall forward with his momentum, he just stopped.

The energy surge had another unexpected effect! Out from his hand appeared the two remaining dragonfly that had made his arm their home. They hovered for a moment, looking at Alex's startled face, and then in a blur disappeared off across the field toward Sophie.

'Sophie, you need to let me go!' Alex yelled. He could feel her through the chains of light wrapped around him. But Sophie felt as though she had no control and wouldn't be able to let him go even if she wanted to. Angrily she shouted at him,

'Together!' Alex rolled his eyes. Not at her, but instead at the realisation at how mixed up his mind really was. His life of being alone, his desire to be alone, did not mesh well with his new desire to be with Sophie. His reaction to run and leave Sophie behind, was completely opposite to the feeling he had of wanting to wrap her up in his arms and keep her safe. The light attaching the two together once again made it possible for them to be in each other's minds. Sophie was pleased to hear Alex's thoughts, his conflicts being consciously played out in his mind gave her hope that he did understand. Alex was also pleased to hear the thoughts of Sophie, that all she wanted was to be with him, to help him help others.

With more strength than she thought she had, Sophie managed to pull her hands from the ground and got to her feet. Walking towards Alex, the powerful ropes of light that were wrapped around him unexpectedly pulled Alex towards Sophie. With every step she took towards him, he was pulled a step closer to her. Back together, the light ropes released Alex, and he fell to the ground, sending a wave of energy out across the grass, causing it to ripple like the water of a pond when a droplet of water falls into it. Face to face again, the two dragonflies that had left Alex were hovering between them. Alex lifted his arm, pulled up his sleeve and with a spark of light, they popped back into the bite doorway that remained on his hand.

'Sophie, something is not right!' Alex said,

'Ok, but what is it?' Sophie asked. He didn't know exactly, so didn't answer. Sophie continued, 'Will you please try to stop reacting! Just take a moment when you feel like leaving me, which you have done twice today!' Sophie surprised herself at how open and vulnerable she was being with him. Alex didn't need to be connected to Sophie or hear her thoughts to sense the hurt in her voice. He heard what she said, felt what she was feeling, but didn't know what to say. Words filled his mind, but for some frustrating reason, he just couldn't say them out loud. As hard as he tried, his mind wouldn't let him. Alex decided to change the focus of his mind from his frustration at not being able to answer her. He thought about the fact that the walk, the time alone from the others, had not given him the insight or answers he had expected from the ancient dragonfly, and that was disappointing. Not even an answer to the question of whether they could get back to Sophie's grandmother, the question she had asked back at the burnt cottage. It worked, the heat that had been building up inside him subsided, and once again he was able to speak.

'And what the heck was that by the way?' he questioned.

'It was crazy right. It was the strangest thing. It felt like I had no control of myself, but then it kind of did!' Sophie's words making as much sense to her as they did Alex.

'Well, guess we keep doing what we have been and just go with it. Did you see them all disappear into the ground?'

'No!' Sophie replied,

'It was like they all went down a hole. I think it was just past those rocks over there. I saw Gracie close what looked like a hatch door. That's when I got the overwhelming feeling something wasn't right,' Alex said.

'Ok, so let's go and find them. But this time let's do it together!' Her tone turning slightly sarcastic, in an affectionate way. It didn't take them long to get to the rocks. Looking around, they couldn't see any sign of a hatch door. Alex started kicking around where he thought he last saw them.

'I am sure it was about here,' he said, just as a hollow sound came from an odd coloured patch of grass beneath Sophie's feet.

'Well, that's embarrassing!' Alex said. Sophie was about ten feet from him. He was looking in the wrong place! 'But well done, that must be it.' Sophie stepped back and as she did, the hidden grass covered door opened to the smiling face of Gracie.

'Come in you two, come on in,' she said. Alex was hesitant. He looked past Gracie, who was standing halfway up the stairs that led into her single room, to see if everyone else was there.

'Hi guys,' Jason said, from a very comfy looking chair, holding a hot cup of tea, the steam rising from it swirling around with the breeze being let in by the open hatch door.

'Everyone alright in there?' Alex asked. Jason looked confused at the question as Ryley and Hanne, the fox cubs, ran up past Gracie to Sophie. She couldn't help herself, and knelt down to welcome their smiling faces with a hug,

'I miss Anchor! But you guys are certainly helping. I hope he is ok back home,' Sophie said. With the lack of haste in accepting her invitation, Gracie's tone changed,

'Come in will you, all my warm air is being let out!' Alex picked up on the change as the feeling of something not being right returned.

'No, I think we will go back to the old house. Come on Sophie,' Alex said. Sophie stood back up. Averie, the cubs' mother, widow of the fox taken mercilessly by Lanny's bears, had also come out of the hidden home to join her babies, whilst Jason and Renga were quite comfortable enjoying the warmth of Gracie's small fire.

'Look at the crystal hanging from the fireplace,' Averie quietly said to Sophie, so that Gracie, who was still holding open the hatch, could not hear. Sophie looked. Picking up on the secrecy of the instruction, she said nothing, just made a face intimating that she didn't know what she was looking at, or for.

'Come on boys, I think it's time for us to go,' Averie said, hoping her awkwardness hadn't been noticed by Gracie. Sophie, not having a clue what was going on and with Alex clearly not happy to enter, decided to go with it.

'We are heading over to your house Jason,' she shouted past Alex, 'you coming?' By this time Jason had woken up to the fact that everyone was trying to leave, so gave up his warm drink and comfy chair.

'Excuse me Gracie, can I squeeze past you?' he asked.

'Why are you all leaving? Surely it's best if you all stay here in the warmth, with a nice hot drink, whilst we figure out what you have to do. I would still very much like to hear more about how you came to be in Heart, and more about that dragonfly of yours Alex.' She moved to the side of her stairs, opening up space for those outside to come in. They didn't, but it gave Jason space to get past her and out.

'I'm happy to stay and tell you everything,' Renga announced from his comfy perch. The frustration in Gracie's face was clear, and confirmed that Alex was right not to remain, as she replied,

'If they are going, you can too you gossiping pest.' Gracie's friendly, floaty demeanour had left completely. With a small hop and flap of his wings, not very happy at leaving the warmth, Renga glided out past her to follow the leaving group. With everyone gone, Gracie let the hatch go. It slammed shut so loudly, her secret home would not have been secret any more if there had been anyone searching for it, even as far as two fields away. Sophie caught up with the fast moving foxes and asked,

'What was so important about the crystal?'

'I was sitting with my babies looking at the fire and it moved. I swear I saw something in it, like maybe the silhouette of a person?' she replied.

'Would have been my reflection I imagine,' Jason said, who along with Alex had caught up.

'No, something made me feel really odd,' Averie said.

'Sounds a lot like what I felt when I ran off from you Sophie,' Alex added.

'So, what we are saying is we were right not to go in there,' Sophie said, happy to be heading back to the old house.

Although Alex had not got any insight from the ancient dragonfly to answer Sophie's question, during the hike back from the burnt dragonfly cottage, he had come up with some theories himself. Walking towards the big, sad looking old house, its front door wide open, the disappearing sun provided just enough fading light for them all to once again see the destruction within. Jason had calmed down since seeing his home ripped apart and leaving in such a rage. He was able to say to himself it was just a shell. A true home was where there was life and love, not just bricks and mortar. Alex was the first to step in. With the front door being open, it pushed the damp smell that had hit him earlier in the day when he had opened the door for the first time, to the back of the house. The crisp, cold air replacing it was preferable. Remembering the poor little tree had gone, Alex said,

'Sophie, in the stories, the legends, they said that the Dragonfly homes were built round an existing tree that Shuing gave the magic to. The stick, or tiny skeleton of a tree that was here when we came in, the one Jason had put there, was not here before this old house was built. But we still brought it to life with a dragonfly.'

Sophie instantly got where Alex was going with his story.

'So what you are saying is we could plant a tree inside this house and make a new Dragonfly home,' she said.

'But the tree that was here was from my Dragonfly Cottage back on Earth. Surely that was the reason for it being able to come to life. It already had magic in it,' Jason said.

'Well, it's just a theory. With the twig you put there gone, it's not like we have anything to lose if we try,' Alex said. With the winter trees leafless and the grass fallen back on the perimeter of the old house's garden, the plentiful tree seedlings were easy to find. Renga's ears were always wide open for information, gossip! Having heard what Alex said, he disappeared out the door and as quick as he left, he returned with one of the seedlings. With the tree clasped in his strong clawed feet, the mud from its tiny roots fell and bounced off the heads of the two fox cubs, as he excitedly flew back in through the open front door.

'Will this work?' he asked, dropping it almost into the exact spot against the wall where the earlier tree had come to life. Sophie made her way over to it, and with the help of an old nail she had seen that had been forced out of one of the broken floorboards, she created just enough space to squeeze the roots and base of the tiny tree into. Alex thought back to when they had first come into the house, how he hadn't even noticed the dragonfly leave him.

'The sharp pain when I came in.' Alex remembered that before the dragonfly had appeared and the tree had come alive, as he entered the old house, he had got the familiar pain in his hand that shot up his arm. 'It didn't happen this time.'

'So that's it then, it's not going to happen here,' Jason said deflated.

'Not necessarily,' Sophie replied. She took Alex's hand and walked over to the door. 'The door was closed when we came in before, you opened it.' She was right. Alex let go of her hand and took hold of the rusty old doorknob and turned it. With everyone watching expectantly, nothing happened. Having waited for an appropriate length of time to give the magic a chance to work, Alex tried turning the handle in the opposite direction. Still nothing. Sophie had thought and took hold of Alex's free hand. As soon as she did, she felt an energy build inside her, and the colours on her body came to life. The dragonflies on Alex's arm began fluttering. The ancient dragonfly on Alex's back woke up and wrapped his wings around Alex's body, under his arms and around his chest, giving a squeeze.

'This is not how it happened before, I can't breathe!' Alex exclaimed. Then the familiar pain in his hand returned, his arm tensed, his hand froze in a claw like shape, and one of the dragonflies flew out from his scar, his dragonfly bite.

Just as the pain from his hand and squashing of his body reached the point of too much to bear, a pulse of light from Sophie surrounded him and the pain was gone. With the tension released, he was able to let go of the doorknob and as he did, the pressure on his body stopped, the ancient dragonfly returning to its usual resting state.

'The tree hasn't changed!' Renga said. The dragonfly that had left Alex was on the doorframe, resting below the carving of the waterfall. Something new had appeared. A carving, with its outlines lit up with a bright, white light of a woman standing on a driveway, surrounded by trees, and in the background was the very house they were standing in. Over the top of the door, in its frame, the words that had not been there earlier when Alex's entrance had brought the first carving to life, the words found on every Dragonfly doorway, were slowly appearing. Faintly at first, they grew, becoming fresh, new, crisp, deep carvings.

'Maybe we don't need the tree!' Alex said. To which Sophie replied,

'The tree is what brings life. The doorway has been given a new life, but the house has not.' She walked over to where she had carefully put the seedling. Still full of energy, the light from the colours swirling on her back shining out from the edges of her clothing, she knelt down. Just as she reached out to touch the tree, she felt a puff of air pass her cheek. The dragonfly had left the doorframe and was now sitting on the highest tiny branch of the tree, causing it to bend to one side. Sophie made contact with the tree as the tiny eyes of the dragonfly looked up at her. Nothing changed,

'Together, remember!' Alex took great pleasure in pointing out what she had to him in a sarcastic way earlier. Standing behind her, he rested his hands on her shoulders, with his thumbs touching the skin of her neck. Instantly his eyes changed to their bright purple, the whites to their supernatural light. There was no pain this time. The experience for both of them was beautiful. They felt all of nature surging through them, every plant, insect, animal, mammal. They felt as though they were in the stars, looking down on the creation of a new world. There was no dramatic explosion, bang, light or spark. Instead, peacefully, life passed into the tiny tree. As the tree's roots grew and spread five, ten, fifty, one hundred times bigger and further than the tiny seedling's, the floor began to squeak and shake as they made their way under it.

Alex, his hands still resting on Sophie's shoulders, whose hands were still holding on to the tree where the dragonfly sat, watched, as the movement of the floor stopped and the tree took its turn to grow. Its trunk was the first part to expand, growing taller and thicker, blending into the wall it was planted in front of. Then the branches spread out in all directions, across the walls and the ceiling. The branch the dragonfly was sat on stretched out towards the doorframe. With the process just about complete, the slow moving growth got slower still, until the only branch left moving was the one the dragonfly was on. As it finally arrived at the doorframe, as it touched it, that's when the dramatics began.

Sophie was thrown back away from the tree's trunk, which in turn knocked Alex on his back, softening Sophie's fall as she landed on him. An incredible dragonfly coloured rainbow explosion, coming from the point the tree and doorframe came together, filled the hallway. Then the most unexpectedly, splendidly, wonderful thing happened. A wave of life spread through the old house like a magical paint brush was being invisibly pulled across its walls, ceilings, floors, doors, stairs, windows. The wrecked, torn apart house, was being replaced with the most familiar of looks. For the first time ever, a Dragonfly home was being born on Heart, not on Earth! From a newly planted tree, in a house that was not built for its very purpose!

The group watched on silently as the house was put back together in a way it had never been. Watching the changing colours head towards where Sophie knew there was a kitchen, an excited thought went through her head. Standing up, she grabbed Alex's hand and pulled him along behind her, as she attempted to catch up with the edge of the colourful wave. Coming to a skidding stop in the doorway, Sophie was not disappointed in what she saw. What had been a kitchen with just a single worktop running along one wall, with a sink and old range cooker, a fireplace on its opposite wall, a window on the third wall and nothing but the doorway on the fourth, was now a kitchen being filled with multicoloured cupboards of all shapes and sizes, covering each wall that surrounded the fireplace, window and doorway.

'Food. Alex, we can actually have some food.' Neither of them had eaten since the night before, during the long drive from grandmother's Dragonfly home to the small Highland village.

'How?' Alex asked,

'Remember what happened back at my place, when grandmother made your mum a hot drink and Vicky got what she wanted? That's how. I am sure of it,' Sophie replied. The remodel complete, Sophie grabbed the first quirky, wobbly handle of a bright yellow cupboard, her favourite colour, and opened it. The shelves were empty. Just as the look of disappointment was arriving on both their faces, food popped out of nowhere - all kinds of breads, little loaves, big loaves, long loaves, short loaves, hard crust, soft crust. The smell was just like one you would find in a baker's shop first thing in the morning. Alex went over to a different cupboard on the other side of the room, where he found jams from every fruit ever discovered, and a couple that haven't been yet. Jason, curious as to what all the exclaiming was about, popped his head round the door to see.

'Wow, this is real!' he said, before dashing across the room to another cupboard, a high up cupboard, from which he produced a sixty-year-old bottle of scotch whisky. 'Well, today just got good.' Renga, Averie, Ryley and Hanne were not far behind. It wasn't long before everyone was pulling open cupboard doors, where they found exactly what they were looking for. Sweets, cakes, seeds, fruits, so much food they could have had a banquet. The table in the centre of the room, which had been laying thrown over on the floor, with one of its legs ripped off by the bears, was standing proudly once again, and took the weight of the food being thrown on it gladly. Squeaks, screeches and sounds of satisfaction as the food was being eaten filled the air. The fireplace, having sprung into life, warmed the room, adding to the guests' comforting experience.

'Could this be any better?' Jason asked, contently sitting on one of the comfy chairs that had appeared, with a small glass of his golden brown liquid and a plate full of oatcakes and cheese. 'I feel like royalty right now,' he said, taking just a sip from the short, stubby glass. He received muffled grunts of agreement from the six full mouths sitting round the table with him.

It felt like they had been there for a lot longer than the five minutes they had been, their initially empty stomachs unable to eat as much as their heads thought they could. Alex, sitting back in his chair, looked out of the kitchen into the narrow corridor which looked similar to the one outside grandmother's kitchen, back at her Dragonfly Manor. The view reminded him of why they came back to the house, why they tried what they did.

'Should we try the front door?' he asked,

'The front door?' Averie questioned. Her eyes were showing hints of happiness as she watched her cubs filling their little tummies.

'Yes. The house is alive, so maybe the front door will take us back to our family,' he replied. Sophie, in her excitement for food, had momentarily forgotten what Alex had just remembered. She almost choked on her food as the realisation sunk in. The thought of seeing her grandmother again got her to her feet. Once again she dragged Alex along behind her.

'What was it grandmother said about the handle?' Sophie said as they stepped into the tree-filled hallway. Before Alex had a chance to reply, the left behind Gracie appeared in the open doorway.

The two cubs who had followed Alex and Sophie, curious to find out what other wonderful things they might see, bumbled their way past them and ran up to Gracie growling, showing their tiny little needle teeth at her.

'I am sorry, but I had good reason for being the way I was!' Gracie said. Jason, having heard the not so threatening growls from the cubs, had reluctantly left his sustenance and come out to see what was going on.

'Tell us!' Jason said.

'If I tell you, I am risking more than I can bear to lose,' Gracie replied, who somehow hadn't registered the changes in the house as she stepped in and caught her foot on a slightly raised, patterned red rug. 'What has happened here?' She looked around and taking in the magic that had been given to the big old house said, 'It's… it's like a Dragonfly home, like my cottage once was! How is this possible?' As quick as she asked the question, looking over at Alex and Sophie, she answered it in her mind.

'You had a Dragonfly cottage?' Jason asked.

'Yes, the one that was set on fire,' she answered. Jason, having known her for some time, had no idea that the cottage that Leilani and Lanny had appeared through had been Gracie's family's for hundreds of years. That she was in fact a descendant of key keepers.

'Why didn't you tell me?' Jason asked.

'I couldn't. She took my family from me. When she came, she didn't know I was there. My mother had hidden me and told me to stay quiet, no matter what happened. All I could do was watch as they took her, my father and my brother. Many years later she came back. I don't know why, but she did and when she did, she did it to me again. She took my own husband and children. She took them all to work in her brother's mines, threatening to kill them if I didn't do as she asked,' Gracie said,

'What did she ask you to do?' Sophie asked.

'If you two have done this, it could be that you could help me. If I tell you, you have to promise me that you will rescue my family, because if I tell you she will know, she knows everything,' Gracie said,

'Ok, if we can we will,' Sophie replied.

'The crystal,' Averie said from the background, 'I heard rumours about her and her crystals, that's how she knows isn't it? Like the one I saw on your fireplace.'

'Yes. After she took my family, she forced me out of my cottage and made me live in that hole in the ground. I am not sure why, but I think it was something to do with the crystals, like they needed to be there. She told me I had to be her eyes and ears, and that if I did as she asked, one day she would give my family back to me. That was many years ago now, too many! I remember the day like it was yesterday. The terror in my children's eyes as the bears dragged them through the doorway was horrific. There was nothing I could do.' Gracie stopped talking, her throat choked with emotion. The fox cubs went from teeth-baring defenders to comforters, as they rubbed themselves against her.

'Do you think they are still alive?' Alex asked. Gracie, still unable to speak, shrugged her shoulders and looked into his eyes. Alex could feel everything from her, each ounce of suffering she had experienced. It took his breath away. He was experiencing her memories, he was in the house watching her children and husband be taken. Then he became aware of something very few were aware of,

'You aren't the only one! Leilani has more like you. You and all the others are her window to see!' Alex said.

'That's how she knows everything. Alex...' Jason didn't get a chance to finish his sentence,

'I know. There is suffering here and back home. The suffering I have seen back home is due to the human condition of greed and power which has taken over like a wave. Here it is far simpler - it's only two people we need to stop, or change. I can feel all around me that those who live here have suffered, but their hearts are still good and full of compassion with the love and respect of nature that is needed. I wish I could say the same for back home. Here is where we shall start. We just have to find a way to stop them. I don't know how yet, but we will,' Alex said.

'I know where to start. Grandmother,' Sophie said. Alex took Gracie's hand and guided her into the hallway, away from the front door, which he closed.

'What was it your grandmother said about the door? Turn it the opposite way to what is natural, I think that was it,' Alex said,

'Together,' Sophie said, putting her hand on top of his. 'Oh, the dragon...' before she could finish what she was saying, the dragonfly who had been wallowing in the energies of the beautiful tree, landed on her hand. The sharp shock of a dragonfly bite went through both their hands as Alex turned the knob. The two images on the doorframe lit up and a pulse of light began bouncing from one side of the frame, following the grain of the wood to the other. On the door itself, a single pinprick of light shone and with a crack of electricity, Alex felt the door-handle clunk. The latch open, he slowly pulled the door free from the frame. Cautiously peering through the small opening they had created, they could see that the view had changed to the one outside the now not so old, big house, in the small Highland village. The garden was tidy, the driveway was not mud and grass. Instead, a fresh looking tarmac glistened as the cold evening's air had frozen the particles of water between each undulation. The driveway was lined with trees, their branches bare, the leaves lost weeks earlier as summer turned into autumn. Alex and Sophie, having let go of the door, allowed it to swing fully open and stepped out.

'Sophie! Oh my goodness Alex!' An excited scream came from behind them. An excited scream that did not come from Jason, Renga, Gracie, Averie or her cubs. It came from Vicky.

Chapter 11

'Why do you need my gold? And what's the point in looking through your window when the ones you want to see are here on Heart?' Lanny asked his smiling sister. He was unaware of many things Leilani was able to do, the opening of a window from place to place on Heart being one of them. A secret now known by Alex, Sophie and their travelling companions.

'Just get me your gold.' Her instruction being in a far less aggressive tone than normal, Lanny was slightly unnerved! So, without asking another question, he left with George and Gregg, down the new wobbly cobbly path, out through the glistening, ornate iron gate and down the dirt track towards his store.

Leilani took a moment to look round her home, allowing herself to feel some enjoyment at its youthful appearance, and on catching sight of her reflection in one of the sparkling clean mirrors, hers too!

'Mistress Leilani!' A squeaking voice came from beyond one of the full of life bushes in her revitalised garden. Leilani turned round and looked out the open door. She knew the voice very well. Her calm demeanour was short lived.

'What do you mean by coming back here you scrawny, pasty-faced, no use to anyone creature?' It was Earl, who having seen her looking so young, couldn't help himself but come out of hiding to see her up-close. It was a decision he regretted almost immediately! Thankfully, he moved quickly enough to avoid a stone Leilani kicked at him off her front step. She may have changed on the outside, but inside she had not!

'Mistress, I was trapped here! You didn't wait for me and the door closed.' For a very short moment, accepting that what he said was possible, she accepted it as the truth.

'Fine. Tell me what has been happening in my absence? What happened to the noises in the...' Stopping mid sentence, she remembered what she had been told about Earl and his running backwards and forwards from the trees, finally not returning. She finished her sentence in a very sinister tone, 'trees?' Her eyes squinting, her lips pouting, tilting her head to one side, her chest lifted as she took in a deep breath waiting for his answer. She wondered if he was going to lie to her once again. Not blinking, she stared into his frightened eyes. Concerned he was being pulled into a verbal trap, Earl replied,

'Like I said before, you left me behind, there was nothing there!' His lie was a big mistake. Having stepped out of the house and joined the cowering Earl in her garden, Leilani moved one of her feet from the path and into the soil to the side of the wobbly cobbly path. Earl was suddenly bounced off the ground with an electric pulse, which caused every one of the hairs of his smooth fur coat to stand up on end. His eyes popped wide open. He feared for his life. With an unseen twitch of her big toe, she sent a massive bolt of lightening up and out from the ground. Making contact with Earl, it threw him out of her garden, across the dirt track and back into the trees he had been hiding in.

'If the trees are where you want to be, there you will go. Do not come back!' she screeched. Happy that she had closure for his treachery, she headed back to her Dragonfly house. Once inside, she headed straight for her damp, gold cauldron room to prepare for her brother's return.

The ability to look around Heart had proved a challenge to Leilani. Unlike looking through to Earth where she could look wherever she wanted, when a window was opened in the liquid gold on Heart, she discovered the same was not possible. As far as her brother was concerned she couldn't look anywhere on Heart of course. However, she had discovered that if she placed a crystal where she wanted to see, she could! It was very limiting, but it worked to an extent, sadly for Gracie, her family and others like her.

Reaching down to the cauldron's trunk, Leilani took out thirteen crystals she had hidden behind a bark door. Unlike she did when looking to Earth where she hung the crystals over the gold, she placed all thirteen crystals around the edge of the trunk. When the liquid gold was poured in, the bright yellow light bouncing off the crystals gave her the ability to see, hear and talk to whoever was with the other crystal - a mystical telephone line.

Leilani, having set the crystals in place, knowing exactly who she wanted to communicate with, left to find out what was taking her brother and his bears so long. Climbing up the couple of stone steps and out of her, untouched by the renewed dragonfly magic room, she heard someone approaching her front door. Assuming it was her brother, she screeched,

'Will you hurry up with the gold.' However! Walking out into the corridor that lead to the hallway and the front door, she realised that the two figures silhouetted, were not her brother and one of his bears. Confused, she screeched 'Lanny!' She couldn't see, but he was actually just coming through the garden gate and also saw the two strangers! Not having heard her screech, he shouted,

'Leilani! it's them. It's the two!' As the realisation of who was in front of her sunk in, Leilani found herself caught in a stare, and fixed to the spot. Unable to move, she was happy to see George and Gregg bounding up the wobbly cobbly path, as the two visitors turned to run back to the doorway.

'Nooooooo!' Leilani, free from her stare, screamed. She was wrong to be happy, to be confident in their capture, as Alex and Sophie completely disappeared, leaving George in full flight, claws out, teeth at the ready! With his intended victims gone, he flew through the doorway, right towards Leilani. Thankfully, his leap fell just short of catastrophe! Landing on the rug, his claws tore into it as it slipped away from under him. Finally, coming to a stop, he crashed into the thick banister of the staircase and not Leilani! 'How is this possible? Where have they gone? Lanny, where are they?' she screamed. Kicking the crumpled rug to one side to clear her path, she made her way to the open door where Lanny was standing as equally confused at what had just happened.

'I didn't see the door open or close, I don't understand,' Lanny said. Once back in the house, he stepped behind the door to check the doorframe and the pinpricks of light for clues. 'There look!' he said, pointing at one particular pinprick of light,

'It's the cottage we just came from. The one you were supposed to have burnt down!' Leilani, in a very cold, accusatory voice, said,

'I did. You saw. You watched it right up until you closed the door.' Lanny replied in his defence. After a moment's pause for thought, he continued, 'Why don't you try it? If they have gone back, then surely we can too.' His observation making some sense, Leilani closed the door, pressed on the pinprick of light, turned the handle the way she always had, and reopened it.

'Why?' she screeched. The view she got was the same as before.

'The doorframe didn't light up. And look, the light on the door where the cottage was, it's fading!' Lanny said.

'What is happening?' Leilani asked, having no idea that back at the Dragonfly cottage, the door had been stopped from fully closing by the fallen rubble. Unseen, it kept the doorway to her Dragonfly manor open just enough for the surprised Sophie and Alex to unexpectedly pass through. Equally unknown to her was that after their escape back through, they had removed the rubble and closed what had remained of the burnt door, rendering it unusable. Having burnt down the tree and the rest of the cottage the magic was gone, there was no way back for Leilani and her brother. Leilani's rage building, in an escalating in volume voice, she shouted,

'This was supposed to be my day!' And then let out a scream that had the bears covering their ears. So loud, so high pitched and full of power, that the branches of the trees as far away as beyond her garden, shook, shaking the lives that had remained sitting on them, hiding, waiting and watching, to the ground. One of the living creatures that fell was Earl, who having survived his electric punch from Leilani, decided not to push his luck any further. He had seen enough, and just as the rest of the living creatures with legs or wings did, he left, across the field beyond the trees, out of and back into other shadows.

'Gold, get me gold!' she shouted at her brother. Lanny had preempted that would be her next order. He was already heading to the discarded stone bucket that George and Gregg had dropped as they went to attack Sophie and Alex. Much to his relief, there was still a small amount of his gold left in it.

'Will this be enough?' he asked a red-faced Leilani. She didn't say a word, just spun round and stormed back to her room.

'Shall we take that as a yes boys?' Lanny said in remarkably good spirits. 'Just bring it in,' he ordered.

The gold poured into Leilani's tree trunk cauldron, which covered the curved bottom with about six millimetres of depth, was just enough.

'What good is the gold going to do anyway sister, they're in Heart?' Lanny asked. Leilani didn't answer. She walked over to one of her drooping shelves and took a vial of blood. Then, making her way round the thirteen crystals, she placed a drop of the blood on each, adjusting them as she did, until finally, from one, an image appeared. Moving right up close, she peered into a room that she had not seen in some time. It was in darkness, with no sign of life. Lanny was confused, he had never seen Leilani use the crystals in such a way, so he wasn't sure what he was looking at. As he opened his mouth to ask a question, Leilani, sensing one was coming, said,

'Patience brother. Now we need to be patient.' Having no idea what he was being patient for, Lanny decided to make himself comfortable on the wonky steps that looked as old and well used as the room. George and Gregg made themselves comfortable on the floor, using each other as pillows, taking what they felt was a well-deserved rest.

'Ha ha ha ha, I knew it.' Leilani saw a face she recognised, it looked older than she recalled but it was definitely Gracie. 'Good girl, you still think your family will be safe if you help me ha ha ha.' After closer examination of the tiny crystal window, she saw that Gracie was not alone. She saw three faces she had seen already that day. The ones that had scurried off after an unimportant and unhelpful fox had had its throat slashed by Lanny's bears. Then she saw two faces she did not know. It was Jason and Renga - the Tawny Frogmouth gossiping bird.

George and Gregg, suddenly woken from their remarkably deep sleep by Leilani's exclamation, were up in automatic pilot. Grabbing the stone bucket, crashing it off the wall and door as they left to get more gold, as that was the normal sequence of events - get gold, use gold, need more gold.

'Silence!' Leilani screeched. She was trying very hard to hear what was being talked about. 'They were with them brother,' having managed to make out the names Alex and Sophie, and a most important fact that they had brought a dragonfly. 'They must be talking about the one that gave us our youth back.' Lanny was beginning to think his sister was going madder than he already thought she was. He heard nothing! He also saw nothing, just his sister bent over, staring into a small crystal. She watched and listened as the conversation moved to what drinks everyone would like, 'How can they be thinking about drinks when there is a dragonfly nearby. This is why we have the power. They really are such stupid beings. They don't deserve to be here on Heart,' Leilani said,

'Sister, I have absolutely no idea what you are talking about. Have you completely lost your mind? And what power are you talking about?' Lanny said without thinking.

'Power you never had brother, and never will!' Leilani responded, taking her gaze from the crystal for a moment. She considered bringing her brother up to speed, but decided that it was best not to enlighten him as to what she was doing and how she was able to it. 'Where has she gone?' Leilani said as she looked back into the crystal. Gracie had left her stove. Leilani moved closer still to the crystal and tilted it slightly. 'There you are,' she whispered, smiling as she did. Turning the crystal to follow her, she watched as Gracie climbed the steps and opened the hatch, letting in the end of daylight as she did. 'Bring them in, come on, bring them in for me to get a better look,' Leilani calmly said, as appearing from beyond the entrance, she saw the young couple that had been standing in her hallway not that long ago. 'I told you brother, patience.' She couldn't make out what was being said, but got concerned when the fox and her cubs got up and left, climbing past Gracie and then disappearing out of sight. 'Get them in!' Leilani said in a firm voice. 'No, no, where are you going!' she said as Jason and Renga also got up and left. 'You better not go with them you little bitch!' Leilani, barking out her unheard order, said. Gracie did not, she came back down the steps and walked right up to the crystal and said,

'I know you are watching! I tried my best.' Leilani took her crystal from around her neck and touched it to the small crystal she had been using as the window. As soon as she did, her brother realised that his sister was not going madder than she already was, as he too could hear a voice. The act of her crystal touching the smaller one, gave her the ability to amplify the conversation and to talk directly to the person on the other side, on this occasion, the person being Gracie.

'You know the reality! Tell me all you know and maybe I might even give you a glimpse of the ones I took from you. If you don't, you will still see them, but be assured they will be in great pain.' Leilani's threats were never just threats, they were promises that had been tested in the past by others, with horrific results, and not tested again. Gracie, with tears running down her face at being the one to give all the information she had, told her all she knew of Alex, Sophie and the dragonfly.

'Now you will go and find them again, watch them, and report back to me all that you find out. I need to know where they are and what they are planning. You know there are others in your position so if you can't get back to your underground hovel, find them and use them.' Leilani had created the network of underground hovels, as they were the only way she could use the crystals on Heart the way she did. Her ability to use the ground's energies were not just for causing injury or harm to others, she discovered they could be used for many things, communication being one of them. With every family she took, every Dragonfly home her brother ransacked, she would force the descendant key-keeper into a hidden home that she created, away from their own Dragonfly home, but close enough to be found if Leilani chose to visit. The irony of the underground homes was that those who knew of them, assumed they were created by the ones who lived in them as hiding places from Leilani and her brother. They were unaware that Leilani was watching and listening, threatening suffering or death to the family she had taken and put to work in her brother's gold mines. Or wherever else she wanted hard labour to be carried out.

It was in that moment that it occurred to Gracie that her fear of harm coming to her stolen family, could very well be irrelevant, and that she could have given up all the information she had, for no reason. She also saw what the future could be for so many, if Alex and Sophie were who all hoped they were. To risk two worlds' peace for her selfish love was not something she could live with, sacrifices had to be made. Gracie sensed that the fear Leilani spread across Heart may be coming to an end, and if there was any chance of her family still being alive, it would be her who would find them, with the help of Alex and Sophie. This led her to say,

'No, you have had enough from me! My family have been lost for over twenty years. I cannot believe that they are still alive. That you would have let them live this long.'

Gracie took the crystal from where it hung by the fire and threw it into the flames. An act of defiance that she hoped she would not regret. With Gracie out of sight and no sounds heard from her home, Leilani was shocked by what had happened. Being defied in such a way was a new experience for her.

'Brother, find her family. I want their throats torn, their hearts ripped out, I want to see their blood filling the vials in this room! I want all to know that there will be no mercy for anyone who dare refuse my demands!'

Lanny wasn't sure how he could do what she asked. He had no idea where they would be, who they even were. No lists were kept of the people and creatures taken as slaves, they were just taken. His largest mine, until he had stopped gathering gold, was the one in south Australia, near the land-locked town of Ballarat, at a place called Sovereign Hills. The slaves that were taken there were many, so many that the town had grown to such a size, he'd had to deploy nearly half of his bear army to make sure all remained under his control.

'George, Gregg, time for a trip,' he said, as he walked out of the room, leaving the raging Leilani behind.

'Master Lanny, how can we without Mistress Leilani?' Gregg asked. Lanny knew he needed his sister to make the short trip through the door, but he also did not want to state the obvious to her, as it would inevitably result in him being the subject of more of her rage.

'You think I don't know that?' was his response, followed up with a back-handed strike to Gregg's head. George couldn't help himself - a burst of laughter shot out, echoing through the hallway, which of course also earned him a blow to the back of his hard, furry head as well.

'We need to appease that not so old and scrawny sister of mine,' Lanny said, as he walked towards the front door with a spark of an idea. 'Earl! Let's go and get that ridiculous creature back. Doing some harm to him may calm her down enough for me to ask her to open the door for us.' George and Gregg didn't need any convincing as they had disliked Earl from the day they met. His lording over them that he was Leilani's favourite, left them fantasising about being alone with him, how they would hang him from a tree and slowly open him up with their razor-sharp claws.

They didn't know exactly where he was, but they knew he had been in the trees before, so that was where they went. Lanny, following not far behind, was very curious to see what was happening, what was being said in the shadows about the two new visitors to Heart and their dragonfly. Out of the gate, some of his bear army still encamped down the dirt track, patiently waiting for orders, realised something was happening. Having seen their generals crash through the brush into the trees, their instincts to follow took over. A loud rumble could be heard from behind, as Lanny looked back to see a sea of bounding, fur-covered, muscular backs making good ground behind them.

'Gregg, go back and tell them who we are looking for. George lead the way.' There was an explosion of noise as the army crashed through the woods, breaking branches and crushing bushes as they did. With no sign of life they broke free out of the thin wood, out into the first open field. Reaching the field's centre point, instinctively, without pause, the army of bears split into three. Each group headed in a different direction. One group south, towards what looked like a river, one north, towards more fields, and the last with George and Lanny, headed east towards a much thicker gathering of trees.

Having escaped Leilani for the second time, Earl was welcomed in by a family who had managed to stay hidden. Surprising, considering their close proximity to the Dragonfly manor. They lived deep in the woods in a home that had once been the home of a dragonfly. It was a quirky looking building with not a single straight wall, all curved, creating a house that looked like a castle's turret, with the same sort of pointy roof a turret would have. The stones that made up its walls were placed unlike any other, creating a visual twisting affect, added to by its slight lean from the hundreds of years of its existence on soft ground. It was quite odd looking in a splendidly wonderful kind of way. Its smiling windows and wobbly cobbly path were still just visible, to those who looked close enough.

The approaching rumble of the bear army could not be missed. There was never any stealth in Lanny and his bears' attacks, or in this case, search. A pigeon who had been flying above the trees, noticed the parting of bushes and the tall trees' branches shaking. Having flown down to take a closer look, she knew that her hidden friends in the quirky dragonfly home were soon to be discovered. With a flick of her tails feathers and a twist of her body, she turned and dove straight for the home. The occupants, already aware of the rumble, were at the front door to see the pigeon's fast descent. Too fast to stop carefully, the pigeon bounced off the floor and into the home. Out of breath, she said,

'Bears, lots of bears, they are coming this way.' A descendant of generations of key-keepers for her quirky home, the dirty faced, short-haired welcomer of Earl, slammed the door shut, grabbed the handle, chose a pinprick of light, twisted the handle and threw the door open. It all happened in a split second. Those standing near the door were hit with heat. The sky of the place the door was opened to was clear blue with a huge, unfiltered sun beating down on the dry land,

'Madam, I believe you have done that one or two times,' Earl said, amazed at the speed in which his option to escape was achieved. She smiled, pushed him through the open door and said,

'You know more than Leilani would wish for any of us to know. Spread what you have told me, do it fast.' As quickly as she had opened the door, she slammed it shut and Earl found himself alone in a not so unfamiliar land.

'He has gone!' The key-keeper announced, as she re-opened the door to Lanny and his hoard of bears to the back of him.

'I have no idea who you are talking about. I was merely out for a walk, saw your home and thought it only polite to be neighbourly. But seeing as you brought the subject up, I can only assume you are referring to my sister's pet. So where exactly has he gone?' Lanny asked, stepping right up to the woman, whose nerve was starting to go. Two little faces appeared from behind her, and happily said in unison,

'Through the door of course.' The voices were of her very young twins.

'Well, isn't that just perfect! Answers and hostages all in the same moment. I am very curious how you have stayed hidden from us. Can I assume you don't have a dragonfly? Actually, right now I don't care!' Lanny said, flicking his head, gesturing for George to do what he did so well. He barged past the woman to round up the twins, whose faces had changed from innocent expectation, to terror.

'Ok, ok. No, I don't have a dragonfly, you took it from me at another place a long time ago. Please, I will show you where he went! Just don't take my babies, don't hurt them!' The key-keeper's shaky words were directed at Lanny, who calmly replied,

'Thank you,' and ordered his bears into the small, quirky Dragonfly home. To get all the bears into the small space, they had to stand on each other's backs.

The heat created by so many piled up furry bodies, was good preparation for where they were headed.

'After you,' Lanny said, gesturing to the closed door, its pinpricks of light glowing and the doorframe's carved stories pulsing with the same white light. This time, slightly slower than in aiding Earl's escape, she went through the process of opening the door, hoping to give Earl a little extra time to move away from the Dragonfly house she had pushed him into.

'Oh, well isn't that helpful!' Lanny said, very pleased with himself, as the door opened and he saw the place of his intended search for the family Leilani had wanted him to find. 'Looks like we will not only be bringing Earl back, we shall be bringing the family as well. Won't my sister be pleased. Oh, you can stay in your home, just shut the door and enjoy the peace while you can. I will be informing my sister of your existence!' Lanny, happy with his parting speech, confidently stepped through the doorway into the heat of the Australian sun, quickly followed by his, happy to be out of the cramped house, bears. Out of the garden with its bleached, wobbly cobbly pathway, he took a deep breath as he stood looking towards a very familiar sight less than half a mile away - the entrance to his mine! 'I feel that my giving up on the gold mines was somewhat premature. Maybe it's time I take home more of that gloriously heavy shiny product again! Once we have found that dragonfly, of course,' said Lanny.

Marching across the dry land, the hot wind causing dust clouds to raise up and wrap around them, the wind was a relief in the heat, although a hinderance at the same time as the dust got in their eyes. It did not take them long to get to the entrance of his mine.

'Seems strangely quiet,' Lanny said. Even though he had stopped mining, he expected the people, the animals, the slaves, to be there. With his youth and strength returned, he was able to kick aside the beam that was holding the large wooden door closed over the entrance with ease. As it fell away, he was hit with a most horrific smell. Behind the door the tunnel was blocked with huge boulders, which he had put in place to guarantee those he trapped in there could not escape, and those who wanted to rescue them, or steal his gold, could not get in. He ordered his bears to clear a way through. It took longer than he would have liked, but finally a way through was made. Unfortunately, it had the unpleasant result of releasing an even more intense version of the smell, the smell of rotting flesh. 'Oh, that is unfortunate. I suppose me shutting them in was not the best idea after all,' Lanny said laughing. 'Our search may take us a little longer than expected George. Also, I am not sure if you noticed, but there was no sign of the key-keeper of the shack we just came through. Maybe send a couple of the bears to check that out for me.' Lanny made his way into the mine, but the bears did not follow. 'What's wrong with you?' Lanny, realising he was walking alone, shouted, his voice echoing out from the tunnel. George tentatively stepped in, his acute sense of smell making it hard for him to breathe.

'Master Lanny, it's bears!' George said, as he stepped over the rotting flesh and bones creating the rancid smell. Lanny hadn't noticed. To that point, what or whoever was causing the smell was irrelevant to him. George's words changed that. If the lifeless, rotting bodies were of his bears, the army he left to keep control, where were the ones who should be laying dead on the tunnel's floor?

'George, where are they, the slaves? How has this been kept secret from me?' Lanny asked.

'Master Lanny, the rotting flesh is only days old. The heat would have accelerated the decay, but I would say two days at the most,' George wisely said. The relevance of the timing was not missed by Lanny. Two days ago was the day of the morning the strange lights appeared in the sky, the day they saw the torso of a strange young man in their Dragonfly Manor. Lanny clenched his jaw. His breath picking up pace, he barked out orders that increased in volume with every word,

'This is not all my bear army, find those who survived. If you can't, find the woman who should be at that shack we just came through, find me any key-keeper. Find me the escapees, find them all!'

CHAPTER 12

'Well, well, well, look who it is!' the very cheerful voice of grandmother said from behind Vicky, as she made her way to the front door to see their visitors. 'If there was any doubt before, there most certainly is not now. I assume you are the reason for this!' grandmother said, looking around the full of life, new looking hallway. 'How did you do it? Oh, I am forgetting myself,' she shuffled her way past Vicky and gave Sophie a very welcome hug.

'I missed you grandmother,' Sophie said, happy to return the loving hug. As she squeezed grandmother as tight as she could, she looked over her shoulder to a perfect replica of the old house she had just left. 'It really is the same!' she said, just as the wet nose and very excited, smiling face of Anchor appeared between them. 'Oh my goodness I missed you!' she said, squatting down and getting a face full of fur as he threw his head over her shoulder, trying to get as close as he could. Alex, who was standing behind Sophie, not wanting to interrupt the reunion, patted Anchor's head. Melissa appeared from the room whose fireplace had changed from a small, barely giving out any heat fire, to what felt like an inferno after its change into a Dragonfly home.

'Hi mum.' Alex calmly said,

'Where did you go Alex? What have you seen? What happened?' Melissa's frantic, quick-fire questions were not said so calmly, which was very unlike her usual considered self.

'It's a long story mum,' Alex replied. Suddenly, everyone's attention was taken by the loud bark of Anchor. A bark so vicious it scared Sophie, who was still at his face height. The hackles up on his back, his fangs fully out. He had seen something.

'Anchor, it's ok, they're with us,' said Alex, having realised who Anchor's aggression was being directed at. It was Jason, along with Gracie, Renga, Averie and her cubs.

'It would seem you have made some friends Sophie,' grandmother said. Alexandria, who had followed Melissa out of the warm room, took a moment to register who was standing in front of her! As soon as she did, she fell to her knees, her head in her hands she began sobbing. Jason pushed past Alex and Sophie, managing to just hold back his own tears and said,

'I can't believe it, your son said you were alive and fine, but I didn't want let myself believe it until I saw you.' He bent down, put his hands under her arms and lifted her up off the floor. Her feet dangling like a child in a high chair, tears pouring down her face, she wrapped her arms round his neck.

'Excuse me, but when am I getting in on some of this action,' Vicky said, with a patiently waiting Bart at her side. Happy to see Vicky's smiling face, Sophie let go of Anchor, stood up and pulled both Vicky and Alex into a group hug. Hug over, Alex thought it would be a good idea to tell Vicky, grandmother, Anchor and Bart who the unknown guests were.

'Ok, so, introductions. The one over there with my other mum, that's Jason, her brother, my uncle! This is Gracie, she has helped us out a bit. The owl looking fella sitting on the door is Renga, who isn't actually an owl and is a very long way from home. This lovely lady is Averie, and with her are her babies. Believe me, they have suffered today.' Finished, Alex totally forgot that the ones he introduced would have no idea who they were being introduced to. So after a short pause to see if Alex was going to go on, which he didn't, Sophie took over.

'And this is my grandmother, Alex's mum and other mum, Anchor is my dopey dog, Vicky is a new friend who like you Averie, has come along for the ride! I think she is mad, but she is fun to have around, and her seeing-eye dog Bart, although he can seem quite serious, he is actually a big softie.' Introductions over, Jason couldn't help himself. Directing his comment at grandmother in a more aggressive way than he had initially intended, he said,

'So you are the reason for Leilani and Lanny's existence!' It was a truth that grandmother had spent over two hundred years dealing with, so she was surprised that her reaction was to become emotional. Her hurt feelings quickly picked up on by Sophie, said,

'Jason, if you think you have known pain, just imagine for a second, living the many years of regret that my grandmother has, before being accusatory!' Sensing the atmosphere taking a dark turn, away from the excited celebrations of coming back together and the meeting of new friends, grandmother put her feelings to the back of her mind and said,

'We have all suffered one way or another, it is not important to what extent. What is important is that we are all here together and that you Sophie, and you Alex, have shown us that things can change. Come on, let's go and see what we can find in the very new kitchen. I am sure there will be something for everyone!' she said with a wink. It was a full house -

many emotions, memories, thoughts flying about. The kitchen, with every treat they could want, seemed like a very good place for everyone to return to a place of calm and focus.

With the cupboards having been excitedly fully investigated, and all present digging into their perfect food and drink; the questions started again,

'Where did you two go?' Melissa asked,

'Heart!' was Alex's initial quick response. He went on to give a quick rundown of what had happened to them in the cave with the lake, the tunnel full of gems, the ever-reducing tunnel and the cave full of trees and dragonfly pods. How he ended up carrying three baby dragonflies, as well as the ancient dragonfly who had made his back its home. How Jason had found them, what had happened at the old house, how they came face to face with Leilani and how they finally ended up where they were.

'So we really do have a very new beginning. I have never heard of a Dragonfly home being brought to life in Heart,' grandmother said. 'I need to have a look at the doorframe.' Everyone followed her out into the hall.

'So what next?' Vicky asked, to which Sophie replied,

'We were hoping, grandmother, you may help with that. We know how to make a Dragonfly home now, but what good is that if once we have, Leilani and Lanny take the dragonfly. Which they did. And from what we saw, they no longer look like the old siblings we had expected.' It was then Sophie panicked, 'Alex, the dragonfly!'

'It's fine. Look.' Alex pointed to a branch of the tree next to the door. And there it was. 'She came with us.' Sophie was relieved. She couldn't bear the thought of losing another one to Leilani and her brother. Grandmother then answered the question Sophie had asked before her panic.

'I am not sure how I can help you. There isn't anything being given away on the doorframe! The words are there, just like all the other Dragonfly homes I have ever known, but there are no stories for me to interpret, just that waterfall and the lady on a driveway. Oh, that's you two isn't it!' she said, looking at Jason and Alexandria. 'And you know what, I think you and Alex are doing a good job by yourselves.'

'Ok. Well I understand that we need to make more of these homes, but the door has only one pinprick of light. So how are we supposed to travel to all parts of the world? We don't have the time to do it on foot, or by car. Also, do you think we can bring the old homes back to life?' Sophie asked. Alex could answer that question,

'Well, we did. Remember your Dragonfly Manor came back to life. It was just the dragonfly didn't stay with me.' Sophie, having forgotten, was happy to have been reminded.

'Erm, Sophie, did you say there was only one light on the door? I think you may be wrong!' Vicky asked.

'Yes, why?' Sophie replied,

'Have another look.' Everyone did, and everyone saw nothing. Even the one pinprick of light had gone.

'You need to hold the handle Sophie,' grandmother reminded her. So she did. She took hold of the handle and sure enough, the one light came back, but it also came back with more tiny lights than they could count.

'How did you see that?' Gracie asked Vicky,

'I don't know, I just did!' she replied.

'It's her eyesight. Her inability to see on Earth is the opposite on Heart, where she can see more than most. And that door is now connected to Heart,' grandmother said, helping fill in the gaps of knowledge. 'The house just needed to grow into its magic, to make its connections with all the other Dragonfly homes here and throughout Heart.'

'Does that mean they will be able to see this place now?' A nervous Gracie asked,

'If they are looking, yes! The only place hidden from them for all time is the island. Only Shuing's ancestors, the protectors, know of it. Well, until today! But they still will not be able to see it or find it. Thankfully,' Alexandria replied.

'So let's go there then,' Gracie said. 'If we stay here, Leilani and her bears could come at any time.' Grandmother explained that it wasn't that easy. Yes, she could get to the Dragonfly house on Heart, but not the one they all stood in. With Sophie being the house's new key-keeper and the dragonfly being with them, they were safe. 'We may be safe, but what about all back on Heart, my family?' Gracie asked.

Sophie, having taken Alex's hand, felt what he was about to say before he even knew he was going to say it, and nodded in agreement.

'We came here for information from you grandmother. We were never going to stay. I, we, know that our purpose is bigger than hiding from the twins. We also made a promise to you Gracie. My heart is telling me that our promise to you should be dealt with before anything else.' That's when Renga got excited,

'That means the mines, doesn't it! My home,' he said.

'If that's where we will find Gracie's family, then yes, that's where we should be going.' Alex, still holding Sophie's hand, turned to the door, 'which one is it?' he asked, looking at the dull lights that covered it,

'That one,' Gracie said, pointing to one towards the lowest of all the lights. Alex touched it. Nothing happened.

'Oh my dears, you can't use the door to get to there from here. First you have to go back to Heart,' grandmother said, in the perfect tone of a primary school teacher talking to her first year pupils. Alex took hold of the door's handle, Sophie placed her hand on his as she had done before and in a blur, the dragonfly left its perch and joined them, at which point they turned the doorknob in the opposite direction to what would be normal. Dancing lights, shooting hand pain, a clunk of the door latch and together they opened the door. Everyone stepped out into the garden, which was still going through the process of renewing. They could see beyond the garden's low wall. The driveway was not the fresh tarmac of the house they had left, it was the dirt track Jason had known for many years, the magic of the dragonfly only extending to the garden walls and its beautiful iron gate of flowers.

Once the train of people and animals were clear of the entrance, Alex closed the door and instantly reopened it, showing off an almost identical hallway, causing him, just for a moment, to question if it was the same house!

'Everyone back in please!' Alex announced. All inside, Alex and Sophie started the procedure again. This time, as Alex touched the tiny light at the bottom of the lights, it lit up. Just as they were about to take hold of the handle, grandmother spoke.

'The dragonfly doesn't usually follow or leave its Dragonfly home, as when it gets older, its the magic from the tree that keeps it young and alive. However, seeing as this little one is young and also that it appears it can rejoin with you Alex and considering there is every chance my granddaughter will find this place, it should come with us.'

As it turned out, Sophie was correct in her assumption that her grandmother may be able to help them in some way, even though she thought she couldn't. She had relayed all kinds of stories from her memory, the books and papers she had read to Sophie and Alex, but the small details, which were obvious to grandmother, were not to them. One simple fact about the door not able to take them to other places on Earth, or directly to other places on Heart from Earth was invaluable.

'Before we leave this place, I am curious! Sophie, have you now become the key-keeper for this particular Dragonfly house? Meaning you can only open the door to Earth through this house, or are you like Alex, who I assume can not only create new homes, but can move between them all on Heart and Earth,' Alexandria asked. Sophie hadn't thought about it. She had been with Alex every time they had travelled between doors, and as they know they are to be together to create the homes, bring the magic to the trees, she answered,

'I don't know, I guess I am probably free to go wherever with Alex.'

'So in theory could I become the key-keeper for this house back in my Highland home?' Alexandria asked. Grandmother interjected,

'I don't see why not my dear, but let's leave that for another time.' Grandmother's flippancy frustrated Alexandria. She had lost her own Dragonfly Cottage because of Leilani and Lanny, her grandchildren. Although she understood it was not directly her fault, she felt that there was a lack of empathy for her situation. After generations of her family having kept the island's location secret, the loss of her home and the most heartbreaking loss of her son for so many years, Alexandria longed for a place she could once again call a family home. She shook it off and did as suggested, in her mind leaving it until another time.

The pinprick of light selected, the door handle turned, the door finally opened. As soon as it did, they were hit with an intense heat. The heat of an Australian summer on Heart. Renga was overjoyed to be flying out of the Dragonfly house hallway, out over the heads of Alex and Sophie into the heat of the country of his birth. He took off flying up into the sky, the invisible heat's currents pushing him higher and higher. Twisting, falling, rising again, it was like being on a rollercoaster in the dark, not knowing which way the next turn will go. He loved it.

Everyone stepped out of the doorway onto the sunburnt wobbly cobbles and garden with no sign of life, just soil so dry it cracked in every direction, creating mini caverns for the insects to find cover from the sun's intense heat. Looking out beyond the collapsed garden wall, more dry land covered in dead brush and the occasional bare tree went on as far as the eye could see. The part of Victoria they had found themselves in was unusually hilly, which made it great for mining, the hillsides creating good access points at the bottom to dig both up as well as down. It wasn't long in the heat before everyone, except

Renga, was searching for a way to cover up, to find shade to protect themselves from the blazing ball of fire that would burn them within minutes. The only ones able to find some relief were the fox cubs, who were small enough to hide in Anchor's shadow.

Renga had found a pocket of cooler air and was happily hovering in it, but then he saw something the group had to know about. Pulling his wings in tight to his body, he dove back down as fast as he could.

'He is here, Lanny, his bears, they are all here!' he exclaimed frantically, circling the group just above their heads.

'Why would he be here of all places?' Melissa asked,

'The gold, it has to be for the gold!' Gracie said, reminding them why they were there, that this was Lanny's main gold mine. She went on to tell them what only she and any other key-keeper that had been forced to spy for Leilani knew - that the ability for her to see to other places around Heart was because of three things - a crystal, blood and gold. 'I don't know whether she ever knew, but as clearly as Leilani could see me through the crystal in my underground home, I could also see her! I saw what and how she did what she did to see me! If Lanny is here, she must need more gold,' Gracie said. She had no idea of the vastness of the store Lanny had, which was full of gold. 'I could be wrong though. Leilani said that she would make my family suffer. I would like to think they could still be alive! Maybe he is here for them.'

Gracie's words sparked a heightened sense of urgency in her, in their purpose for travelling to the mines. Alex wanted to say something profound and helpful, to come up with a plan, but he was distracted by Vicky. Having walked off towards one of the dry hills, she had stopped at a large pile of rocks. Over the couple of days she had known Alex and Sophie, she'd had the ability to see as clearly as anyone with healthy eyes could, and to hear without difficulty on Heart. Having arrived in Sovereign Hills, she had stayed silent. Which was unlike her. The reason for her silence was that she had been enjoying taking in all she was able to see. From the tiniest detail on each singed blade of burnt grass, to the curve of the horizon in the opposite direction of the hills, the flat land spreading out as far as she could see. She was hearing as sharply as she could ever remember, which was why she had stopped where she had. She had heard the sound of something moving in a pile of rocks.

'Be careful Vicky, remember we are in Australia! Snakes, spiders and the like could be hiding in there!' Sophie shouted over, as Vicky bent down to the rocks.

'It's Heart, not Earth!' she shouted back. It didn't take long for her clear-visioned eyes to see what had created the sound. A scorpion! Peering into the shadows, she quietly said, 'Hi, I am Vicky.' Because of grandmother's stories, along with being able to understand Anchor, Bart and all the other animals she had come across on her strange journey, she was confident that she would get a response. 'It's ok little guy, I'm not going to hurt you!'

'Little guy! I will have you know I am probably the largest of my family.' The stern voice came from the jet black scorpion who scurried from the shadows out into the sun, his eight legs a blur.

'I meant no disrespect,' Vicky said. Her words seemed to do the trick. The stern tone to the scorpion's voice was replaced with one less so,

'I haven't seen you in these parts before. The old shack is definitely up and running again, seeing as you are the second ones to arrive today. It's been a long time since we have had visitors that aren't just him.' The 'him,' the scorpion referred to being Lanny.

'We are here for my friend. Her family were taken from her some time ago. She thinks they were probably brought here to be used in mines,' Vicky said.

'The mine hasn't been used for quite some time. If they were there, if they are alive, your friend is correct, they would have been in the mine, as the brother trapped everyone inside before he left! But, what he didn't take into consideration, was that all the living things he trapped in there had been digging for him for years! So they found a way out! If your friend's family are here, it's not the mines you need to go to. Head up over that hill, you will find the land not so dry and dusty. You will also find more life than there is this side, or it will find you!' Vicky, taking in what she had been told by the very helpful scorpion, said thank you, and returned to the group who had been nervously watching from a safe distance. Renga, still hovering above their heads, said,

'That's the opposite direction to where I saw Lanny, so that's good news.' Then, with a flick of his tail feathers and repositioning of his wings, completing an impressive sharp turn, he took off up the hillside. Alex, Sophie and the rest of the ever-growing group followed. After a long, very hot and sweaty hour's walk, watched over by their eye in the sky, Renga, they made it to the top. Pausing to catch their breath for a moment and to see what their descent would entail, they looked down the hill. What they saw was a far steeper descent than the gentle rise they had just completed. There were pockets of shade given by various steep, rocky drops, which they were all very happy to see. It was grandmother who suggested a route which made full use of the shadows, to escape the oppressive heat of the blazing sun, to the forest which sat at its base. Looking across the incredibly tall, almost white tree trunks, with their branches at their tops having some green but dry looking leaves, the forest seemed to have no end.

'I thought your scorpion friend said there was more life this side,' Renga said, returning to the group after having flown some distance over the forest. He could find no sign of life, let alone a gathering of people, a village, or even a house.

'Maybe they are hiding in the trees,' Vicky replied. Her always optimistic self not being deflated by his report.

'Well, only one way to find out,' Melissa said, leading the way down a part of the hill that wasn't too steep. She took Alexandria's hand, which didn't go unnoticed by Sophie, nor was the very affectionate smile shared between them. The descent took them half the time of the climb up. It would have been even quicker if it hadn't been for the steep parts that required a little more care. But they made it down safe and sound, just hot and thirsty.

'Hello!' The greeting, heard by all, came from a shadow behind a tree.

'Run!' Gracie screamed. The volume of her scream, and the fear in her voice, meant everyone did as she ordered without question. They all took off along the tree line, in the opposite direction of the voice. Averie ran behind her cubs. Their small legs were not quick enough to keep up with everyone, and they were being left behind. Averie was beginning to panic but Anchor, who had been out in front, came to the rescue. Having taken a glance back to check everyone was with him and noticing their loss of contact with the group, he turned and ran back to his new young friends. One at a time, he gently grabbed them by the fur on the back of their necks and threw them up on his back. Once they were in place, he said,

'Hold on tight. Just grab my neck, don't worry it won't hurt.' He was wrong. Their needle-like teeth made his eyes flutter and his ears go flat as he tried to block out the sharp shock. Thankfully, it was no different to any injection at the vet, so as quick as the pain was there it was gone.

'Thank you Anchor,' Averie said in her soft, gentle voice. Her babies were having the time of their lives, bouncing all over the place as they caught up and passed the group, Bart nodding his approval at Anchor's help as they passed.

The heat and their thirst meant none of them could run as far as they would normally, so they were thankful when they came across a small opening in the trees with a track that led into the forest. Having taken it and gone a short distance, they stopped, thinking they had made their escape, that they hadn't been followed. They were wrong! The body belonging to the voice that had said "hello" to them, had scurried along inside the tree line, following their every step, unseen. This time, hoping not to frighten the group, he came out from the trees with his front paws raised.

'I am completely alone here, I am here to help!'

'Don't trust him, he belongs to Leilani!' Gracie said, instantly recognising who he was. She had seen him by her side in the crystal, in her home under the ground.

'Like you, I belong to no-one, I am just like you. I am here to help you two as much as I can.' He couldn't believe he found himself standing in front of Alex and Sophie. He had seen them through Leilani's window. He had seen Alex's torso on the Dragonfly Manor entrance. He knew how important they were. Somehow circumstance had taken him to just the right place at just the right time.

'You must understand our hesitation here!' grandmother said. Renga, flying much lower than he had been, just feet above the trees, confirmed he was alone by saying,

'I have seen no-one else.'

'Well, you said there was no life here at all and you were wrong about that!' Gracie said. Renga couldn't argue with that, but pointed out that he was very high before.

'I can't run any further anyway. So it's probably worth at least speaking to the funny-looking thing. What are you?' Vicky asked. Earl could have taken offence to her question, but was just happy not to be run away from again, or worse, hurt by the group that greatly outnumbered him. Gracie wasn't convinced. She stepped behind the group and put her back up against a large tree, looking past Earl into the forest for other eyes, which if he was with Leilani or Lanny, would be bear height. Ignoring Vicky's question, Earl decided to tell them how he ended up there, hoping that would help them trust him. How he had been talking to the humans and animals in the trees outside Leilani's Dragonfly Manor, how he had managed to escape Lanny and his bears with the help of a key-keeper, how he had discovered the mine was closed, how he had seen Lanny arrive with his bears and how he had managed to get away without being seen.

'I am here to help! I can tell you all you need to know about Leilani, what she does and how she does it. What she wants and what she is willing to do to get it,' Earl said,

'I think we know what she is willing to do!' Gracie said, still unimpressed they were entertaining his presence.

'I understand Gracie, that you would not trust me, but remember, like your family, I was once free. Being in her control was not a pleasant place to be, but having stayed has meant I know more than she would want me to. I know this will be hard for you to hear, but there is also a side to her that isn't as evil as everyone sees.' Earl's words took Gracie from her safe place. She stormed across the solid ground and despite the length of his claws, she picked him up by the neck,

'That woman is pure evil! She has taken everything from me, just as she has from so many others. She has turned Heart into a place of fear and pain, not freedom and love. Do not tell me there is another side to her, don't you dare!' Averie stepped forward, rising onto her back legs she rested her paws on Gracie's hip and said,

'Leilani and her brother ordered my life partner to be killed, and the bears opened his throat. This happened today in front of my babies. I know what she has done, but Gracie, please let Earl go.' Her calm voice and sad story got through to her as she dropped him to the ground.

'How do you know my name?' A slightly calmer, humbled Gracie asked.

'I know all the key-keepers names that have had the misfortune to find themselves controlled by Leilani. I know who you are, and I know that your family still lived when Lanny closed the mines years ago. I also know that they all escaped,' Vicky interrupted Earl,

'We know that as well, a scorpion told me.' Words she never thought in her wildest dreams she would be saying.

'Young miss, I would imagine that would be the same scorpion that I spent time with. If they are still alive, they will be somewhere in there, in the forest,' Earl said. With everyone now able to relax and with no sign of an imminent attack, Earl expanded on his story. How, having managed to not be seen by Lanny, the scorpion had got his attention and quizzed him for his reason for being there. How, happy that he was no threat and that he was there to help, the scorpion had decided to help Earl, which he hoped would help everyone.

The scorpion was part of an early alarm system for those who had escaped the mines. The alarm system hadn't been needed or used for many years as far as the Dragonfly shack was concerned, but it was very helpful for avoiding the bear army Lanny had left behind. Earl told the listening group that the scorpion described how the slave miners had escaped, and where they all now lived.

'I don't know why I have ended up here, but I am glad I have. I want to see Heart returned to what I have been told it once was, as I imagine like all of you who have never known what a beautiful place it could be. Respectfully, apart from you, who I know will know very well the reality that once was Heart,' Earl said, looking at grandmother. He knew who she was. He also knew that there were times he had heard Leilani talk to herself in conflicting ways, going from the twisted reality that her brother had trained her to believe, to the reality that was the faintest of memories when she was young and grandmother would read her stories. 'She is young again. As is Lanny. Somehow they found a dragonfly. Can I assume that was from you?' he said, turning his attention to Alex.

'Us!' the firm voice coming from Sophie. Alex took hold of Sophie's shoulder and walked her away saying,

'I don't think we should be giving more information than we need to right now.' Sophie agreed. Turning back to Earl, Alex asked, 'So, where will we find everyone then?'

'We need to go back to where you ran away from me. I was told to look for a fire that was no more, that should be again. It was like dealing with Leilani again, the scorpion kept talking in riddles.' If Earl thought that would get a laugh, he was wrong. It was far too early for making familiar jokes.

'You can lead the way then,' Gracie said. The group followed, staying inside the forest, using its shade to stay cool and hidden from anyone who may see them.

'You are being very quiet!' Alexandria said to Jason.

'I'm just taking this all in. I cannot believe we are together again! There is so much I want to ask you, to tell you. But honestly, right now, I am just happy to be with you. I have missed you so much.' He put his arm around her and hugged her into his side as they walked, fitting her nicely under his arm. The feeling of being back together as brother and sister, twins, it was intense. 'And you have your son back. From what I have seen, he really is quite an impressive young man.' Alexandria agreed with him. She was amazed at his maturity in dealing with being who he had only just found out he was, and at meeting her, his birth mother.

'And I chose the most perfect of mothers for him. She is beautiful in so many ways.' Alexandria realised she may have spoken a little too lovingly about Melissa, and too loudly! She was concerned that Alex may have heard and not react as kindly as grandmother and the others had to the blossoming relationship. Out of respect, she wanted to give Melissa the chance to speak to him. She was his lifelong mother after all.

'A fire that is no more. Surely it's just where there was a fire,' Vicky said as they arrived at roughly the area they had run from. After a short time looking around the floor away from the trees and further into the forest, they found no fire pits. Anchor was playing with the cubs, not taking the search seriously at all, kicking up the dusty floor and making far more noise than the cautious Gracie would have liked. Bart on the other hand was dutifully at Vicky's side. He caught Gracie's eye and pulled a face as if to say, yes, I know it's ridiculous behaviour. Eventually, unable to stay quiet, Bart shouted at the trio who were spinning round a tree,

'Will you just grow up!' It was the first words he had uttered since arriving on Heart, and it took everyone by surprise. The trio stopped in their tracks, looking like scolded children as they dropped their heads.

'Actually Bart, I think it's you that should lighten up. You do realise I am completely capable here. I can see, I can hear, and it's wonderful. Enjoy yourself.' Bart was a mixture of confused, hurt and lost. Having been trained so well, he loved what he did, he loved being responsible.

'Er, could that be what we are looking for,' Bart said. The dust settling around the tree that the trio had been dashing around, was showing not a pale trunk like all the surrounding trees, but a tree that looked as though it had been on fire. There were burn marks rising six metres up from the ground.

'You see. If they hadn't been having as much fun as they were, we may have missed that,' Vicky said.

Jason and Alexandria made their way round the burnt tree trunk, looking for some clue to which way they should be going.

'There is nothing here,' Jason said. Everyone else, having carried out their own checks, had come to the same conclusion.

'Oh hang on, you said "a fire that was no more, that should be again" right?' Jason asked. Earl confirmed that he was correct. 'Then maybe we need to set it on fire again,' Jason suggested. With no sign of any other fire nearby, they all agreed. The only problem was how they would start it!

'Not a problem,' Vicky piped up. 'Bart get over here.' Always prepared, the harness on Bart was not just for her to hang on to whilst being guided. Vicky had created a little kit for surviving the city. In it were plasters as she often bumped into things, a tiny torch because even if the light was good, an extra bit helped her to see if she dropped something. There was also an emergency chocolate bar, which she had forgotten about and had melted in the heat. And finally, most importantly for their situation, a multipurpose tool. Included on it were screwdrivers, a knife, a saw, a few other things and a tiny magnifying glass. 'We can use the sun to start a fire with this,' she said, removing the harness from Bart and going on to say, 'You don't need this now, go and enjoy yourself Bart.'

'Vicky, your preparedness is most impressive.' The admiring voice came from Renga, who was sitting on one of the branches of the burnt tree. Vicky and Alexandria quickly gathered some dried grass, which was plentiful at the edge of the forest, found a spot in direct sunlight with no breeze, and took turns in holding the magnifying glass. It took longer than they thought it would, but finally smoke rose from the ball of grass. Within moments, the tiniest of orange sparks crackled and the grass burst into flames.

'Quickly, quickly, before it burns your hand,' Alexandria said.

'Careful, don't run. Take your time, we can't risk this fire spreading,' Averie said, as she saw the two running back towards them. The thought of a wildfire hadn't crossed the excited Vicky's mind, which could happen so easily with devastating results! So she slowed to a shuffle. She would rather risk being burnt herself than cause the destruction of the forest and its inhabitants.

'What now?' Vicky asked, having got to the tree. 'If I put it down, it will spread into the forest.' The grass was getting hotter and hotter,

'We need to go that way,' grandmother said.

'How do you know?' Vicky asked.

'Lift your hands up my dear and look through the flames,' grandmother replied.

'It's hot, it's really starting to burn.' Vicky wanted to look but was too busy panicking as she was feeling the burning pain grow in both her hands.

'Put the fire on this!' Alex said. He had found a rock which had a deep crack in it. Having thrown it against another larger rock, it fell open, leaving a nice flat surface for Vicky to put the burning grass on. Panic over, Alex held the fire in front of the tree. The group all around and behind him saw what grandmother had. Looking through the flames, an intricate picture of a large town surrounded by forest could be seen. Below the picture was a small burn mark in the shape of an arrow which pointed into the forest.

'We are looking for burn marks low on trees. Earl, they are at a good height for you to find, plus if you lead the way we can keep an eye on you,' Gracie said. Vicky pointed something out.

'If we had to see the picture within the burns on this tree with fire, it is safe to assume it will be the same with the others.'

'I am nervous about taking fire balanced on this rock any further to be honest,' Alex said. Then a voice he hadn't heard for a while echoed round his head,

'You are part of nature, as all things are. But unlike all things, you have a connection with me. You don't need to use fire, you just need to learn how to see.' The ancient dragonfly's words were carefully used to guide, not to give all the answers. Alex shook his head.

'I need to learn to see!' He said out loud.

'What?' Jason asked,

'The dragonfly said I don't need the fire, I just need to learn to see,' Alex replied.

'This voice in your head thing is going to take some getting used to young man. But ok, let's figure this one out,' Jason replied. No one said a word for a short time as they all tried to come up with a way to see.

'Oh come on, it's simple. We don't all see with our eyes do we, I can read brail, my hands would do the seeing,' Vicky said.

'Not just a pretty face are you,' Alex said, his complimentary words causing Vicky to blush. Alex walked over to the tree and touched the burnt trunk. As soon as he did, he felt a surge of energy pulse from his back down his arm and into the tree. Just as he was able to sense, see, feel what those around him were, he felt the power and energy of nature. He was connecting with it. Initially, out of nervousness, he resisted, but as soon as he let go, the image of the village and the tree with the arrow on it lit up, not just for him to see, but everyone.

'And that's how you see,' Vicky said. The way to continue in the correct direction now clear, the group headed where the arrow pointed, into the woods.

Grandmother hung back from the group as she had a question for Averie,

'When you spoke to Gracie, you referred to Leilani and Lanny as old. Was Lanny as old as his sister?'

'I would say older,' Averie replied. Grandmother was confused. Everything she knew, and all that she had been told, had said that Lanny was much younger, having consumed a dragonfly and not sharing it with his ageing sister.

'Are you sure?' grandmother said again. Earl, walking not too far in front of the quizzing grandmother, had been listening and couldn't help but join in,

'They are both not so old now, quite the opposite I would say. They are both younger than I have ever known them. Also, I have never felt so much power from Leilani when she threw me out of the Dragonfly Manor garden. I think it surprised her as well. The good thing was, as painful as the landing was, I was thrown so far I was able to escape easily, until Lanny and his obnoxious bears nearly got me.' Grandmother took it all in, went over what Earl, Jason, Alex and Sophie and now Averie had told her, in an effort to find a reason for the change in their age, for Lanny to become old. She came up with nothing.

'Did you see the old Lanny Alex?' She had to shout as he was getting ahead of the group, looking for more burn marks on the trees to guide their way.

'No, but he is young now anyway! Like your granddaughter, well, they were when we were in their house!' Alex replied.

'So you don't know how they got old? Does anyone?' grandmother asked. She wanted to find out, as if he could get old once, he could again.

'Zachariah said he had taken them, or rather he was forced to take them to the loch with the Dragonfly island. I think it happened there, as that's when he escaped. And before he escaped, they looked like you describe, Leilani older than Lanny!' Alex said.

'Zachariah?' grandmother asked.

'Yes, an amazing stag who also helped us,' Alex replied. Grandmother finally put the pieces together. Dragonflies who have lived many years beyond what they should naturally, who leave the magic of the Dragonfly home, become nothing but dust as they leave the magic given to the tree. The Dragonfly island did the same thing in reverse. Her theory was that the island, which had given Alex and Sophie the magic of the ancient dragonfly in an effort to restore balance, must have used the balance in nature to take back what Leilani and Lanny had taken from it. She let out an excited shout which got everyone's attention. With everyone looking at grandmother's smiling face, she said,

'I know how we can stop them!'

Chapter 13

Left alone in her Dragonfly Manor, waiting for her brother to return, with no way of tracking where Alex, Sophie and the rest of them were, Leilani, unsurprisingly, was getting extremely frustrated. To get any information outside her four walls, she had always relied on the whispers heard by Earl, but she had literally thrown him away, and with no fresh gold to use in her tree trunk cauldron, she also had no way of watching or contacting any of the key-keepers she had forced into underground homes with her crystals. Several frustrating hours having passed, stuck, frustrated in her beautifully revived Dragonfly Manor, she couldn't wait any longer, she had to take action. So, leaving the comfort of her library, Leilani headed for the front door, pressed on a particular pinprick of light, turned the handle, opened the door and for the first time ever, stepped away from her home on her own. No support, no bodyguards, out into the same blazing Australian sun her brother and the group heading deeper into the sparse forest were baking under. She wasn't alone for long!

'Well, that's convenient!' The voice was Lanny's. Having sent a selection of his army in different directions, and with he and his generals having searched the mine as much as they could be bothered doing, they'd had no success or answers to where Earl or the family were. He decided to return to the Dragonfly shack, which he thought was the most likely place to catch a break in his search. Leilani's eyes, adjusting to the brightness, took a moment to realise who was walking towards her.

'So you haven't found them then?' Leilani said.

'No, I have not! It would appear that they have escaped from the mines.'

'Escape, or they all died in there? I told you there was no way for them to survive being trapped, with no food and no water,' Leilani angrily said,

'Well, actually, there was plenty of water deep down in the mines, and I suppose there were enough species of animal in there they could have eaten! Either way, no they are not dead, they are just gone,' was his response. Leilani was both happy and annoyed to hear his report. Happy, as it meant there was still a chance of finding Gracie's family alive, for her to sacrifice for her greater good, but annoyed that they had escaped.

'Where are your army of bears?' Leilani asked. Lanny explained what had happened. How he had searched and how he had sent them all off to find the escapees, or any key-keeper to get him back to Leilani. 'So what do we do then?' Leilani asked. She had hoped that coming to this place would reduce her frustration, and the uncomfortable feeling of helplessness, not make it worse.

'Erm, wait!' Lanny replied. That was not something Leilani was willing to do.

'They have to be here somewhere! Every living thing here, not your bears clearly, will know where they are! Wait, how did you get here? Actually, it doesn't matter!' Leilani said.

'If you can find any life, I will be impressed. I don't know how anything survives in this heat!' Lanny said, which got Leilani thinking.

'So where could they survive then?' she asked herself out-loud. Her second thought, also spoken out loud, was, 'And how did they escape the mine?' She wasn't looking for an answer, but got one anyway!

'I don't know, but it wasn't through the entrance I blocked up,' Lanny replied.

'Well, let's go and find out,' she said. Her thought was, that with the amount of slaves, the people and animals, they would at least need a good source of water, and as her brother had said there was a good source of water at the bottom of the mine. Figuring that over hundreds of years, the water would be sure to have cut its way out of the mine, out into the daylight, somewhere at the base of the tall hill, the mine was the best and first place they should look for the escapees exit.

Leading the way with purpose, she strode across the dusty fields and arrived remarkably quickly at the mine's entrance. Stepping into the shade, Leilani was hit with the same death smell Lanny and his bears had been. 'What is that?' she asked, covering her mouth, the smell so strong she could taste it.

'Bears. I don't know how they got there though. They were behind the rocks inside,' Lanny said. Leilani came to the same conclusion Lanny and his generals had, that the strength of the smell and their decomposed state meant they had only been dead for a few days. Stepping over and round the corpses, Leilani made her way down the slippery slope into the dark. George and Gregg had found a discarded lantern which, with a spark from the solid flint stone that hung from its side, burst into life.

'Most helpful. Now you can find yourself one!' Leilani said, snatching the lantern from George's claws. There would have been no way Leilani would have been able to make the journey the age she was earlier that day. She was thankful for her physical youth as she made her way down the uneven tunnel to the top of a wooden staircase that hugged the walls as it descended. She positioned the lantern to get a better look at how far the spiralling staircase went down. There was no way her one lantern would give enough light to see to the bottom of the cavern, hundreds of feet down. She could only just make out the first of many platforms and entrances to new tunnels, that spread out in equal distances, as the staircase went lower and lower.

With all the years of gold mining and all the tunnels that weaved under the ground, Leilani couldn't help but wonder how it was possible the ground hadn't collapsed. Looking around she noticed a system of ropes to the side of the spiralling staircase. Attached to them were heavy looking square wooden buckets, which had been used to bring the gold to the surface. The ropes were showing signs of their age, fraying, having held on to the weight of the buckets for so long. The wood of the buckets were equally tattered, corroding from the damp that filled the dark air.

'Lanny, are these stairs safe to use?' Leilani asked. Lanny didn't want to say categorically yes, but also didn't want to suggest that they may not be, so took the easier option,

'George, Gregg, make your way down a few levels!' he ordered. The bears looked at each other, knowing they didn't really have a choice. Slowly and carefully they placed their paws on to the wooden platform which led to the first step. The old wood and nails let out squeaks that echoed throughout the open cavern. However, for all the noisy protests, the platform and the stairs stayed in place. Their cautious steps getting progressively quicker as they disappeared round the first twist of the staircase, their confidence growing, the two bears reached a full on bound. Having made their way down four levels, they stopped, and George shouted back,

'They seem to be strong enough.' Leilani, not looking to take any chances on the bears' report, had pulled up the least frayed looking piece of rope from the seemingly bottomless mine. Happy that the rope she had found was strong enough to hold her, she untied it from the wooden post it was attached to. Pushing it through one of the many holes that had been chipped into the rock wall, created to secure the ropes and their pulleys, she tied the end in place. Then Leilani took the free end and tied it around her waist. Confident that if the stairs gave way, she would be saved from hitting the bottom of the mine, she made her way down to the first level.

'There are so many tunnels leading off everywhere. The escape tunnel you are looking for could be any of them. So what is your plan here?' Lanny asked.

'Listen for water. We find the water, we find the exit,' Leilani replied, giving up her plan. Many flights down, the bears had kept the gap of four levels between them and Leilani, until they couldn't go any further. The wooden spiral stairs having ended, still no sign of the bottom of the mine, the bears waited for the siblings to arrive.

Having not reached the bottom of the mineshaft by any means, although it looked like they should have, seeing as the ropes which held the buckets went no further than where they stood, Lanny took Gregg's lantern and dropped it. They all watched as the light got smaller and smaller, until finally it disappeared into the darkness. Waiting, watching and listening,

Leilani was about to give up her idea of continuing down, when she heard the faintest sound of breaking glass. The lantern had found the bottom.

'Did anyone think to count?' Leilani asked,

'Count?' a confused Lanny replied,

'Yes count, we would have been able to estimate how far down the bottom was.' That was far too intelligent for Lanny. Thankfully, he had seen something that would take his sister's mind off the fact that no one had.

'There are steps carved into the wall over there.' Just a short jump away was a very uneven, differing depth with every step, set of stairs that disappeared into the wall.

'Looks like that's where we are going then!' Leilani said. Her youth and strength holding strong, her impatience to find who she was looking for stronger than her fear for her safety, she removed the rope from around her waist and led the way, leaping with ease from the rickety platform that was just holding all their weight, to the first jagged step. Not hanging about, Leilani was soon out of sight of Lanny and his bears as the stairs disappeared into the rock face. Lanny was not as confident as his sister in the mine's safety, so waited for a sign that it was safe to follow. A few minutes passed before he saw a light appear much further down the mineshaft.

'Leilani, is that you?' he shouted.

'Of course it is. What are you still doing up there, you stupid man?' she shouted back as she carried on. Deeper and deeper she went, so quickly, Lanny and his bears had no chance of catching up with her. Occasionally she would appear back in the mineshaft, but most of the climb down was done in natural pockets, caves, that whoever had created the descent had used with great effect, lessoning the work required to carve out steps on and behind the rock face of the mineshaft.

Finally, having reached the bottom, Leilani looked around. To her annoyance, it appeared that there was no way out, no tunnels leading off from the bottom and no water.

'I don't understand!' she said to herself, her brother still having not caught up. Her impetuousness had replaced her usual clear-thinking self. She questioned if she had missed something on the way down, maybe a tunnel off the descent that could have taken her where the water may have been. No, she had not, she was sure of it. She walked around the edges of the mineshaft, her lantern on the verge of going out, giving only just enough light to make sure she didn't trip on something. Although, the light being dimmer enabled her eyes to adjust more to the dark, the contrast not being so dramatic between the bright light of the lantern when she began her descent and the pitch black of the mine.

Having made her way round the walls, she was back at the tunnel she had popped out of when she arrived, just as Lanny and his bears appeared.

'I can't find a way out down here,' Leilani said.

'Well, I can assure you, as fit as I feel, I am not climbing all the way back up. There has to be some way out down here!' Lanny smartly said. Leilani had walked out from the edge and towards the middle of the area. 'Aaaaa!' she screamed, as one of her feet disappeared, her leg following, her hip crashing off a solid jagged piece of rock as she just managed to catch herself, before the rest of her followed. The situation had caused her to drop her lantern which smashed and went out.

'Leilani!' Lanny shouted. George, having heard the scream, had already left his side and with four huge bounds was at Leilani's side, pulling her out of the hole she had fallen into.

'I would have rather someone else found this hole! But at least we have another way to go,' Leilani said, as she rubbed her leg that was sure to bruise.

Down to two lanterns, throwing one down the hole would not have been sensible, so instead, Leilani, holding on to Lanny's lantern, peered into the hole.

'It's only about five foot down, and there is a tunnel that leads off beneath us. Lower me down,' she instructed. As soon as she landed on the uneven rock, she heard it. 'Water!' she shouted back. 'Pass me your lantern,' Leilani ordered up to her brother. Which he did. Once again, Leilani was off by herself, leaving the others to make their way down into the tunnel themselves. This time she could see an end, a light in the distance. The further she went, the wider the tunnel got. From being close to her shoulder where she had dropped down from the main mine, it was the width of four people by the time she reached its end.

'So here we are then!' Lanny said, having caught up with her and stepped around her, to look at the source of the running water sound. The walls of the open area they found themselves in were smooth, worn away from thousands of years of water rushing through. Looking up at the worn away rocks, seeing the colourful lines, the beauty impressed the self-centred, self-focused Leilani. Her pause for taking in the cave's beauty short lived, with a smug look on her face she said,

'I told you!' as she pointed towards the opening where the water was gushing out into the daylight.

Stepping into the water, Leilani's breath was taken away by its coldness. She hadn't expected that. It didn't slow her down though, as she made her way to where the water joined the daylight. Enjoying the hot air that was mixing with the cave's cold, Leilani paused in the perfect temperature as she looked to see where the rushing water was landing. Just a very short climb down from where she stood, was a rocky river that snaked its way into a forest of almost alive trees.

'We can't jump then,' Lanny said, peering round his sister. 'We would break a leg.' Leilani had already figured that out, but had also already come up with another way down. She had seen a very steep path that ran off to the side of where she stood. Lanny followed his sister, who once again took the lead.

Down what looked like a very well-used path, Lanny said,

'Now we will get them! Every last one of them!' Passing his sister, he ran off towards the forest. For a man who was incredibly talented at twisting people's minds and generally being twisted, Leilani was often amazed at his stupidity. Although his stupidity, combined with his attack first without thinking approach, and her intellect long since surpassing his, had meant that she had become the one in charge, the one with the power. Even when she was physically much older. Leilani was a strong believer that brains outwit, and ultimately outlive, brawn. She was living proof. She shouted after him,

'No brother, we wait. If we go to them, there is every chance they will see us coming. We wait here, we hide. We will be the ones seeing who comes.'

Chapter 14

'Oh my goodness!' grandmother exclaimed. Having taken a turn around the twelfth tree with a burn mark, the group was faced with a barrier of spider webs.

'I know we are in Australia, but it would have taken a lot of spiders to do that. Can I also add, there is no chance I am walking through them, no chance, no way!' Vicky said. The wall of webs spread between the trees as far as they could see. After a look one way and then the other along the wall of webs, Alex noticed a tree that had branches lower than the others.

'I am going to see if I can get a look over the webs,' he announced, dashing off toward the lowish lying branches.

'Do you need a hand?' Jason asked, seeing the branch Alex was heading for, although lower than the others, was still just out of his reach.

'He will be fine!' Sophie said, answering for Alex. Having witnessed his rock climbing skills back in the Dragonfly island's cave, she had no doubt he would manage. He quickly proved her correct, as he was up and on the first branch with ease! From there he was able to reach the next ones without jumping, so he could make his way up to the point in which he could see over the web in no time. Thirty feet up from the ground! Surprised at how high the trees' webs had gone, he was even more surprised when a huntsman spider, with a body as big as the palm of his hand, its legs as long as his forearm, came swinging towards him. Trying to avoid its advance, Alex fell! But not back to the watching group. He fell to the other side of the webbed wall. Sophie screamed as she saw him lose his balance. Vicky screamed at the sight of the huge spider! As he fell, he bounced off the webbed wall. His weight and gravity's pull made it impossible for the web, which would normally grip anything passing with its stickiness, to stop him. However, it had the very helpful effect of slowing the speed of Alex's descent, just enough for him to land on his feet with very little discomfort.

'I am ok!' Alex said, loud enough for the others to hear. Looking away from the wall, Alex couldn't see any more spider webs. Instead, he was now facing a wall of snakes. 'Oh come on!' he said.

'What is it?' Vicky asked,

'Snakes. A lot of them!' Alex replied. He had no escape, there were no tree branches low and close enough for him to climb. Although having looked up, he saw that even if there was, the one spider that had swung at him had become countless spiders, all hanging on threads of web staring right back at him. Alex was not the biggest fan of spiders, but snakes he was ok with, normally! but the quantity that faced him was making him very nervous.

'Fire, water, earth, air and animal are all connected by the energies that flow through them.' The voice of the ancient dragonfly broke the stand off silence.

'Yes, ok. But you know what?' The snakes and spiders getting closer paused, confused as to who Alex was talking to. Then he did something that was quite surprising. With no fear, full of confidence, he removed the clothes that covered his torso, chest, shoulders and arms. He dropped them to the floor, lifted his arms out to his sides and slowly turned, so that every set of eyes staring at him could see what was on him.

'You continue to surprise me Alex. I can't remember being taught something in a very long time. You are correct. To see is a connection just as strong as the energies,' the dragonfly said.

'Move aside, out of my way. Come on, shift will you.' A friendly looking face appeared. A jolly man with a nose as round as his belly, a head of thick, grey, curly hair. His skin painted with white, elaborate aboriginal designs, as bare chested as Alex was. 'G'day. Well mate, you are far from the visitor we were expecting today, but good god, you are welcome.' The happy man walked up to Alex and gave him a welcoming slap on his back. 'Come on in.' He gestured to the group stuck the other side of the webs. 'Oh yes, sorry. Open it up if you don't mind boys,' he asked, looking up at the spiders. Two of the huge insects dropped down, jumped onto the web, and just like opening a set of curtains, pulled the web apart. 'Quite a good trick, don't you think? Come on, come on through, the snakes and spiders won't hurt you. We're all mates here.'

The group hesitantly made their way through, and joined Alex. Earl was the last to enter. He was more nervous than the rest of the group. The quantity of spider and snake guards on and beyond the web wall was disconcerting. As all knew of Leilani, they would all no doubt know of him. Once through, the spiders dropped the web curtain back into place.

'Let's get you lot some water, you all look like you could do with a drink.' This was an offer they were all very pleased to accept. The snakes cleared a pathway, the group nervously passed through.

'My name is Iluka, I'm thrilled to meet all of you, especially dragonfly boy here,' he said as they walked through more dead looking trees, followed by the snakes and more spiders than Vicky would have liked. Alex introduced himself and then everyone else. 'So the strange lights in the sky a couple of days ago, am I correct if I say you were the reason for them?' Iluka asked.

'I don't know whether it was me directly, but it was the day things changed for me. I think for the better!' Alex replied.

'We know of the dragonfly legends here, we never forgot them, unlike all you lot back on Earth,' Iluka said.

'What do you know of what has been going on on Earth?' grandmother asked.

'Working in the mines, being close enough to Lanny, his bears and Leilani, more times than I would like, we heard things,' Iluka said. Gracie, hearing he was from the mines, couldn't help herself.

'Do you know of a man called Nicholas? He would have had two children with him - a boy called Eric and a girl called Ella?' She held her breath waiting for his answer.

'I do, good mates of mine. In fact, Eric is involved with my daughter.' The emotions of years of clinging on to hope washed over Gracie. Her face went red, her eyes bloodshot. There was no holding back. The floodgates opened, and streams of tears ran down her face. Jason made his way over and gave her a hug.

'They are alive Jason!' she said,

'And very close. So come on, save the water, you need it in this heat. Dry those tears and let's go and find them,' Jason said.

The walk through more trees, thankfully for Vicky, without spiders' webs, was not a long one. The trees having got taller, with foliage at their tops becoming thicker, meant that the sun was completely blocked. A big relief to the group. Then, having made their way round more trees, they came across piles of rocks, rubble and a wall.

'All those years of mining, the rock we dug had to go somewhere. Have to say has been very helpful for us,' Iluka said. 'This way!' The rubble wall looked flat, with no way through from where they stood. It wasn't. The way the wall had cleverly been built, helped by the lack of sun, meaning there were no shadows, meant that the way through was hidden. To the first-time visitors, it looked like Iluka just vanished into the wall. Alex was the first to get to where Iluka had disappeared, and after running his hands along the wall, found a very obvious opening.

'That's so cool! It's an optical illusion guys!' Alex said, as he stepped part way inside the, to him, not so invisible gap. To the group, Alex looked like he was part of the wall, half in, half out. He could see the painted Iluka walking off and disappearing again. 'Come on, we'll lose him,' Alex said. The group was quick to follow.

'You won't lose me, don't you worry,' Iluka said, popping his head round the next hidden gap he had taken. The snake and spiders did not follow. As much as they wanted to see what was to come with Alex and his dragonfly, they had an important job to do where they were. Six more invisible gaps later, Alex, the first to step out, couldn't believe what he was seeing. He was looking down on an entire town, built in a valley, created by all that lived there. A place to stay hidden from whoever may have been looking for them. Equally amazing was what was above him. Clear of the trees, he expected to be hit with heat again, but he wasn't. A most unusual roof cooled the direct heat of the sun.

'What is that?' Alex asked.

'Clever isn't it. It's spider webs. Just like the wall that stopped you. The spiders created the roof of webs to keep us hidden. The birds helped by dropping branches on top to make it more in-keeping with the rest of the forest. A good all round team effort, don't you reckon?' Iluka said.

'That explains why all I saw was forest,' Renga said. He was thankful that his searching skills hadn't failed him after all. When he had flown over the forest earlier, trying to find signs of life, they were just well hidden. It was a masterpiece. The strength in the spider webs, stronger than any steel roof, had been stretched from tree to tree around the town's edges. Cris-crossing over and over until the huge town was covered. The light that made it through, cast all kinds of interesting shadows over the town, playing amongst the streets as the sun moved across the sky, lighting up all the amazing variety of homes that had been built from what they could find, mainly rock. There were small ones, tall ones, round ones, square ones, and every other size and shape in between. At various points there were tall plinths of land that had been left as they dug down. On these plinths were tall trees that helped to hold up the web canopy. It was a marvel.

Alex looked across the town, and as soon as he did he was hit with the lives, thoughts, memories and emotions of every single person, animal, insect and plant that lived there. It knocked the wind out of him. He closed his eyes, trying very hard not to allow what he was seeing and feeling to take over, as he could feel the explosion of energy that came from him and had sent his mother, the two police officers, the suited

'A Legend Remembered' 245

officer, the weasley man and every other thing in its way flying, outside grandmother's Dragonfly Manor.

'You are learning fast Alex,' grandmother said, placing her hand on his still exposed shoulder, having recognised what he was doing. 'You will need that strength and calmness as this journey continues. Open your eyes.' As he did, he saw hundreds of eyes looking up at him. Sophie took his hand, and instantly, the dancing colours on her back rose up around her neck. Bright oranges, reds, pinks, every warm colour imaginable. Alex's eyes turning to their shade of purple, the ancient dragonfly left his body and rose above the two of them, staying connected by a colourful light that wrapped them up, and then fell into the valley like a tsunami. Unlike the fear experienced when a tsunami strikes, the light that flooded through the streets, wrapping round their houses and touching the feet of all the onlookers, filled them with love.

'Embracing each other, respecting each other and nature. Here is proof that all can live together. Proof that there is hope in all corners of our worlds.' The ancient dragonfly's words, as always, heard by Alex, and on this occasion, as they were hand in hand, Sophie. The dragonfly lowered itself back on to Alex. The light from them fading, a cheer from more voices than could be counted filled the air with excitement.

'There are faces from everywhere,' Vicky said.

'Acceptance is how we live here. There are challenges, but all, no matter what their species, colour, race, or sexuality, are welcome. No one is judged. As it says right there, respect for all and all are respected,' Iluka said, pointing to the wall they had just passed through, which had the very words carved into it. Iluka's spoke with so much passion. Alex felt his energy.

Standing, looking down on the cheering town, Alex felt another new experience! He felt as though he was leaving his body. He was suddenly floating down, in amongst every face, experiencing who they were and where they had come from. Each creature, each human, was from a different part of Heart, brought to the mines by Lanny as slaves. He felt the pain all had experienced, but most importantly, he felt the love each one of them had for each other. The acceptance Iluka spoke of was real. To Alex, it felt as though he had been floating amongst the dry streets for hours, learning, witnessing, embracing true companionship and seeing that no-one saw any physical difference, just the soul that lived within. Love between every species, woman with man, woman with woman, man with man and everything in between. It was truly beautiful. He could feel nature and its pureness everywhere, no laws or beliefs created by humankind for the benefit of humankind. Instead, an understanding that to survive and live in happiness, all should be together in positivity and understanding. True happiness comes from a focus on what is good, not what is bad. In the small things that can make a difference, that could ultimately change the large things that otherwise would not.

'This is what Heart is. Leilani and her brother may have brought terror, fear and so much loss, but love remains. Our Earth is the same. Potential for love, selflessness and acceptance of others is still there. Alex, the dragonfly keeper, now you can see what could be.' The ancient dragonfly's words brought a feeling of humbleness to Alex. They also brought his mind back to his body.

No-one had noticed his absence. The group, embracing the positive energies, were not used to being the centre of attention, a place none of them felt comfortable in. However, they were happy to be there. The cubs, Anchor, and surprisingly Bart, were excited, running about, barking, having fun. Even Renga was getting involved, landing on and jumping from furry dog back, to furry dog back. Earl on the other hand, who had not long become part of the group, was not. He had seen a large number of creatures he knew well, mixed up amongst the faces. Lanny's bears. He hoped that Alex, Sophie and the dragonfly's display had been their focus, and that they had missed his presence.

As they made their way down a slope leading to the town, in an attempt to stay hidden, Earl used Jason's height and size. Arriving at the first crowd of smiling faces, it was only then that Gracie, who had been too busy looking for her family, noticed what Earl had.

'Lanny's bears!' she said in a panic, grabbing onto Jason's arm and moving behind him to take up Earl's hiding place.

'It's fine mate. They were as much slaves as we were in the mines. Oh, although being honest, there was a group who got spooked with the lights the other day. They started talking about how the twins were coming and they took off back to the mines. Again, being honest, I think they may have got bitten by a snake or two during their change of loyalty, so not sure how far they may have got. But don't worry, the bears that are here want to see the end of Leilani and Lanny's reign as much as I do,' Iluka said. Gracie cautiously accepted what he said. It wasn't long before her caution changed to acceptance, when one of the bears caught sight of Earl.

'Grab him!' he shouted, and a group of six ran straight at Jason, round him, and took hold of Earl, whose fears had come to pass.

'Wait, wait, wait. He is with us!' Alex shouted,

'He is a spy, he is Earl, Leilani's,' the bear was interrupted,

'Let me stop you there. If we are to trust you, what makes him any different?' Gracie calmly asked. It gave them pause to think for a moment. Sophie stepped into the middle of the six bears and pushed them aside.

'He is with us. He has helped us, and as far as I am concerned, is a friend. You don't need to know anything more. Now step away!' Vicky said, also getting involved along with Anchor, Bart, Averie and the cubs coming to Earl's aid, circling the six bears. The group had become a family, when one stood up they all did. The crowds, which had fallen silent with the commotion, talked amongst themselves.

'You heard the lady, let him go,' Iluka said. The bears did as he asked, and calm was restored. 'Let's get you that water I promised,' he said, leading the way through the crowds. Another five minutes of walking found them at a stone house larger than any they had passed. Standing on the front step was a man and woman with very familiar features. Gracie instantly knew who they were, much older, but they were still her babies. She ran up to them and took them both in her arms, each one of them squeezing the other so tight, breathing was hard to do.

'Your father, where is he?' Gracie's question changed the mood. She could see in their faces something was wrong, and that the answer to her question would not be a good one. Her children, Eric and Ella, couldn't bring themselves to say the words. The awkward silence was thankfully filled by Iluka,

'Your husband was a brave man. He kept us strong and positive when Lanny trapped us in the mine. He never gave up. He was the one who found the way out for all of us. I am afraid with the risks he took in the darkness, searching for our way out, he fell. He survived long enough for us to find this place. But Gracie, I am sorry, he died from his injuries.'

Deep down, Gracie had known for some time he was gone. She felt it, she just didn't want to admit it. She hugged her children even tighter,

'You are my world,' she whispered.

'Urgency is required here. We cannot pretend that my grandchildren will not find this place,' grandmother said, cautioning the group, making her way up to the stone house Gracie's children had appeared from, past the last of the crowds of interested and excited faces. One of the smiling faces stepped out from the crowd, walked up to Eric and took hold of his hand.

'Mother this is Jedda, Iluka's daughter,' Eric said, introducing the sweet-looking girl with the most infectious of smiles. As Gracie looked her up and down, she couldn't help but be envious of her incredibly long, dark, wavy hair, glistening in the light and her fresh, flawless skin. Then she saw something that got her very excited!

'Is that what I think it is?' Gracie said, placing her hand on her stomach,

'Yes mother Gracie, I am having a baby. And yes, it's your son's!' Jedda replied, laughing. Gracie threw her hands up in the air, spun round on the spot and grabbed Jedda, giving her a hug like she had never experienced.

'Yes, it's all lovely, all life is precious, but there could easily be death here if we do not act!' Grandmother couldn't help herself. Her tone was not as excited as she knew it should be at the news, but she was nervous. 'Please, we need to make a new plan, and I have an idea. Iluka, can we go in?' she said, standing outside the thick tree trunk cross section which made up the front door to the stone house.

Iluka nodded, made his way past the group, patted his daughter on her head as he did, and led them all inside. They found themselves in a large room filled with chairs, and a fireplace in its centre. No corridors or entrance halls, just a communal area which was refreshingly cool in temperature. The inner walls looked no different to the outside ones, they were stone. There was one window on each of the two walls that didn't have the entrance door on, and on its fourth wall, opposite the group, four closed doors.

'Water, let's get you all some water,' Iluka said. He was always happy being a host. Grandmother was not happy, she wanted to get on with her plan, so ignored his kind offer,

'Alex. How do you feel about using that last dragonfly you have on your arm?' she asked. The thought had already crossed his mind. 'Do you think you two could add some dragonfly magic to this place?' grandmother asked.

The strange lights two days earlier, the rumours reaching them of the ancient dragonfly returning, Eric, Ella and Jedda were still in the dark as to who these people in their home really were. But they were getting an idea.

'A Legend Remembered'

'I think this home would be a wonderful place to start!' Sophie said.

'Start! But what about the big old house back in the Highlands?' Melissa sarcastically asked. Sophie felt a little silly. Alex, sensing her discomfort, said,

'This would be the first house in the heart of a town, not hidden, not on its own! Everyone here should have the chance to return to where they had been taken from. So yes, this would be a good place to "start".' Melissa was not used to Alex defending anyone but her, let alone against her, but it gave her a warm feeling inside to see him growing the way he was.

'Alexandria, you have been very quiet! If Alex and Sophie do what they do, could they go anywhere, I mean here and on Earth. Oh, also, will they need to have key-keepers for each property?' grandmother asked, knowing that Alexandria and Jason, being descendants of Shuing and having been guardians of the island, would have far more of an understanding of what the ancient dragonfly could make possible.

'What exactly are you asking me?' Alexandria replied.

'Well. I am wondering, could they go to the island?' grandmother replied. Alexandria looked at Jason,

'I have never heard of that happening before.' She was nervous and looked at Jason again. His jaw clenched, and his posture straightened, before saying,

'Yes, it could happen!' Alexandria's eyes popped wide open, and she stared at him,

'No, it cannot!'

'I have missed you sister all these years, but let's be real here. There is no way things are going to get better without some risk-taking on our parts. Your son and his friend have quite proved themselves capable.'

'We are supposed to be the protectors of the island!' Alexandria angrily said,

'Lexi, we could end up the protectors of nothing. They are young again. We could be facing decades of their invigorated anger. At this point in time Earth is lost, and Heart without Earth is lost. It's time to do something different. Yes, Alex and Sophie can open the door directly to the island, if they bring the dragonfly magic to this house, and I believe that they should!' Jason, finished, sat down on a very uncomfortable chair. The room fell silent as everyone took in the monumental truth that had been shared. It wasn't long before the silence was broken with a knock at the door, and without waiting for an answer it was thrown open.

'I am sorry to interrupt, but there is news you must hear. Leilani and Lanny are here! They are at our water hole,' an out of breath, young Asian girl announced.

'Are you sure?' Iluka asked. The young girl nodded her head and ran off as quickly as she had arrived.

'I do not wish to be the one to say I told you so. But this is why we need to act fast,' grandmother said. Vicky, Bart and Anchor had followed the young girl out of the big, heavy front door, and disappeared out of sight.

'We need a tree of some sort,' Sophie said,

'Sorted!' Vicky announced, arriving back almost as soon as she had left. A clever girl, she had already figured out what was required. In her hand was a two foot tree, with three leaves barely hanging on. She had been careful to make sure there was plenty of soil round its roots, as dry as it was. She handed the tree to Sophie, who looked round the room for a suitable place to put it.

'I guess here is as good a place as any,' she said, as she bent down having found a loose stone, one of many which made up the cool, wobbly floor. She pulled it up, put it to one side and placed the tree in its place. The process they had both experienced, more than once, began again. Sophie, staying knelt on the floor, touching the soil at the tree's roots. Alex, standing to her side, resting his hand on her shoulder, his eyes turning into their mystical light of white and purple. The dragonfly came out of his hand and made its way to the tree. With light bouncing off every wall, heat filling the cool room, the tree came to life. The sound of creaking and cracking wood echoed, as its branches spread across and into the stone walls, spreading towards the doorframe. Grandmother watched in wonder at what was happening, and held her breath as the tip of one of the branches finally made contact with the frame. There was a moment of inactivity, and then a pulse, dull and slow at first, which built up into a strong heartbeat of light, bouncing backwards and forwards over the frame. Alex lifted Sophie up and pulled her in to him. He kissed her on the cheek and asked,

'Are you ok?' She looked up at him and smiled. The experience was not without pain for both of them, but she replied,

'Yes, and you?'

'Equal, balanced, Sophie and Alex, I can see why you are the ones to bring hope back to us all,' Iluka said, marvelling at the selflessness of the pair.

'There are no lights on the door!' grandmother said.

'Give it some time, they will come,' Alexandria replied.

'We do not have time!' Grandmother's out of character impatience was unnerving Sophie, so she decided to change the focus altogether, as there was nothing they could do but wait. She had seen something, and wondered if Alex had missed it! She thought he would have said something if he had, as it was something positive and happy.

'Do you have something you would like to share, Melissa?' she asked with a smile.

'Erm, no, I don't think so!' Melissa replied.

'It's ok mum, I know,' Alex said. Melissa felt uncomfortable. She knew what they were both referring to, but she had so wanted to choose the time to talk to him about it, not have it forced on her. That time was not going to be in front of the group and their new friends, as far as she was concerned.

'Let's have a talk outside,' Melissa said.

'Honestly, it's ok mum, I am happy for both of you. Being in love is what you deserve and the fact it happens to be my birth mum, makes it even better,' Alex said. The feeling of acceptance that washed over her was not something she had expected to feel, having shared a truth about herself that she had kept hidden for so many years. A strong woman, letting people see her heart and emotions was not usual for her, but on this occasion she couldn't help herself as she broke down into tears. It was a release that she had needed. A breaking down of a wall of emotions she had kept solid for far too long. She looked so small and alone, standing in the middle of the room. She wasn't alone for long as Alex, Sophie, grandmother, Vicky and finally Alexandria, dashed over to her, and wrapped her up in a hug that saw all their emotional walls come down as well. The tears that ran down their tired cheeks left streaks as they passed over the dust from the dry land that covered their faces. Alex felt the dragonfly on his back moving, enjoying the experience of such unconditional love.

'Look,' Ella said. She felt bad for interrupting the moment, but the door had suddenly flashed with thousands of pinpricks of light. By the time everyone looked at where she was pointing, the lights had gone. Alex knew what had happened and walked over to the door, hand in hand with Sophie. He touched the handle, and sure enough, the door came to life.

'Now, I have a plan. It will not be easy, but if it works, we could bring about a change that will bring Heart and Earth back together,' grandmother said.

She went on to explain what her plan was. With Lanny's visit to the island having resulted in his youth being taken from him, leaving him older than he had ever been, she assumed the same could happen again to both him and Leilani. From the stories she had heard in her short time on Heart, both Leilani and her brother would seem to have been inactive for some time, which grandmother put down to them growing old. She suggested if they could return them back to being old; they could save Heart and Earth from what would be sure to come if they remained young. All they had to do was get them back to the island.

'Earl, this is where you come in,' grandmother said. 'You will go to Leilani and act as though you have been working for her all along, that you have found us, and this house.' She explained how he would lead them to this hidden town, how, when they arrive, Alex and Sophie would open the doorway to the island, and let them chase them through it. And that is when balance could, should, be returned.

'Do you know what you are suggesting? To take them to the island where it all began, with the ancient dragonfly! Are you insane?' Gracie, in a panic, said.

'Yes, there is a risk, but no, I am not insane. I am showing us a way to bring these two hundred years of misery to an end. Also, if what I recall is correct and what we saw on the island, by bringing this house to life, I would suggest Leilani is already well aware of where we are, and what has happened to this house,' grandmother said. Alex and Sophie realised at the same time what she meant,

'The light, it has gone up into the sky every time we have done something!' Sophie said.

'She is right!' Alexandria said.

'You two, can you see if you can open the door to the island. If you can, we will go through and stay there, wait for you to arrive,' grandmother said. For an old woman, her brain was working well.

'I will not leave my children again, I am staying here to make a home with them,' Gracie said.

'She will have this home!' The voice of the dragonfly surprised Alex.

'How?' Alex asked, and as quickly as he did, he felt a weight being lifted off him. The ancient dragonfly under his skin, seen by all on his uncovered back, spread its wings and slowly passed through Alex's outer layer of skin, and out into the once again cool air. The wings were followed by its body, and finally its legs. Free from Alex, its wings a blur, the dragonfly made its way over to Gracie, moved behind her, landed on her back, and with the strength of its buzzing wings, pushed her forward to the door. Gracie didn't fight it. She knew all about the ceremony that took a young daughter, trained in the ways of the Dragonfly homes over the five years between their sixteenth and twenty-first birthday, where the daughter would finally become the key-keeper. Arriving at the door, the young dragonfly, who had been sitting on a branch of the tree, flew down and landed on her hand. At this point, the ancient dragonfly left her and hovered over her as she placed her hand on the handle of the door. A mystical array of vibrant lights came bursting from the handle, as the young dragonfly disappeared, sinking into her hand with a momentary, sharp pain. The ancient dragonfly returned to Alex, back to his home.

'A long time coming. She is the first to become a key-keeper in far too many forgotten years,' the ancient dragonfly said in Alex's mind, before settling down and becoming a motionless tattoo of itself, on his back, once again. Gracie stepped back from the door as the young dragonfly left her hand and made its way back up to a branch on the tree. With the lights on the handle and the door disappearing, new lights appeared on its frame. What was blank, was now full of story. Not like the old house back in the Highlands with just two pictures. This frame was covered.

'I recognise them!' Ella said. The pictures were the stories of those who lived in the hidden town with them, 'How is it even possible?' she asked,

'There is so much possible that has been forgotten child. Like the dragonfly, which has at last been remembered, all other things that have been forgotten shall also be,' grandmother said. Everyone in the room was struggling with the conflict of feelings, from happiness for Gracie and the birth of a new

Dragonfly home, to the feelings of fear of what was to come.

'It is time. Alex, you must open this doorway to the island. Jedda, Ella, Eric, Gracie, Averie and you two fun bundles of fur, come with me. We shall clear the town. Get everyone into the forest so that when you, Earl, bring the twins here, everyone will be safe. We will leave the webbed doorway open and mark your route through the walls' hidden entrances. I wish you all good fortune and hope we meet again very soon,' Iluka said, as he ushered his group out the door.

'I will stay my friends, I feel I can be more assistance here,' Renga announced, as he flew out the door.

'That leaves us then,' Vicky said. Alexandria stepped forward to Alex,

'To get to the island is not how you would pass to any other Dragonfly home. Do not take hold of the handle. Place your hands on the door itself.' Alex did what his birth mother instructed.

'Together!' Sophie said, arriving at his side, putting her arms round his waist. As soon as she did, the pinpricks of light came to life.

'Now what?' Alex asked.

'Move your hands, like hands round a clock,' Alexandria replied. It seemed odd to him, but again he did as instructed. A most unexpected thing happened. The pinpricks of light began following his hands.

'Faster!' Alexandria said. Once again, he did as he was told. Faster and faster he went. The colours started to change from the supernatural white, to that of the greens, purples and blues of the dragonfly. As he was running out of energy, the swirling lights overtook Alex. His arms tired, his hands sore from the friction on the rough wood, Alex stopped and stepped back. The colourful lights continued to swirl, creating a hollow in their centre, where the wood of the door could be seen. Then in the hollow, a familiar Dragonfly home, with its tree growing out from its centre, appeared,

'Now you can open the door!' Alexandria said with urgency. The room had fallen deathly silent. No sounds of the hustle and bustle from outside. No sounds of the fireplace in the centre of the room crackling. No sounds of breathing. It was as though they had become deaf. A feeling Vicky knew very well, back at her home on Earth. As soon as Alex reached down and opened the door, the sounds of the loch's water splashing up to the Dragonfly island's shore, the trees and their leaves rustling in the gentle breeze, the birds flying overhead and the creaking of the island's Dragonfly cottage roof, filled their ears with joyful familiarity.

'Stay safe you two. If you think this will not work at any point, trust your instincts and run!' Melissa said, as she stepped through the door, back onto the Dragonfly island. She turned and looked back at Sophie and Alex, feet away, but in fact, thousands of miles away in Earth's mirror of Australia in Heart, and smiled.

'You guys have got this,' Vicky said, along with Bart, who was becoming more and more vocal with his newfound freedom. Understood by everyone, he barked his agreement' and dashed through the door with Vicky. Grandmother had been the first one through. Keen not to waste any time, she had forgotten herself. Wrapped up in the reality that she could soon be face to face with her grandchildren after two hundred years, she had said nothing to Sophie or Alex. The fact that she had been forgotten hurt Sophie, however Anchor made up for it. He hadn't forgotten about her at all. In fact, he didn't want to leave her behind, and had stayed at her side.

'Come on you big monster,' Alexandria said, the last of the leaving humans left in the new Dragonfly home. Anchor was having none of it. He was going to stay. Alexandria took hold of his collar and tried to direct him to the door. He just sat down. 'Yeh ok, I get the message. You two are so special, and I don't mean just because of the dragonfly. Having lived through what you both have - sixteen years of being unaccepted, never fitting in, being abandoned. Despite all of this and your unpleasant experiences with people, you are still here, sacrificing everything, to help those same unpleasant ones. My boy, we will see each other soon, without this heavy cloud over our heads. I love you, I always have.' Alexandria closed the door. Sophie, Alex and Anchor were finally alone.

Alex didn't wait long to reopen the door to the hidden Australian town in Heart. Joined by Sophie and a whimpering Anchor, he stepped out into the eerily quiet, abandoned street. Iluka had done as he said he would. No living thing had been left behind. With an audible nervousness in his voice, Alex said,

'I hope this works!'

Chapter 15

The town's occupants made their way south into the forest, the opposite direction to which Leilani would potentially enter from. Earl began his walk to where he had been told to find her.

'I have your back.' He was both surprised and pleased to see Renga, perched on the branch of a tree where the spiders had left the web wall open.

'Thank you. I have been with Leilani for more years than I have not, and know her well, so believe me when I say she is capable of more than most realise. Honestly, I am not sure how well this plan of the old woman's will go,' Earl said,

'Why didn't you speak up, tell them your concerns?' A slightly annoyed Renga said, rethinking his choice in staying.

'I know I should have, but I felt it wasn't my place to say anything and after all, we have to try don't we?' Earl thoughtfully said. Renga could not disagree and at the very least, his wings would take him to safety much easier than Earl's short legs.

'Let's do what we have to then!' Earl said, heading through the webs and back into the forest. He marked every fifth tree with his razor-sharp claws as he passed, to make finding their way back as easy as it could be. He was slightly uncomfortable hearing hundreds of tiny feet, belonging to the spiders, above him. They had not headed south with the rest of the town. Instead, they chose to stay, confident enough to remain and follow Earl, to keep track of his mission. The snakes had found hiding places in holes in the ground between the web wall, the trees, and the stone wall that hid the town, ready to act if needed.

'Are we going the right way?' Earl shouted up to Renga,

'Yes, indeed we are. I can see the pool of water. It's quite a distance away still, but we are heading the right way,' Renga shouted back. Suddenly, the slow moving taps of hundreds of spiders stopped! The sudden silence alerted Earl to something not being right. He hid behind a tree and fallen branch.

'It cannot be far from here!' The words echoing around the silent forest were Leilani's.

'Maybe your eyes didn't benefit from the age reversing dragonfly like mine did, as I didn't see any lights!' Lanny said. Leilani didn't care for his sarcasm, but didn't care enough about him at that point to do anything about it. Grandmother had been correct. The light from the new Dragonfly home's creation had been seen by Leilani, and she had left the pool of water she had been waiting at. Earl took a deep breath and made his move.

'Mistress Leilani, I have found them and a doorway that will take you to the island!' The response was instant - he was pounced on by George and Gregg. Pinned to the floor, Earl felt their claws pass through his fur and pierce his skin. There was no way he could fight back, not without the claws sinking deeper. Leilani knelt down on the hard forest ground, inches from Earl's face, and menacingly whispered,

'You treacherous, untrustworthy creature! Do you think I would believe a word that comes from that tiny mouth of yours? Do not worry, I know exactly where they are!' Renga, high up in a tree, could see the terror in Earl's eyes as he looked up at him. With

Earl's years of experience of Lanny and his bears, he knew what was coming next. Closing his eyes, he felt the claws that had him pinned down, press further into him and tear at his skin. Standing up from bedside him and walking away, Leilani said.

'Slowly. Make him suffer!' Earl, her companion for so many years, was too insignificant to her to have even given him a second chance, let alone a second glance, before Lanny's bears took his life. Witnessing the cold-hearted evil he just had, in a panic, Renga did not leave the tree as quietly as he would have liked, as he headed back to the hidden town to warn Sophie and Alex that they were coming.

'I have seen that bird before!' Lanny said. He paused for a moment as he racked his brain. Finally remembering, he said, 'In the woods, when I was old. After we had left the loch, and we had that fox. He was in the trees there.'

'Good, then they are all more than likely to be where I saw that light. And look! Apparently Earl has been of some use.' Leilani was pointing at one of the freshly made marks Earl had scratched on the trees, to help him find his way back. As they walked past the mark, she saw another, then another. 'Looks like we are going this way,' she said, leading the purposeful team.

Continuing further into the forest, following Earl's marks, a thought popped into Leilani's head. If the boy and girl she had seen were there with the ancient dragonfly, why had Earl come to find her. They would surely have offered him safety.

'There is a chance we could be walking into a trap here,' Leilani said.

'Gregg, you take the lead. I want a twenty bear gap between you and George,' Lanny ordered.

'We really could have done with more of your bears, brother,' Leilani said. Lanny was well aware of that. He also would prefer to have had an army around him. He knew the challenges that such a part of Heart tended to throw up. If it was not for the gold that he mined, he would not have been back. Far too many poisonous creatures and humans who were hard to control, who had a tendency to fight back, even on Heart. After some time, and no traps being sprung on the nervously leading Gregg, they found themselves at the open web wall.

'They are expecting us,' Leilani said.

'Or could it be they have run because we were coming?' Lanny suggested. That did make more sense. After all, all on Heart knew she was capable of more than just setting an army of bears on them.

Having returned to the town, Renga, not having had a chance to warn Sophie and Alex, had at least managed to warn the remaining spiders and snakes around the town's perimeter of what had happened to Earl. Knowing that he would not be any use, Renga flew back up to the web canopy to watch, hoping he would not be seen, and live to tell the story to those hiding in the forest if things went wrong, or right!

Leilani sent the bears through the web wall to investigate first. Having found the tall stone and rubble wall, they were back quickly.

'There is a worn path to a wall, and a well camouflaged opening, Miss Leilani. There doesn't appear to be anyone guarding it,' Gregg said.

'Well, lead the way,' Lanny replied. He and his sister followed the two bounding bears. Not being the biggest fans of spiders, they were happy to be getting away from the web wall. Through the wall maze and standing where Alex and Sophie had, the four looked down on the empty town.

'Clever,' Leilani remarked. She was very impressed with the ingenuity of what had been created, dug into the hard forest ground. 'Looks like you may have been correct brother. They have run!' Leilani said.

'Let's hope the separation of Earl from his life was not a mistake, and not all have run away,' Lanny said. The thought had crossed her mind already, and she was mentally kicking herself. So as not to show weakness, and having remembered the reason they were heading to the hidden town, she replied.

'That was not a mistake. A new Dragonfly home, that I know we can find, was created here.' As with all Dragonfly homes, she was sure it would have similar features - a wobbly cobbly path, a flower-filled garden, a big, red front door and smiling windows. Truly, the most unexpectedly, splendidly, wonderfully inviting of homes. A sight to behold for those who could see. Leilani took the lead from the bears, striding at speed down the slope into the streets of the ghost town.

'It really is empty isn't it!' Lanny said,

'Yes, but newly empty. There is smoke rising from some houses, doors are open and wet clothes are hanging out of windows. Whoever was here cannot be far away, so keep your eyes open,' Leilani replied.

The dusty streets gave them an indication which way the ones living there had made their escape. They also gave an indication as to which way the new Dragonfly house could be, as the feet and paw trails led away from the town's centre. It wasn't long before they were standing outside a new-looking wall with an ornately decorated, red iron gate with flowers, beyond which was the wobbly cobbly path that Leilani had expected. Shorter than she was used to, but it was there none the less. And of course, the tall single-story house at its end, did indeed have a big red front door. Not as refined as hers, instead showing every lump and bump of the tree it had been made from. The windows to each side of it, they were smiling.

'There is movement inside!' Lanny said, having seen the silhouette of a person pass several feet away from the window.

'I saw. Get a closer look,' Leilani replied. Lanny crept up to the window.

'It doesn't look like there is anyone in there, it looks empty. Just one big room,' Lanny said, having walked backwards and forwards to get a better view. Leilani wasn't about to burst in without a little more thought. She knew the wonderful and powerful magic given by nature that had created it. She also did not want to send the bears in first. She found herself in quite the dilemma.

'George, go and get me a chair from that house,' Leilani said, pointing to a small, open-doored cottage. A neighbour to the Dragonfly home. 'I think I shall have a seat for a while.' He did what she asked, and quickly produced a solid wood chair, beautifully carved. Its legs flower stems, its seat a flower in bloom, its back leaves.

'Nice chair,' Lanny said. He was inclined to barge right in, but took his sister's lead and came back out of the garden. He waited patiently, standing behind her as she sat calmly, directly in front of the closed iron gate.

Still hovering high above the town, Renga was getting tired. Not only did he need a rest, but he was conscious that he had also been away from anyone who would listen to his gossiping for far too long! So he began a circular glide towards the edge of town. Eventually, spying the perfect landing place - a branch sticking out of the stone and rubble wall that surrounded all sides of the town, he landed. Settled and getting his breath back, he was happy that he was just able to see the dot that was Leilani in the distance, still sitting, waiting on the chair. All he had to do now was find some living thing to talk to, who was equally curious as to what was going to happen, rather than so scared they had vanished deep into the forest.

'Are they still there?' It was Averie. She had left with Gracie and her family, but her cubs being far too curious to see what was happening back in the town, had slipped off from the group and found their way back to the wall.

'How did I not see you there?' Renga said,

'Well, I am not surprised at all, you were looking back more than forward! At one point I thought you were going to fly right into the wall!' Renga laughed and then proceeded to update Averie and her curious cubs with what had been going on, right up to Earl's death. Just as he was on the verge of giving too much detail, Averie stopped him before her cubs heard.

'She is still there, just watching the house. Who knows what she is planning,' Renga said.

'Does she have an army of bears with her?' Averie asked.

'No, actually she doesn't, just two! I assume they will be Lanny's loyal ones, George and Gregg,' Renga replied. After a moment of reflection, Averie said,

'The two who killed my partner!' Her cubs, hearing what she said, suddenly took off to find one of the camouflaged entrances, to get back into the town and avenge their father.

'Get back here right now!' Averie's usually calm and quiet voice was raised and full of panic, with the fear that they may find a way through.

'Don't worry, the gap they are looking for is far from them, and actually the other way,' Renga said, having a good view from where he was perched.

'What are they waiting for?' Sophie asked.

'Honestly, I don't know. But I would like those two bears to leave,' Alex said.

'What is the plan if they come in?' Sophie asked.

'I have been thinking about that. There are four rooms at the back, and I think there is a high chance they will start searching the rooms from the left, as that's the closest to the front door. If we hide in the far right one, when they come in to look, we should be able to get to the front door and open it to the island before they realise,' Alex said.

'A good idea in theory. But what about those bears!' Sophie replied. Alex knew something Sophie didn't. He had seen something she hadn't, and just replied with,

'I don't think they are going to be a problem. Just be ready when I tell you to run to that room, and do it as quick as you can.' Alex had found a place to stand where he was sure he could not be seen. A place that he could see what was happening out the front windows, to where Leilani was sitting, and to the side windows, which looked out to the pathways each side of the house.

To the side of the Dragonfly house was a house made of tree trunks. Having got bored waiting, Gregg was investigating one of its open windows.

'Now! Take him!' From the shadows of the window, four bears, quietly, swiftly, appeared, grabbed Gregg, and before he had a chance to react, pulled him inside. Not all living things had left the town for the safety of the forest! As the four bears pulled Gregg into the shadows, the face of Iluka appeared. He quickly checked out of the window to check Leilani, Lanny or George hadn't seen what had just happened. Iluka caught sight of Alex who had seen the abduction, and after a smile and a wink, disappeared back into the shadows. Nearly an hour passed. Leilani, still happy to wait, finally noticed the absence of Gregg and asked,

'Where is your companion George?' He also hadn't noticed his absence. Instead, being so hot in his thick fur, George was fantasising about swimming in the water hole they had left on the edge of the forest. Preempting the order that was sure to come, he slowly got to his paws and went to find his companion. Remembering that Gregg had gone off down the side of the new Dragonfly home, George decided that was the best place to start his search. Out of sight of Leilani, out from the same shadows, the same four bears with the same precision, carried out the same silent abduction. This time of George. Once again, witnessed by Alex.

'Sophie, Anchor, run to the room now!' Alex said assertively but quietly. Happy she was out of sight, Alex went to the front door and threw it open. Having looked Leilani right in the eye, still with no top on, he turned his back to her and shouted,

'Is this what you are looking for?' showing off the ancient dragonfly. Lanny couldn't control himself. If he got to him first, he would have the power, not his sister! Before Leilani had a chance to get to her feet, he crashed the gate open, was up the steps and in through the open door.

As quick as he was, Alex was quicker. He had made his escape and joined Sophie in what they hoped would be the last room searched. Leilani was furious. She would have waited, stayed in her chair until Alex had left the house. Knowing her brother, she had no choice but to follow him.

'Where did he go?' Leilani asked.

'I didn't see, but one of those rooms I would think,' Lanny replied. Leilani was not about to let her brother take the lead, so made her way to the first room. The first room on the left! Throwing open the door, she saw that it was a storeroom, full of beautifully made wooden toys.

'I will wait here, you can go and search,' Leilani ordered. She wanted to be the one to keep an eye on the other rooms, just in case this was not the room they were hiding in. Lanny didn't need to be asked twice and ran past her into the room. With his usual chaotic technique, his search began with toys being thrown everywhere, along with the shelves they were stored on.

With all the noise Lanny was making, Alex knew that was their chance to make their move. He grabbed Sophie's hand, and after a quick glance at each other, he pulled her so hard as he took off, Sophie felt like her shoulder was about to come out of its socket. Anchor was quick at their heels! Arriving at the open front door, Sophie slammed it shut as Alex placed his hands on it and began his clockwise circles.

Somehow, Leilani had missed their dash, and hadn't heard the door slam with all the noise her brother was making, but when the white lights came alive and started their transformation into the dragonfly colours, she noticed.

'Lanny!' she screamed, as she turned and ran away from the destroyed room and past the fireplace, just in time to see Alex remove his hands from the door, and an image appear in the swirling colours' centre. 'Don't you move!' she shouted at Sophie and Alex. Her order was ignored. Alex reached for the door handle and calmly opened the door, revealing the old, wobbly cobbles, and lush green grass of Dragonfly island!

Aware Leilani was fast approaching and hearing Lanny crashing out from the room he had turned upside down, remaining calm, Alex stepped to one side and gestured for Sophie to make her way through. Anchor didn't wait for his gesture. He was already past Sophie and through! Once Sophie had joined him, Alex followed, and they both stepped to the side of the doorway, out of sight of Leilani.

'Lanny!' Leilani screamed again, as having passed through the doorway at great speed, she was faced with more than the two young ones she had been chasing. Stopping himself just before crashing into his sister, Lanny exclaimed, with just an,

'Oh!' as he looked to see what his sister already had. Standing in a line, staring at them in silence, was Alex, Sophie, grandmother, Melissa, Alexandria, Jason, Vicky and the two growling dogs, Anchor and Bart.

Leilani let out a laugh that filled the air. Shaking her head, with a smug look that took over her face,

she sunk her bare feet, covered in the ropes of gold and diamonds, into the soft ground and said,
'Oh, you foolish creatures!'

Chapter 16

'Don't let them go! We need to give them as much time as we can to get through,' Iluka shouted, struggling to keep hold of George. It was easy to control Gregg when it had been the four bears and Iluka, but now having George as well, they were struggling. Even though they outnumbered them, they were just no match for the, well seasoned in battle, bears. With one swipe from George's sharp-clawed, powerful arm, two of the bears were thrown across the wooden house, crashing off the furthest away wall.

George, having set himself free, turned his attention to helping Gregg. He dragged Iluka, who had avoided his claws by spinning round behind him and grabbing him by the neck. Gregg, now only being held by two, was already getting the upper hand. With George's arrival, the last two bears, once commanded by George and Gregg themselves, let go, before suffering the same critical claw attack the other two bears had. With their paws raised, they backed off.

'We will be back for you!' George menacingly said. He'd heard what Iluka had said about someone needing time to get through, so didn't want to waste any time on his abductors. As he left the house with Iluka still hanging onto him, he spun, crushing him into the sharp-edged doorframe. Iluka couldn't hold on.

Out the house, George and Gregg bounced back up the pathway, back round to where Leilani and Lanny should have been!

'There!' Gregg shouted, pointing at the open, new, Dragonfly home door.

Her foot firmly in the ground, the soil between her gold covered toes, Leilani theatrically raised her hands and shouted the words,

'Hold them where they stand!' whilst using her connection with the ground to send plants to wrap themselves around Alex, Sophie and the rest of them, to trap them where they stood, so she could remove the ancient dragonfly and have her victory.

'Who are you talking to granddaughter?' grandmother asked a confused looking Leilani when nothing happened. Lanny's smile dropped from his face, when he realised that whatever abilities his sister normally had, seemed to have gone. 'Are you beginning to feel old granddaughter?' grandmother asked in a very sarcastic tone. Leilani's face lost its arrogant smile, as the realisation that she may not have thought her plan through as well as she should have sank in. Yes, she was on the island in the presence of Alex and the ancient dragonfly, but she was also in the area that took her brother's youth. Looking down at her hands, after a few moments, confident that nothing was changing, with an evil glint in her eye, she looked back up at the group standing in front of her and said,

'It would appear not grandmother! I would like to say you look, well, young, but you look as old and tired as the day I watched you vanish from Heart. The day I stopped your daughter from doing what she was going to do to me, the day I was supposed to take control of the dragonfly!'

'My dear you are so wrong. The only plan we had that day was to celebrate your wonderful twenty-first birthday. The day you would have taken charge, not control, of our Dragonfly Manor and yes, its dragonfly,' grandmother said,

'Confusion is contagious. Your old eyes deceived you then, as they do now. It was I who stopped my parents from taking my life, I who cracked both their skulls open!' Before Leilani had a chance to finish, grandmother interrupted, saying,

'He really did a good job on you, didn't he!' looking over at Lanny. Leilani paid no attention. She was once again concentrating on her connection with nature through the gold, the diamonds and her feet. As hard as she tried, nothing happened.

'I know you have come here for me. But as you can see, you are outnumbered!' Alex said,

'And whatever magic you had seems to have abandoned you!' Alexandria added. Lanny had stayed silent, but let out an uncharacteristic,

'Yes!' as he heard the voice of George, coming from inside the island's Dragonfly Cottage,

'Miss Leilani, Master Lanny, are you in here?' Leilani let out a cackle that travelled across the loch, sending shivers down the spines of every living creature within a mile of where she stood, as she turned to see her brother's generals!

'I believe the tables have turned once again. Get him!' Leilani screamed at the bears. The order given, even as unsure of where they were and who was the other side of Leilani and Lanny, George and Gregg were out the door and past the siblings in a blur of fur, in the blink of an eye. Alex had no chance to react and found himself pinned to the floor, like many had been before. George's left paw and claws were clasped round Alex's neck, his other arm pulled back like a slingshot. Just as he was about to slash down, Leilani shouted, 'Stop! Do not kill the child you dim-witted bear, I have use for him.' Jason ran forward, followed by Anchor and Bart, to attack the attackers. Seeing their charge out the corner of his eye, Alex calmly raised his hand and said,

'No, it's ok.' Anchor, in full bound, wasn't able to stop in time and was caught with a massive blow from Gregg, throwing him across the island, back to where the rest of the group stood. 'She needs me to get to the dragonfly. Probably best not to be together!' Alex said, with extra emphasis on "not to be together." Sophie knew exactly what he was getting at.

'Did you think bringing me here was going to end any other way? Grandmother, I thought you were supposed to be a wise woman. I do not know you young man and you do not know me, but be in no doubt, you will give me what I want,' Leilani said as she approached Alex.

'What are we going to do,' Sophie whispered to Alexandria, who was standing next to her, with her arm protectively around her. She didn't say a word, but gently pulled Sophie back towards the loch. The rest of the group noticed what she was doing and with Leilani focused on Alex, followed her lead, edging themselves away from Leilani, Lanny and the bears, leaving a remarkably calm looking Alex pinned to the floor.

'So young man, how do you think this is going to end for you?' Leilani asked.

'I imagine very well!' he replied. His words unsurprisingly angering her, she ordered George to get him to his feet. She wanted a closer look at what was on his back.

'Quite beautiful,' Leilani said. As she touched Alex's back, the ancient dragonfly moved away from her. 'Now to getting you out of there!' she threateningly said.

'I have a better idea,' Alex said.

'Yes!' Leilani replied with a raised eyebrow.

'How would you like as many dragonflies as you could ever want, or need?' Alex asked. His words stopped the retreating group, horrified at what he was offering her.

'No Alex, you can't!' Sophie shouted.

'Well, that seems to have got a reaction,' Lanny said. A fact that increased Leilani's interest in his question. Stepping around Alex so she could look him in the eye, confident in her ability to tell whether he was just buying time or telling the truth, she said,

'Go on!' Alex described the cave of trees filled with dragonfly pods in great detail. How he and Sophie could bring them to life, how she could live forever and open as many doorways to and from Earth as she wanted. She listened intently, with a cautious scepticism as to why he would be offering such a possibility, but could not stop herself from getting excited, which her face could not hide at all.

'Maybe together is better after all,' Alex said, looking over at Sophie. She wanted to scream at him and run away. How could he want Leilani to have them both? How could he let her learn how important the two of them being together was? How could he have given away the secrets that could have kept them, along with Heart and Earth, safe?

'Bring her over here!' Leilani's order, directed at Gregg, was redundant, as Sophie, having broken free from Alexandria's protective arm, was already walking over towards the captured Alex. As confused and angry at him as she was, Sophie felt she knew him well enough after their few days together, and the many years of dreams in which they were unknowingly connected. She trusted him. Another most important fact Sophie knew, was that together, touching each other, there was a chance that if he and the dragonfly had a plan, she could hear exactly what it was.

'Pretty little thing aren't you,' Leilani said, grabbing her arm and pulling her to line up beside Alex. Leilani had no idea who she really was, that she was in fact her relative! Not that that would have made any difference to how Sophie would have been treated. 'So where is this place of wonder?' she asked, being overly dramatic and throwing her arms around, mocking Alex. Alex didn't respond, he reached out and took Sophie's hand. As soon as he did, just as she had hoped, Sophie was being shown something. In her mind, she was back in the dark tunnel, somewhere beneath the island, with the noise of thundering paws and growls coming towards her. Now knowing why he had been so calm and why he had told Leilani so much, Sophie let go of his hand and loudly said,

'In there, through the inner doorway.'

'Wonderful. Show me!' Leilani said, her tone turning menacing. Turning to go back into the Dragonfly island's cottage, as the door had not yet been closed, the large room with its fireplace in the centre, back in the Sovereign Hill's forest town, was still visible. In the shadows behind the fireplace were several sets of eyes, watching what was going on. The first belonging to Iluka and the two bear kidnappers that hadn't been injured by George and Gregg's escape. The others were eyes Sophie and Alex were surprised, but glad, to see.

Arriving at the wobbly cobbly path, a few feet from the front door, Sophie smiled a smile that was translated by the hidden onlookers. They knew she had seen them and they knew they could act. Completely unplanned, shouting and screaming and giving up their hidden status, they all ran through the doorway. Sophie stepped aside and pulled a startled Alex with her. Leilani reacted just in time, unlike Lanny and George who were knocked to the ground with the speed and strength of Iluka, two bears, Averie and her cubs, Gracie, Eric, Ella and Jedda. Gregg, who was shielded by George, who took the full blow of the attack, had managed quite a graceful spin and dodged the full impact. Bouncing off the charging rescuers, he got to Alex and grabbed hold of him!

With the charge past her, Leilani reacted quickly. Grabbing the front door, she slammed it shut and as quickly as she had closed it, she reopened it, revealing the inside of the island's Dragonfly Cottage, with the tree in its centre and the cinematic walls, showing the moving images of places all over Earth. Gregg, having a good hold of Alex, pushed him past Sophie. As he did, he grabbed her arm and dragged both of them into the cottage. Leilani was quick on her feet. Right behind them, not giving her brother or George a chance to catch up, she slammed the door closed and locked it!

'Show me!' with rage in her eyes, the out of breath Leilani demanded. She did not want to waste any more time, knowing fine well the lock would not hold for long with the deafening thuds she heard, as the ones outside tried to break it open. She also knew that as hard as they would try, there was no way George and Lanny were going to be able to overpower so many.

'It's ok Iluka. You don't need to get into the cottage, they will be fine,' grandmother said to the powerful, charging man. 'You don't look so good!' grandmother said, turning her attention to Lanny. Iluka, having stopped his assault on the locked door, lifted Lanny up from the soft grass. The focus having been on Leilani, her loss of abilities and the fact she had not aged, meant that it was only now grandmother noticed that returning to the island was affecting her grandson. He was becoming old once again. A fact that had not been missed by Lanny himself. His reactions, not being as good as they should have been, resulted in him being easily knocked to the ground. He looked down at his changing hands, the skin becoming patchy, his knuckles becoming thicker, his fingers thinning. As he stared at them, he felt something round his ankles - a thin mist had arrived and was gently swirling around them.

'I don't understand!' Lanny said, nervous, not at what they would do to him, as he had a good idea that they were not the type to hurt anyone, but nervous because his sister was out of sight and with the ones he had hoped he would be alone with himself! Questions flew through his mind. Would she come back with dragonflies for him as well? Or would she let him age and die, surplus to her requirements? Thanks to grandmother, who had planted the truth into Leilani's mind about the day they had taken their parents' lives, he concluded that it was more likely that she wouldn't be back to help him.

'I think you will find the island has other ideas for you. Even though your sister never received the bite from the dragonfly, being a key-keeper provides her with a certain amount of protection. She has and always will have the magic of the dragonfly in her, whereas you, as the son, did not, do not and will not!' Alexandria happily said. The thousands of years of knowledge being passed down to her had given her insight, but more than what had been told by her mother or what she had read. Consciously and unconsciously, in dream whilst asleep or awake, she had access to the genetic memories of all the Dragonfly island protectors, the daughters of every key-keeper, the direct descendants of Shuing were always there for her. Standing in front of Lanny on the island she was born to protect, Alexandria was accessing more than even she knew she could.

'Come on, I really think we should get this door open,' Jason said,

'No, my long-lost brother, as grandmother said, we do not need to!' Alexandria joined him at the locked door. 'My son and that young woman are where they need to be. I know I was the one who was trying to prevent this inevitability, but it was, after all, inevitable! Surely you have seen they have a wisdom and connection to nature greater than even I can understand. We must trust them. We must wait.'

'Are you sure about this?' Sophie asked, as she and Alex placed their hands on the tree together.

'Too late to go back now!' Alex replied, as the wobbling, twisting, bright, colourful lights appeared in the grooves of the bark of the tree, just as they had the first time they did what they were doing now. Then the voice of the ancient dragonfly was heard, by both of them. It asked the same question it had before,

'Where do you want to go?' Picturing exactly where he wanted to go to, Alex replied,

'The tunnel filled with sparkling gems,' hoping his request would mean they would avoid the awkward climb up the rock face of the cave beyond the underground lake. The location requested, the cobbles that made up the floor began to wobble, as bright white light shone around each one of them. Just as before, the room began heating up. The door's lights, the doorframe's lights, the tree's lights, the floor's lights, swirled around the room, dancing between Alex, Sophie, Leilani and a nervous-looking Gregg.

'This better be what is supposed to happen boy!' Leilani angrily said. He paid no attention, he was too busy soaking up the loving energy that was wrapping them up, building to the point Alex knew would have them taken to where he had asked to be. Finally, at the perfect time, Alex reached out and grabbed hold of Leilani. Before she could challenge his action, Alex and Sophie took their hands off the tree and they were exactly where Alex had hoped. In the tunnel, looking out of its entrance across the underground lake.

'Gregg, where are you?' Leilani shouted, looking around the tunnel full of light from the gems.

'He was not in contact with us, so he is not here!' Alex calmly said.

'Do not think that gives you the upper hand. Being underground is where my powers have always been their strongest. Show me where these dragonflies are or you will find out just how powerful I can be,' Leilani warned.

'If you are so powerful Leilani, how was it your bears had to rescue you back on the island?' Sophie asked sarcastically. Leilani turned away from them, looking past the gem coloured walls, down the tunnel into the darkness.

'I have been here before!' she thoughtfully and quietly said. There was something familiar to her about the place. She didn't know what, but she was sure she had been there. Sophie looked up at Alex,

'Could she have been?' she whispered.

'I don't know how!' Alex replied. Leilani paid no attention to the gems, which was very out of character, considering she had spent so many years searching for them for her experiments back in her Californian laboratory. There was enough in that tunnel to keep her busy for a very long time.

'I know this tunnel, I have been here so many times, but...' suddenly a spark of a memory caused her to stop mid-sentence.

'It was you!' Leilani spun round and looked right at Sophie. 'You have been here before as well. With me. You always ran and...' she stopped again. This time she walked back and up to Alex and looked deep into his eyes. She saw what she was looking for, 'You were the one, the bright-eyed silhouette, you took her from me every time!' Leilani felt a weight lifting from her. Sophie was not the only one who had suffered nightmares for as long as she could remember. Leilani had suffered similar ones, going back long before Sophie's existence. Just like Sophie, she was looking for an escape in them! She found herself trapped at a dead end and also saw a silhouette with bright eyes, who she assumed was there to help her get out.

'Who are you to me?' Leilani asked.

'I am the great, great, great niece to your grandmother. How could you not know this?' Sophie replied. Leilani was being flooded with all kinds of emotions, some she didn't know she was capable of. Beginning to question her own reality, the words grandmother had said about Lanny doing a good job on her came back. Over two hundred years of death, suffering, mistrust, searching for a way to get back to Earth and take the Dragonfly Manor and her rightful place as key-keeper, had filled every waking moment of her long life. She took so much pleasure in causing the suffering of others as she took control of every Dragonfly home, consuming what she thought was every last one of the magical dragonfly.

'But you call her grandmother! How can that be?' Leilani asked.

'Everyone calls her grandmother. I am her brother's great, great, great granddaughter, a fact that I was totally unaware of until a couple of days ago.' Alex listened to the unexpectedly calm and honest conversation. His plan was to take Leilani into the caves, to where the terrifying growls and heavy, bounding paws echoed. To leave her there in the dark, trapped with whatever the monster was whilst they made their escape. 'You are the animal I was running from! Who was chasing me in my nightmares!' Sophie said.

'Not in my nightmares. There was an animal though, even when I didn't see you, it stalked me with its heavy breathing, its growls, its claws scraping the rocky tunnel ground,' Leilani said, as she relived her petrifying, recurring nightmares. Sophie, sensing a negative energy build in her, stepped back and away. As she did, she fell into the wall of gems, which instantly exploded with light and colour. Sophie's own colours reacted to Leilani's negative energies, her fall into the wall and the realisation Leilani had been part of her nightmares. They were swirling with reds and blacks as they made their way up her neck.

'What is that? Are there two dragonflies, do you have one living in you as well?' Leilani asked. Alex, having sensed a change in Leilani's demeanour, from anger to something less frightening, decided to risk sharing the secret that would have kept the dragonfly and Earth safe, if she was never to know,

'No Leilani. I am the direct descendant of Shuing,' Leilani interrupted,

'Yes, I know that!' A hint of the Leilani all knew too well returning in her voice, didn't stop Alex from continuing,

'This time it is different. What you and your brother have done here and on Earth, along with humankind's desire, selfishness and continual self-destruction, has left Heart and Earth sitting on a cliff's edge. With one gentle breeze both will fall. Heart will be gone forever, and Earth will be overrun with humankind until it ends. Much sooner than all that live there realise. Selfishness, a lack of compassion for others, humankind's assumption that it has power over all living things, has left them, as well as animal kind and all of nature, without balance. A loss of balance that started the day you and your brother killed your parents. You by accident, Lanny most purposely. Closing the Dragonfly Manor door and that of every other Dragonfly home on Heart, with your selfish consumption of every magical, beautiful dragonfly, is the reason Earth and Heart find themselves on that cliff edge. What I have learnt on this short journey, is that true balance cannot be restored as it was thousands of years ago, when nature gifted us the dragonfly with Shuing. Today, more than one is needed. Sophie and I have been bound together for as long as we can remember, we just didn't know it until the day we met outside our dreams, our nightmares. So no, there are not two ancient dragonflies, just the one, that this time, requires both of us to do what Shuing did alone.' Sophie, surprised that Alex had shared so much, was pleased he had, as she saw something in Leilani's eyes that she had not expected to - warmth.

'The dragonflies, take me to them!' Leilani said,

'I cannot!' Alex replied. Leilani turned and walked out of the light of the gems into the darkness, leaving Alex and Sophie behind.

'You will take me to the dragonflies! My goal here has not changed,' Leilani said firmly. Alex said to Sophie,

'We cannot change what she has become. Whether or not there is vulnerability inside her. We also cannot let her find those dragonflies.'

'But we can't leave her to die down here either,' Sophie replied. Alex didn't know what to say or do. 'I am going after her. Our dreams may not have featured the monster we thought, but there is one in these tunnels, you know it! That's why you brought her here.' Sophie walked away towards the dark, leaving Alex hoping for some advice from his ancient companion. The dragonfly stayed silent.

Shaking his head and taking a deep breath, there was no way he was going to let Sophie go alone. Running his hands down the wall of gems as he did, their light crackling behind him, he followed them into the dark. Strangely, as far as he walked, Alex didn't catch up with the dark. There were no gems on the walls, but the light stayed with him. Realising, Alex stopped to look. He soon wished he hadn't. As soon as he did, it went dark. Having gone from such light to such dark, Alex couldn't see anything!

'Oh, hang on!' he said to himself, having come up with an idea. Reaching back to the wall he had stopped touching, he turned to look and see how the tunnel was still lit. He placed his hand back on it. 'Yep, just like the trees and their arrows!' The wall was lit back up brightly, the veins of various minerals that ran through it pulsed with light. Alex's connection with nature was the reason for the light.

'Well, that's very helpful.' Sophie had returned to him, having seen the light go out and then come back on.

'Yes it is,' Alex replied.

'She moves fast, I can't hear her anymore,' Sophie said.

'Well, let's see if we can change that,' Alex replied. One hand on the rocky wall, the other in Sophie's hand, they headed off in the only direction available to them, other than going back.

Having realised it was his connection with the mineral veins in the walls that was lighting them up, Alex's acknowledgement and focus on them, had the effect of the light getting stronger and moving away from him, down into the tunnel. It wasn't long before the lights were so far ahead, they couldn't make out what they were lighting up. It was also not too long before the light caught up with Leilani, its arrival causing her to stop. She reached out to touch it, curious how it could be and what it was. Her touch had the opposite effect to Alex's. The section she rested her hand on went dark, as did the veins that went beyond her. As soon as she removed her hand, just like pressing a vein on an arm to stop the blood flow, then removing it and watching as the blood filled the empty vein back up, the light returned and moved ahead of her. She looked back down the tunnel she had walked through, and could just make out the silhouettes of Alex and Sophie making their way towards her.

During her time alone in the dark searching for the dragonflies, Leilani's mind had been reliving her nightmares, looking for something that would help her understand why she was the one running away from the monster, and how it was possible to have been in the same nightmare as both Alex and Sophie, years before they were even born. As frustrating as it was, she accepted that what was, simply was, and changed her focus on to the monster. What or who was it? Why did it chase her? And why, although she could never escape the tunnels, was she never caught by it? As much as she wanted to do what she was doing by herself, she needed more answers to that one question. The only ones who could help, the ones she had left behind, were getting closer and closer, so she waited.

Finally, Alex and Sophie caught up with her and as soon as they did, she asked them to describe their part in the nightmare. In particular, their experience of the monster. Sophie was happy too. As terrifying as the nightmares were, they were never too long once she had learnt how to wake herself up. But Alex chose not to. There was nothing he experienced that could add to what Sophie had already said.

'Did you ever see the monster?' Leilani asked.

'Animal, not a monster. I never saw it, but for some reason I thought it was a very large cat, like a panther, a tiger or a lion,' Sophie replied. Alex could not believe where he found himself. By his own actions, he was in a tunnel with the woman who was the reason for him not growing up with his birth mother. The cause of so much death and separation, and Sophie was talking to her like they were friends. It made him feel very uncomfortable.

'Did you hear that?' Leilani said. Sophie stopped talking, and they all stood motionless. 'That!' Leilani said again.

'I can't hear anything,' Sophie said.

'Are we near the dragonfly cave with the trees you described Alex,' Leilani asked with urgency. He was so conflicted. She was not the woman who had been described to him. She was not old and her voice was getting softer with every conversation they were having. But still, she was the one who had done what she had. He couldn't risk telling her that actually the light ahead, reaching its end, was where the rocks had fallen and trapped whatever had been stalking Alex and Sophie on their last visit. And to the side of that was the entrance to another tunnel, which led them to the dragonfly cave. Then he heard what Leilani had. It was the sound of tiny bits of rubble falling. It was coming from the tunnel's blockage.

'I think we should leave! Remember what happened last time - the cave collapsed. It's happening again!' he said.

'Leave! I don't think so,' Leilani said. She sensed that he did not want to answer her question, and that they were close. The quiet falling of loose rubble suddenly turned into a thunder of falling rocks.

'Sophie, we need to go!' Alex said, grabbing her hand, trying to direct her back down the tunnel towards the cave with the underground lake. Sophie pulled her hand out of his and said,

'No. Can't you see, she is more than what we have been told.' Alex lowered himself down to Sophie's head height and quietly said,

'Whatever was trapped behind those rocks, it's found a way through. It's coming.' Sophie saw the concern in Alex's eyes. His eyes had turned more purple than the blue that usually lived in them.

'Aunt Leilani please, if Alex is right it's not safe to stay here.' Sophie's familiarity touched something inside Leilani. At no point in her life did she experience the feeling of trust towards anyone. It was new to her, but in that moment, she did. Leilani was torn between going with them and what was potentially ahead of her, so close to what would give her all the power she ever wanted, youth, strength and the ability to control all on Heart and on Earth.

'Nooooo!' she screamed. The power in her voice made the ground shake beneath them, and as they watched her run towards the collapsing cave, the lights Alex had made possible on the walls went out.

'Alex, do something,' Sophie said. He put his hand back on the wall, but nothing happened. He placed both hands on the wall, still nothing. Then, as the sound of falling rocks got louder as they got closer to them, Alex pulled Sophie again,

'Come on, we need to get out of here!' he shouted. Sophie did not move, in fact she had moved in the opposite direction, with every intention of trying to get to Leilani. But then, she was stopped by a cloud of gritty dust, which pushed out towards them with such force, it was impossible to see anything. Its thickness was making it impossible for them to breathe. Alex, giving up on trying to pull Sophie away, bent down, judged roughly where her legs were, and in a quick sweeping motion, grabbed her, picked her up, and ran faster than he had ever run before, towards where the light given out by the gems was being swallowed up by the same dust cloud.

As Alex ran, he felt Sophie go limp. She wasn't fighting him any more to stay. Every time he took a breath, he choked from the dust, so he sunk his face into Sophie's hair. It worked. It gave him just enough of a filter to get to the end of the tunnel. Not stopping at its end, he jumped with the unconscious Sophie in his arms, out of the tunnel, into the cold underground lake. He threw her forward as he was in the air, so as not to land on her and cause her further injury. As his feet hit the bottom of the lake, he pushed as hard as he could to get back up as quickly as possible to find Sophie. She was floating, face down, several feet from him. With one strong kick of his legs, he was at her side. He spun her over and dragged her back to the rocky edge, exactly where he had been looking down at her as she lay underwater, in the dream they had shared.

'Sophie, please no!' he said, having checked her for signs of life. She wasn't breathing, and he couldn't find a pulse. 'I don't know what to do! Help me, please help me!' Alex said, directing his plea for help towards the ancient dragonfly. He didn't get an answer. Alex had seen resuscitation done, but had never done it himself. He bent down and tried blowing air into her. It didn't work. His breath just puffed out her cheeks. He thought maybe something was stuck in her throat, so he lifted her up and spun her round. Facing away from him, he tried to force it out by squeezing her into him, below her ribs. She remained lifeless, limp, with no signs of life.

'Do something!' Alex screamed. Becoming lightheaded in his panic, his vision blurring, he tried hard to focus on Sophie's face. She looked as beautiful as the first time he saw her. Sitting back on the cold, wet ground, he pulled her on to his lap and held her tight.

He felt more alone than he had in his entire life, more so than having been abandoned as a baby, more so than being alone and tortured in every school he attended. Not being able to help Sophie, despair took over. Unable to hold on to her any longer, his body going as limp as hers, Alex fell back onto the hard ground.

At the point of complete physical and conscious shut down, unable to stop her, Alex felt Sophie slide from his lap, back into the lake, and with the gentle sound of parting water, he heard her float away. Paralysed and the world fading, for what he thought would be the last time, Alex softly said her name, 'Sophie.'

Chapter 17

'Sophie! Is that you?' Alex said, assuming the female figure in the distance in the dark tunnel, with her back to him, long, red, curly hair cascading over her shoulders, was her. Getting no answer, Alex walked in her direction. The sound of his feet on the loose rubble breaking the silence, echoed through the tunnel, but was quickly hidden by the sound of a scream for help. It was Sophie! 'Sophie, it's me, Alex!' His confirmation of who was approaching did not help. She continued her scream, so Alex began reversing away from her. It worked, the ear-piercing scream came to an end. In what seemed like a very strange position to be in, a stand-off of acquaintances, Alex stood quietly, watching the motionless Sophie, standing with her back to him.

Five, ten, fifteen minutes passed as he waited for something to change. Then it did! Alex spun round as he heard the thud of heavy paws and the heavy breathing of a large animal, but saw nothing!

'Listen to what you are hearing.' It was the voice of the ancient dragonfly, 'Your ears are hearing what your mind understands. Listen again, not with your old mind, instead with the one that has experienced Heart.' Alex, getting used to the strange advice in his head, closed his eyes and began taking deep breaths. The tunnel went silent.

Opening his eyes, he once again headed towards Sophie. This time she did not scream. This time she turned to look at him. Focused on her bright green eyes, Alex, still some distance from her, heard the sound he had moments earlier. The same horrific sound he had heard in his nightmares, the same sound he had heard during their first visit to the gem-covered tunnel.

'Listen beyond what you think you hear!' The dragonfly spoke again, a little more assertively this time. He didn't stop, he didn't look back. Pushing the fear aside, Alex stayed focused on Sophie and carried on walking towards her. As he did, he tried as hard as he could to challenge his mind's translation of what he was hearing, to clear his mind, to hear the sounds beyond the sounds. It worked. Feet from Sophie, he felt the oppressive atmosphere lift, and the sound of heavy breathing became the sound of wind, pushing its way through the tunnel, bouncing off the undulations and imperfections of the tunnel's walls, ceiling and fallen rocks. Finally, face to face with the silent and motionless Sophie, the thumping sound from heavy paws also changed. They became a heartbeat!

'You are in the Heart of Heart Alex. The Heart of Earth. Your Earth and Heart's beginning, nature's beginning. A beginning I truly hope does not end.' With a flash of light, Alex was no longer in the tunnel. He was standing in the water of the underground lake, looking down at Sophie, just as he had in the dream he'd had, sleeping in the old camper van, on their journey to the small Highland village. There for a fraction of a second, as quick as the first flash came, a second one did, and Alex was awake, laying on the rocky edge of the underground lake, looking up at the tree roots of the Dragonfly Island's cottage. As real as it felt, realising what had just happened to him was some sort of dream, reality hit him and he called out,

'Sophie!' He went to push himself up to look for her, but as he placed his hands on the rocks, a bolt of energy from them, the plants, soil, water and cold damp air around him, shot through his entire body. So powerful, as it left his body it sent a pulse into the lake, which created a wave that rolled across it, crashing into the walls on the opposite side to where Alex was now sitting bolt upright.

After an athletic jump to his feet, he followed the wave and ran into the cold water to look for Sophie. Looking across the water's surface for her floating body, he lost his balance as his foot caught something! Someone! Sophie. Her eyes wide open, bubbles of life coming from her mouth, Alex reached down and pulled her up, out and back into his arms. No longer limp or lifeless, Sophie's eyes were full of life, and her face was lit up with a smile that lifted her flushed cheeks, and squinted her eyes as it spread across it. In Alex's arms, her legs dangling in the water, Sophie looked up at him, lifted her hands to his face, gently placing them on his jaw, and pulled him down to her. Without saying a word, she gave him a long and soft, loving kiss. As the tears from Alex's eyes made their way down his cheeks and joined their kiss, Sophie let him go.

'You are alive!' Alex said, full of emotion, carrying her out of the lake.

'Was I dead?' Sophie asked, as Alex placed her down on the slippery rocks.

'Do you remember anything?' Alex asked,

'Not really. Well, erm we were up there, right?' Sophie's mind was beginning to clear, from the jolt of energy that had brought her back from being nowhere.

'Do you not remember the tunnel collapsing? That I grabbed you and carried you out. You stopped breathing! I tried to help, honestly I did, but I didn't know what to do. It was all so weird, I lost all my strength, and you ended up back in the water and I...' Alex stopped as the dream he had woken up from, jumped back into the forefront of his mind.

'What is it?' Sophie asked.

'I was back in the tunnel I always dreamt about, with you. You didn't recognise me and just screamed when I walked closer. The sound of that awful, stalking animal and its breath was there as well. But it wasn't an animal at all. As soon as I realised it wasn't, I was awake. Here. And now you are alive! These few days just keep getting stranger,' Alex said. Sophie tried hard to recall what had happened in the collapsing tunnel.

'I do remember not being able to breathe. Something blocked my throat, I think, maybe the dust. Leilani!' she exclaimed. 'We must help her!' she said, looking over to where the walls covered in gems, were not shining as brightly as they had before, hidden by dust, fallen rocks and rubble. 'Oh no, she must be trapped in there!' Sophie said. Alex grabbed her arm as she made a dash to Leilani's rescue. Turning her back round to look at him he said,

'Sophie. She ran into the collapsing tunnel. There was nothing either of us could do. You are safe, we are alive, it's time to go back to the island and make sure everyone else is also ok. Remember we left them with Lanny and his bears.' Sophie knew he was right, but she had recalled a feeling which made it hard for her to leave. A feeling that made little sense, having heard all the stories about Leilani.

'Her compassion for all, is why great things will be, with you two together,' the ancient dragonfly said to Alex. Sophie sat down on one of the rocks and looked up at the blocked tunnel. A single tear ran down her cheek, for the Leilani she felt, and could not save.

'Sophie, we need to go,' Alex softly said.

'I know,' Sophie replied, in an equally soft voice. She stood back up and looked about. 'We can't get back to the cave with the dragonflies, how will we get back?' she asked.

'Look over there.' Alex pointed to the other side of the underground lake. 'The roots of the tree above us, make their way all the way down to the rock face on that side. If that is the tree from the cottage on the island, I think it should take us back as quickly as it brought us here.' Sophie was impressed at his deductions and concurred with his conclusion.

Thankfully, no climbing was required this time. Instead, they made their way downstream, away from the gem-covered tunnel entrance. With a small jump, they easily crossed over the trickles of water overflowing from the underground lake, and found a way along the bottom side of it to the cave wall, where the roots grew down.

'Gotta hope this works,' Sophie said. She placed her hand on a thick, damp root. Alex placed his hand on hers, and it did! A stream of light pulsed up the root, and travelled to the centre of the cluster of roots that spread out across the ceiling of the cave. The light then spread into every other root, lighting up the cave in a most spectacular way.

'Take us back to Heart's Dragonfly Island,' Sophie asked. She didn't need to be reminded by the ancient dragonfly this time!

'Clever Sophie, I would have missed the Heart part!' Alex said,

'Specifics are always important,' replied the academic Sophie. As though they had been sucked into the roots, using them like nature's highway, they were quickly returned to back inside the island's Dragonfly Cottage.

'Oh!' Sophie exclaimed. Sitting against the main door, was a very bored looking Gregg, who, getting a surprise at their sudden return, jumped into life, asking,

'Where is Miss Leilani?'

'I am sorry, I don't think she survived,' Sophie replied.

'Well, that's that then!' Gregg said, very matter-of-factly, as he turned and unlocked the door. Once open, he politely stood back and gestured for Alex and Sophie to go first. Everyone was there as they made their way out into the fresh air. However, there was no celebratory dash over to each other, hugs or squeals of excitement to welcome them back. The expectant faces had learnt too well, where Leilani was concerned, not to get excited until they had heard the full story. Lanny and George, still captives, had made no effort to escape. There seemed little point on two counts. Firstly, the odds of having a successful escape with just the two of them were not great, and secondly, they were confident that Leilani would be back, once she had got what she wanted from Alex and Sophie. Finally, close enough to the expectantly waiting crowd, Alex said,

'Leilani has gone!'

'Gone?' Lanny aggressively questioned.

'Well, we don't really know for sure, but she ran into a tunnel that was collapsing. I can't see how she could have survived. I tried to get to her, we tried to warn her not to go, but she didn't listen,' Sophie said, with a hint of emotion, that surprised the onlookers, considering who it was for.

'Why would you try to save that woman?' Jason asked, with a frown on his face.

'Because she was family,' Sophie replied. Knowing that they were safe, and that Leilani was not about to jump out from the cottage, grandmother shuffled her way over to Sophie and gave her a hug.

'Are you alright?' she asked.

'Yes, of course. I am fine,' Sophie replied, thoughtfully.

'So, what do we do next?' Vicky asked.

'We do what we are meant to do,' Sophie replied. She walked over to Lanny, squatted down in front of him, looked into his eyes and said,

'She was remembering what you did to her. She was remembering that it was you that took your father's life, that her mother's death was an accident. I just wanted you to know that!'

'Are we going to have to swim the loch then? You know, so we can get back to my big old house in the village, or are we getting there some other way?' Jason asked, hoping there was another option. Totally in sync, Anchor and Bart looked towards the loch's cold water, and then made their way in the opposite direction, back towards the cottage. Vicky laughed and said,

'I am with them thanks.'

'Can I ask what we are going to do with these three?' Iluka asked, pointing at Lanny and George who were still tied up, and the passive looking Gregg, who was standing beside the two prisoners, free from fear for the first time in many years. As he stood and hoped that he would stay free, visions and memories of what he and George had done over the years rushed through his mind, and found their way to his heart. A sadness washed over him, as he was forced to acknowledge the horrifying fact that he had begun to enjoy the destruction and murder he had carried out under orders. The youth and innocence he once knew a forgotten dream. He looked over at Lanny tied up, ageing with every passing moment, and a spark of light pierced the dreadful images. This was his chance to be free of the viciousness that had become his life.

The two bears had been together since birth, taken as cubs from their families to work for Lanny. George could feel what Gregg was feeling. He was reliving his own memories, his own nightmares. He knew what his brother in species was thinking, even though not a single word had passed between them, and he agreed.

'If you don't mind, we would like to go back to the gold mines, meet back up with our army, no, our friends! And tell them they are free. That they can return to their families if they still live. Further to this, we would very much like to take him with us, to keep him under our control!' Gregg said. Averie was quick to respond.

'Do you really think you are going to be free to carry on your death march across Heart? You took my partner, my cubs' father. You should be in the cave, crushed with that evil woman!' Averie was shaking with anger at his request. Sophie walked over, wrapped her arms around her furry neck and whispered in her ear. No one heard, but it was enough for her to turn and walk away.

'You will all remain right there until we have done what we have to,' Sophie said to the captive Lanny and his bears, guarded by the two deserter bears, who had come to the island having joined Iluka.

'Before we begin what I know we have to, I want to go back to my home. I assume you would all like to do the same?' Sophie asked. The response from everyone was emphatic. Nods from each one of them could be seen, and mutters of agreement filled the air. 'So let's get you all home then. Iluka, Gracie, Eric, Ella and Jedda, you will be first. Let's get you back to your new Dragonfly home in the forest.' Gracie interrupted,

'I wanted to ask - it is wonderful to have my new home, but born in Heart, will there be a home mirrored on Earth?' Alex answered her question. He knew the answer the moment he and Sophie brought it to life.

'Sadly, no. Only those created on Earth are mirrored. But we will reawaken your cottage back over the hills. You can use your new home's door to get there and return to Earth, if you want.'

'It's not that I want to go there, but it would be a dream come true to be able to share with my children, and one day, grandchildren, the wonderful visitors we have from Earth, and how we can help who needs to be helped,' Gracie said. Sophie took her hand and led her into the Dragonfly cottage, followed by the others who wanted to return to the Sovereign Hills forest.

'Oh, I'm sorry, is it ok if you two stay for a little longer to watch them?' Sophie asked the two bears guarding Lanny and his bears. They were happy to. Alex, the last one in, closed the door.

The process of finding the correct pinprick of light on the light covered door took no time at all. With the door reopened, having said their goodbyes, Alex and Sophie, who remained inside, waved to the group as they stepped out of the Dragonfly Island cottage, back into the warmth of the Australian sun. With one last goodbye, they closed the door.

'Kind of looking forward to your grandmother's kitchen!' Alex said with a wink, as together they re-opened the door, revealing the Dragonfly Island again.

'Alexandria, where do you want to go?' Sophie asked. She looked at her brother Jason, smiled and said,

'I hope you understand, but I want to be wherever they are! I want to get to know my son and his mother.'

'I completely understand. With these two, we will be able to see each other whenever we want from now on anyway. Of course I can't open the door to Earth, I am no key-keeper, but I am sure I will find someone to help,' Jason replied. After a quick hug, Jason, followed by Averie and her cubs, walked into the cottage to join Alex and Sophie. The door closed once again.

'Thank you Sophie. Your words are, and always will be true. Love is what I shall hold on to. I will never forget what you have done for us,' Averie said, as she ran out the door, off into the woods that hid the big old house from view, with her cubs. Jason took Alex's hand and gave it a firm squeeze as he shook it.

'Nephew, don't stay away too long. Now get yourselves back and leave me to enjoy my magically renovated house. Oh, please remember to send another dragonfly, obviously need my sister for that though!' Alex nodded and watched as Jason stepped out on to his front step, turned back and with a smile, pushed the door closed, letting Sophie and Alex once again return to the island.

'I have missed our Dragonfly Manor,' grandmother said.

'So have I,' Sophie replied.

'What are we waiting for then? Let's get on our way,' Vicky hesitantly said. She was thinking about how much she had enjoyed being able to see, to hear, without restriction, but she so very much wanted to see her parents. She knew they would be worrying about her.

'And us Miss Sophie?' One of the bear guards spoke up.

'Don't worry, I have not forgotten about you.' She looked at Alex, 'Do you think they can be trusted?' she asked.

'You are the one that can see something beyond the memories, feelings, emotions and visions of others I do. You saw in Leilani something I hadn't. The only one who can truly answer that question is you,' Alex replied.

'Then back to the mines it is.' Sophie gestured for the four bears and Lanny to walk over and join her and Alex in the cottage. The door open to the wrecked shack back on the hill, overlooking Lanny's mines, Gregg and the two bears disappeared in a cloud of dust, bounding across the dry fields. George remained by the slow moving Lanny's side, where he had always been.

'Do not concern yourself Miss Sophie, I will keep him out of trouble. Heart has changed today, well actually, it changed a few days ago, everyone sensed it here. He has too!' he said, gesturing at Lanny.

'Thank you, I believe you will,' Sophie said. As Alex closed the door with all the bears and the very old Lanny out, Lanny turned back, and just in time for Alex to hear, said,

'I still feel her. She is not gone!'

'What did he just say?' Sophie asked. The door closed and as it was about to be reopened back to the island, Alex chose to do something he wasn't used to - lie. Thankful she was not holding his hand, as she would have instantly known the truth, he said,

'I have no idea.'

Opening the island's cottage door, Sophie stepped out on to the Dragonfly Island's wobbly cobbly path, to join the much smaller group. Alex didn't follow, he was looking across towards his two mothers. He could sense the love between them, and it made him happy. Sophie, realising there was an Alex-sized space beside her, turned back. She took his hand and pulled him out into the cold winter's setting sun.

'Come on then guys,' Alex said. Anchor nearly knocked Alex to the ground, with the loving force in which he excitedly launched himself at him. Bart was not as excitable, but was a long way from the very serious puppy that had begun the journey. With everyone in the cottage, Alex took hold of the door's handle. Just as he was about to invite Sophie to put her hand on his to turn it, Sophie said,

'You do know you need to choose a light?'

'I've got this!' Alex replied. That wasn't good enough for Vicky, who piped up,

'I am sure you know exactly what you are doing Alex, but grandmother, or Alexandria of course, seeing as you have lived a life with these doors, can you explain to me how this door thing works? I mean, where will we end up? Will we be back in Australia, back at the old house here on Heart? If we choose to go to grandmother's Dragonfly Manor, how will we know it will be hers and not Leilani's? Honestly, I have got a little lost with what these two do, how they do it, who needs to be there etc.!' Grandmother laughed at her openness, and lack of any inhibition, at asking the questions she was sure more than one would have liked to ask.

'Alex, I feel you have a knowledge greater than mine at this point. Why don't you answer this intrepid young lady?' grandmother said. She was correct, he did. Having joined with the dragonfly and experienced what Sophie and he had experienced over the last couple of days, more and more knowledge was coming and being made available to him. It wasn't conscious knowledge where the Dragonfly homes were concerned, he just instinctively knew what was to be done, what was needed.

'This is how I understand it. If you remember, grandmother told us that visitors to Heart, could travel between the Dragonfly homes on Heart to travel the world. Well, that is still the case. In that scenario, to do that, you need a key-keeper, but you do not need a dragonfly. However, if you are at a Dragonfly home on Earth, then you can only travel to the mirror of that home on Heart, nowhere else on Earth or Heart, and along with a key-keeper, you also need a dragonfly, the key. Does that make sense?' Alex asked. Vicky replied with another question,

'Ok, so that explains that, so how are we getting back to grandmother's Dragonfly Manor from here?'

'Because the Dragonfly Island, combined with Sophie, me and the dragonfly, are the exception to every rule. From this doorway we can travel anywhere on Earth, or Heart, we just have to ask. There is no need to choose one of the lights on the door here, but we could if we wanted to. If we had never been there, it would be impossible to ask to go there! Do you follow me?' Alex asked Vicky. Alexandria interrupted,

'Really? That explains why Leilani was so desperate to find it. Not that I imagine even she knew how much power she could have had!' She was surprised. Having been a direct descendant of Shuing, she thought she knew everything there was to know. She didn't! She then went on to ask, 'And the baby dragonflies, the cave and tunnels where they live, you can get to them through the doorway as well?'

'No, the tree,' Alex said, turning and pointing to the beautiful old tree, growing at the cottage's centre.

'So, when you took the others home just now, how did you get there and back so quickly?' Vicky asked.

'Because we never left the cottage. To leave, you have to step out from the doorway and close the door. It really is as simple as that. Open a door, close a door,' Alex said.

'I am still totally lost. So just get us home will you,' Vicky said, laughing. Something else had occurred to Alexandria during the pause in returning to Sophie and grandmother's home. Before Alex had time to turn the handle, she said,

'No. Alex wait. Take us to Leilani's Dragonfly Manor.'

'I don't think so!' Melissa replied,

'There will be secrets there that could give answers to a lot of things. We can't miss that opportunity!' Alexandria said. Vicky didn't like the idea at all,

'I just want to go home. Please, can we just go?'

'It's important we take this chance to look!' Alexandria said.

'We all need a rest, a shower and change of clothes. Things are different now, there really is no hurry. She has gone,' Melissa said, hoping to calm the tension that was rising.

'I understand that, but it's important we don't miss any opportunity, just in case,' Alexandria said, firmly,

'in case of what?' grandmother asked in a very soft voice.

'I don't know,' Alexandria replied. Looking round the room at the group who clearly did not agree with her, Alexandria finally conceded, 'Fine. But I will be going there later.' The secrets Leilani had in her home were safe for a little longer - her tree trunk cauldron, the vials of blood and the crystals no-one knew existed.

'So again, just get us home will you!' Vicky said.

'I was trying to,' Alex jokingly replied, taking hold of the handle. As soon as Sophie joined him, colours from the dragonfly on Alex's back, and the swirls of colour on Sophie, filled the room. In his mind, Alex asked to go to grandmother's Dragonfly Manor. Hand on hand, his question heard by Sophie, together they turned the handle. As soon as they did, the doorframe lit up with the thousands of stories of so many visitors to Heart, and Alex's blue eyes with the hint of purple, turned to their now familiar full purple, and the whites, their supernatural white.

The energies rising to explosion, the cottage's walls, which had been a still image of Jason and Alexandria's new Dragonfly House in the Highlands, began to change. Slowly at first, images of unknown places, homes, people, animals, plants, oceans, moved around the walls, until they were passing so quickly they were hard to make out. With one final, bright flash of colourful light, the pictures stopped moving, and the place Alex had asked to go to, appeared.

Alex the empath, the direct descendant of Shuing, looked down at his beautiful, red-haired, freckle-covered companion, as she looked up at him and said,

'And we are only at the beginning!' Although the future was not guaranteed, looking into her eyes, he saw the excitement and possibilities that together, could be. The destruction of Heart, its inhabitants, its nature and humankind on Earth, which was a real reality, had changed. A small step back from the cliff's edge had been taken. The magical dragonflies purpose - the helping of those who were ill, in physical and or emotional pain, had returned. The helping of those who have suffered or continue to suffer at the hands of bullies, the ignorant, the evil, the selfish. The bringing of balance to both world's beauty in nature, and in all living, breathing creatures, was more than a beginning, it was a legend at last remembered. Together they opened the door.

'We are now arriving at Dragonfly Manor, I repeat, this stop is for Dragonfly Manor. Come on guys, everyone out!' Vicky said, in her best train conductor's voice.

Having done as Vicky ordered, Alexandria, Melissa, Vicky, Bart, grandmother, Anchor, Sophie and Alex found themselves standing in a familiar garden. Behind them was a lovingly made, red iron, flower-covered, decorative garden gate. Which led to the gorgeously red, wobbly cobbly footpath they were standing on, each wobble and cobble framed by the most unexpectedly, splendidly, wonderful display of flowers, with every shape, colour and smell their minds could conjure up. And in front of them, was a friendly, perfectly formed, incredibly inviting, bright red front door, with its completely oppositely crooked windows, that gave the unexpectedly, splendidly, wonderfully perfect home its most inviting of smiles. They were home.

THE END

Printed in Poland
by Amazon Fulfillment
Poland Sp. z o.o., Wrocław